WESTON FIELDS

Fail-Safe

Sign up for my newsletter at weston-fields.com to receive regular updates on future titles and get a free copy of the previously unreleased short story "Quill's Box."

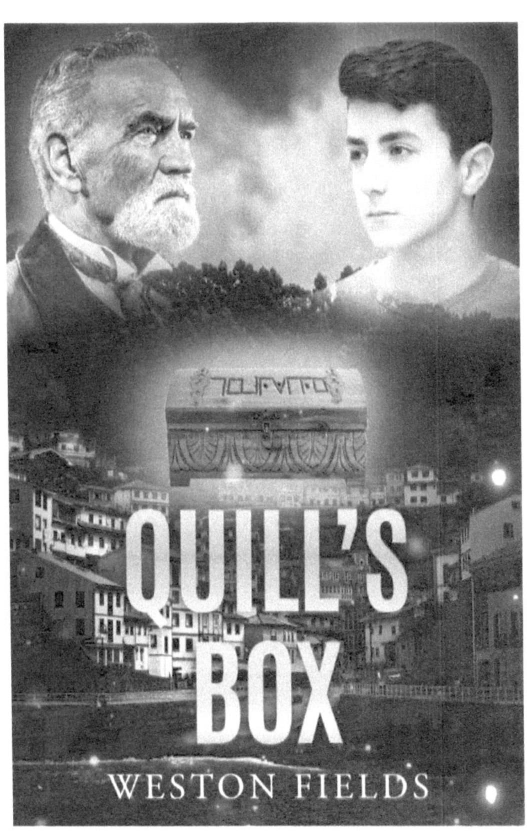

Chapter 1

"I can't thank you enough for what you've done for Alpen," the feathered mutant Congressman said, looking back and forth between Quill and Timothy. It had been only hours since the mountain nation of Alpen had been freed from the iron-fisted control of the Council, but the recently reinstated government had wasted no time in throwing a banquet to celebrate their liberators.

"I didn't really do all that much," Quill said, shaking his head. At sixteen, he was one of the youngest of the Guardians of Kawts, beating out Timothy by about a year. He was also one of the newest members of the group—the fight for Alpen had been his first as a full member of the team.

Quill gestured toward Timothy. "Timothy was the one who came up with the plan that helped us turn the tables on the Council."

Timothy bit his lip, suddenly uncomfortable. "The only reason my plan worked at all was because we got lucky," he said. "And because there were so many recently discharged soldiers still in Blancstadt. It was Alpen's own armies that really turned the tide."

"Well, whoever's ultimately responsible, I know that you both still played an important role," the Congressman said with a kindly smile. His attention drifted to something over Timothy's shoulder, and he added, "Excuse me for a moment. I have to speak to President Draagetsew."

The Congressman hurried off across the banquet hall, leaving Timothy and Quill alone for the moment.

"This is beginning to feel like Kawts all over again," Quill said with a smirk, his blue eyes glinting with amusement. "People were stopping by to thank us for weeks!"

"I'd rather be thanked by random strangers than risk getting brainwashed by the Council," Timothy said, laughing. "It seems like a fair trade to me."

Quill laughed. "It's hard to argue with that logic," he said. "It does kind of make me wonder, though…"

Quill continued talking, but Timothy was no longer listening. On the other side of the room, Jewel was standing in the middle of a cluster of Alpenite dignitaries. For a moment, their eyes met, but then Jewel quickly looked away.

Timothy sighed inwardly.

With everything that's been going on, we still haven't had a chance to talk about what happened back in the Weather Belt complex. We've just been avoiding each other for the last few days.

And the worst part is, Crystal was right. I really do have feelings for her.

"Don't you agree, Timothy?"

Timothy looked up at Quill, startled. For a moment, he had the thought that Quill had somehow read his mind. Quill stared at him, waiting for him to say something.

"I'm sorry. What were you saying?"

Quill raised an eyebrow. "I was just saying how we should go talk to Aksell," he said, jerking his head in the direction of the doorway. "He looks like he could use the company."

Timothy followed Quill's gaze to see Aksell standing just inside the doorway of the banquet hall, looking around at the crowd with a mixture of regret and confusion. As the son of the head Councilman, Aksell had initially sided with his father during the Battle of Kawts, fleeing the city along with the rest of the Council. He had since come to regret his decision, but only after his father had ordered him to execute his former friends.

Timothy nodded. "You're right. He looks a little lost."

Weaving their way through the crowd, Quill and Timothy made their way over to where Aksell stood. Aksell's face brightened when he saw them, a look of relief washing over him.

"Quill!" he shouted, embracing his friend. "You're not dead!"

"That's thanks to you, you know," Quill said, grinning.

A shadow flickered across Aksell's face, but he said nothing.

"Where've you been?" Timothy asked. "I feel like I haven't seen you since the battle."

"I was… visiting my dad," Aksell said at last. Timothy nodded sympathetically. Aksell's father was the head of the Council who had invaded Alpen, and during the fighting it had been Aksell who had taken him down.

Aksell looked up at Timothy. "I don't know what to do with myself now. All my life, it's been expected that I would one day take my dad's place as a protector of Kawts. But that's kind of off the table at this point."

"You don't have to be part of the Council to protect the city," Quill said. "Come back to Kawts with us. Everyone back home misses you. I'm sure we can figure something out."

"Thanks," Aksell said, although his face said that he wasn't totally convinced.

"In the meantime, why don't you tell us what you've been up to for the last few months," Timothy suggested. "We have a lot of catching up to do."

Aksell nodded, grateful for the change in topic. The trio continued chatting, hardly noticing what was going on around them. It seemed like they'd hardly begun before Draagetsew's voice cut through the chatter.

"Food's ready!" he bellowed. "Everyone, take a seat!"

Slowly, the Guardians of Kawts and the surviving Alpenite Congressmen made their way to the table. Spread out before them were a variety of dishes that Timothy had never seen before, ranging from what looked to be white asparagus to thin, breaded slices of meat.

As everyone took their seats, Gearwire, who was seated at the head of the table, stood up on his chair.

"If nobody has any objections, I would like to lead us in prayer first."

Timothy noticed some of the Alpenite Congressmen frowning at this, but none of them said anything. Gearwire allowed his request to hang in the air for a few moments longer, then lifted his hands and began to pray.

Everyone bowed their heads, and, after a second of hesitation, Timothy followed suit.

Gearwire finished his prayer, and everyone began to eat. As Timothy reached for a piece of asparagus, Samuel leaned across the table toward him, notebook in hand. The elderly former librarian looked almost giddy, his eyes sparkling with excitement.

"So," he said, looking at the trio seated opposite him. "Now that the Council's been defeated once and for all, what are you three going to do now?" When none of them answered right away, he added, "This is for posterity, you know. I'm compiling a first-hand account of what happened here today."

Even so, the silence lingered for a moment longer. *We've been fighting the Council for years*, Timothy thought. *What do we do now that they're in custody?*

"Honestly? I'm not sure," Quill said at last. "It'll be nice to be able to rest for a while. But after that, who knows?"

"I think I'm with Quill on this one," Timothy said, smiling at his mentor's enthusiasm. "It'll be nice to rest and hang out with everybody without having to look over my shoulder all the time. And once things settle down, I need to finish my expedition to figure out what happened to Maurice. I owe him that much," he added, remembering how his brother had disappeared in the months leading up to the Battle of Kawts. Timothy had tracked him as far as the site of a Council attack on a nomadic camp, although his body was never found, nor were the bodies of his two companions, Ally and Maverick.

"What about you, Aksell?" Samuel asked, looking up from his notepad. "It's good to see you again, by the way."

Aksell opened his mouth to respond, but whatever he was going to say was cut short by the sound of the door slamming open. Timothy turned to look at the source of the sound and saw Dr. Maddium standing in the doorway. His hair and lab coat were more disheveled than usual, looking as if he had just run all the way from the site of the last battle with the Council.

As Timothy watched, the time-traveling scientist made his way over to Gearwire and said something to him that Timothy couldn't quite make out.

Gearwire's eyes widened, and he said, "Are you sure?"

Dr. Maddium nodded. What he said next was heard by everybody, despite his attempt to stay quiet.

"We have only sixty hours until the Orgwar arrive."

Chapter 2

Orgwellis Space Station
Orbiting the Planet Threye

"Sir? There's a ship approaching."

The Orgwarian High Command ignored the messenger, instead staring at the screen in front of him, which displayed Councilman Ethos' frantic message.

I wondered how long it would take that gullible fool to reach out, High Command thought as he read. *He actually thinks that the Orgwar would seriously consider a partnership with a human.*

With a few deft strokes, High Command closed out of the transmission, replacing it with the coordinates of Earth as he turned to face his subordinate.

"Who is it? It had better not be the new Defender."

The messenger hesitated. "It could be. It looks like Flarouna's ship."

"He's a clever one," High Command said. "I never said anything about sending one of the others in his stead. But it doesn't matter. Fire a warning shot. If they persist, shoot them down. And send someone to kill the prisoners."

"Right away, sir," the messenger said, disappearing again into the belly of the ship.

High Command stared at the coordinates on the screen. He felt the old space station shudder as the cannons fired.

A fitting end to our little game, he thought, recalling the Defender's origins. *I'll take out you and your people in one blow.*

A wicked grin tugged at the corner of his mouth as he reached for the radio.

"Orwog! R'goar! Ready the flagship! We're making a trip to Earth."

* * *

Blancstadt, Alpen
Sixty Hours Remaining

Dr. Maddium's words hung in the air. For a long moment, no one spoke. Then chaos broke out, everybody talking over each other as they tried to make sense of what was happening.

Out of the corner of his eye, Timothy could see Gearwire's mouth moving as he tried in vain to calm the crowd. Finally, he turned to Draagetsew, who nodded.

"QUIET!" the four-armed mutant bellowed, his voice echoing around the room. The banquet hall fell silent, and he continued in a slightly softer tone, "I'm going to request that the room be cleared except for the Guardians of Kawts." One of the Congressmen started to protest, but Draagetsew cut him off. "I assure you that as soon as I know what's going on, I will make a full report to the Congress of Alpen. But until then, we have to have a place where we can figure this out without having to worry about all the official red tape."

Slowly and begrudgingly, the members of the Alpenite Congress stood and left the room. As the door swung shut behind the last of them, a moment of silence stretched out over the group.

Finally, Gearwire spoke.

"I don't know how much you heard of what Thomas said," he began. He fell silent once more, looking out at the faces of his crewmembers and companions. "For those of you who weren't able to hear it, the Orgwar are on their way to Earth as we speak with an army."

"How?" Quill asked. "We stopped Ethos. We defeated the Council! We won, didn't we?"

Dr. Maddium shook his head. "I'm afraid our victory wasn't as complete as we thought. It appears that Ethos was able to activate his transmitter before Aksell froze him. And it seems to have worked."

"We don't know the exact details of the Council's arrangement with the Orgwar," Gearwire said. "But what we do know is that it included a provision for military assistance from the Orgwar in the event that the Council needed it."

Timothy glanced over at Aksell, who was standing beside him. "Do you know anything about this?" he whispered. "Anything about the details of the Council's deal, I mean," he added quickly, seeing the flash of hurt in Aksell's eyes.

Aksell shook his head. "Dad never told me about most of his backup plans. He played things pretty close to the vest, even with us."

"Based on what we know about Orgwarian technology and how long it took for Ethos' message to go through, Dr. Maddium has calculated that the Orgwar will reach Earth in no more than two and a half days." Gearwire looked out at his crewmembers, his face grimmer and wearier than Timothy had ever seen him before. "If they reach us before we can stop them, they will wipe us out. Or worse."

"Not if Alpen has anything to say about it!" Draagetsew said, fire blazing in his eyes. "We have almost three days. With your help, we can turn Blancstadt into an impenetrable stronghold! What's the best way to defeat these guys? Swords? Missiles? Grenades?"

Gearwire shook his head. "Our weapons would be of limited use against an Orgwarian warship," he said. "The Orgwar invaded Earth once before—back before even the Robot War. The firepower of all the world's militaries hardly made a dent in their forces. The only thing that saved us then was the combined might of the world's superhuman heroes. And even then, most of them gave their lives in the battle."

"That was a full-scale war!" Draagetsew protested. "The Orgwar aren't going to send an entire fleet just to bail Ethos out."

"Even a single Orgwarian warship might prove too much for us to defeat," Dr. Maddium said. "The global infrastructure still hasn't recovered from the Robot War. Many settlements and countries don't even know of the existence of the others. And as far as superhumans go, neither Gearwire nor I are aware of any other than Crystal and Jewel."

"The first time the Orgwar invaded was before mutant kind was born," Draagetsew said. "The Orgwar won't know what hit them!"

"I realize my knowledge on this subject might be rather outdated," Penn said, steepling his long, gecko-like fingers. "Having been trapped inside the Weather Belt complex for a few hundred years and all that. But unless Alpen's technology has progressed dramatically since my time, I don't think we have any weapon in Alpen that could even reach such a warship if it remained in our upper atmosphere." He glanced at Dr. Maddium. "And I assume they would probably have some way of attacking us without having to come all the way down here."

Dr. Maddium nodded. "An ordinary Orgwarian ship would be capable of vaporizing a city from orbit. And from the looks of this transmission, this isn't an ordinary warship—it's the flagship of the Orgwarian fleet."

"Orgwarian technology is far more advanced than ours," the Mysterious Man said, adjusting the brim of his battered fedora. "Despite what the old legends say, they're the ones who created Marathon's rings. It's light-years ahead of anything we have."

There was silence for a moment as everyone digested the Mysterious Man's proclamation.

"Actually, that's not strictly true," Gearwire said reluctantly. "The way I see it, there is only one thing in the entire world that would stand a chance at destroying an Orgwarian Battleship." He stared up at the carved stones mounted over the door of the banquet hall. Timothy followed his gaze, seeing the engraved sun crest that matched the one carved throughout the Weather Belt complex. With sudden clarity, he knew exactly what Gearwire meant.

"The fail-safe devices," Timothy breathed.

Gearwire nodded. "They were made from the best technology available in the wake of the Robot War, combined with superpowered relics from the heroes who fought off the Orgwar the first time. If combined into their intended form, they would be strong enough to blast right through any Orgwarian vessel. Or create a protective barrier around the earth should that fail."

"This is crazy," Crystal said. "We spent almost a month trying to retrieve just one of those things! And you want to try to collect *all of them* in less than three days? We don't even know where the others are!"

"I know it seems like an impossible task," Gearwire said. "But we've done the impossible before. The fact of the matter is that I know where the devices were hidden after they were first made. As long as they haven't drifted too far from their original spots, we have a fighting chance."

"That's a pretty big if," Crystal said, shaking her head. "And even if we *do* know where the rest of the devices are, we still have to physically travel all over the world to retrieve them. There's no way we'll be able to gather them all in time."

"Actually," Howard said, chewing on his lower lip. "I might have a solution to that. I've been working on plans for a booster engine for the ship for a few months now. It's still untested, but it should theoretically be able to increase our maximum speed by a substantial margin."

"I don't see why time is even a problem, anyway," Aksell said. "Didn't you guys say that Dr. Maddium is a time traveler? Why can't he just hop back in time a few days and collect the devices before the Orgwar are even called? Or prevent my dad from calling them in the first place."

"I'm afraid it isn't that simple," Dr. Maddium said, shaking his head. "When I travel back in time, I still experience its passage at the same rate. So even if I traveled back in time to get the devices, I would still only have two and a half days to pull it off. And making a jump to anywhere closer to a hundred and fifty years from a time you've already been is far too dangerous. You risk destroying the fabric of reality itself."

"So, we're doomed, then," Crystal muttered, shaking her head.

"Nonsense!" Penn said, pounding his fist on the table. He rose to his feet, his tattered brown cloak making him look almost kinglike. "Every one of you in this room are heroes! You've already done the impossible by retrieving the Weather Belt. And from what my old partner-in-crime, the Golden Knight, tells me, this isn't the first time. Two of you are among the great heroes of the Robot War. You defeated the Council twice—and on each occasion, they possessed one of the most powerful fail-safe devices. And now you have myself and the robot, Jeff, on your side as well!"

There was silence for a moment as Penn's words hung in the air. Finally, the Mysterious Man spoke. "I hate to be the one to bring this up, but there's still one major problem with this plan. The Weather Belt is gone. It'll take us days to find it in that ravine."

"If you have sufficient technological capacities, there is an alternative," Jeff said, his processors whirring to life. "The blueprints for the

Weather Belt are still in the compound."

Dr. Maddium scratched his chin. "If we take a small team back to the ruins, we can retrieve the plans through the hole in the ceiling. And if we can do that, I have a few friends who might be able to help us rebuild the device."

Gearwire nodded slowly. "That should do the trick. While we're doing that, I need everyone else to help prepare for the journey. Our top priority is getting Howard's turbo-booster up and running. Crystal and Jewel can help with that—and Revenant, if you can get ahold of him. Everyone else needs to start gathering supplies. We can't afford to stop to restock halfway through."

The room was silent for a moment, then the Guardians of Kawts began to disperse, making their way back to their temporary quarters in the castle to retrieve their gear. Timothy turned to follow them, but someone grabbed his arm. He turned around to see Dr. Maddium standing behind him, his face unusually concerned.

"Timothy. May I have a word with you? In private."

Timothy nodded slowly, alarm bells ringing in his head.

What does Dr. Maddium need to tell me that he doesn't want anyone else knowing? Does he know something about the Orgwar that the rest of us don't?

His apprehension growing, Timothy followed Dr. Maddium out of the banquet hall and into a maintenance hallway a short distance away. Only once he was sure that they were alone did Dr. Maddium speak.

"I need you to keep an eye on Gearwire while I'm gone," he said, looking Timothy directly in the eyes.

Timothy frowned, his forehead furrowing. "What do you mean, 'keep an eye on him?' Are you saying that Gearwire is working with the Orgwar?"

Dr. Maddium shook his head. "Nothing like that." He hesitated for a moment, then went on. "There's a lot of this that I probably shouldn't be telling you. And under normal circumstances, I wouldn't be." He hesitated again, then sighed. "Look. I know Gearwire seems like he has it all together. But the fact of the matter is, his mental state is going to be in a very precarious place. If something goes wrong on this mission, it will destroy him."

"What do you mean?"

"Gearwire blames himself for all of this," Dr. Maddium said. "During Milkop Quawz' rebellion, a shopkeeper named Ayrton was killed by the Council. Gearwire blamed himself for convincing the man to join his crusade. He's been holding himself responsible for the deaths of every person the Council has murdered since then. And there have been quite a few. Some have been good friends." Dr. Maddium sighed. "He's going to blame himself for the Orgwar's attack."

"Why are you telling me this?"

"Because if somebody gets killed on this mission—or worse, if you aren't successful, I need you to take over for Gearwire. This mission will strain him to his breaking point. If the worst comes to pass, he's not going to be in a fit state to lead."

"I'm not sure I will be either," Timothy said. "Remember how I was after Henry died?"

"I know. And I'm sorry. I wouldn't be putting this on your shoulders if there was any other way. But if Gearwire is unable to lead, you are humanity's best hope for survival."

"I'll try," Timothy said at last. "But I can't promise you that I'll be any better off than Gearwire."

"That's all I ask," Dr. Maddium said. "I just need to know that if Gearwire starts to unravel, someone will be there to finish the mission."

Timothy nodded. "I'll try," he repeated. Dr. Maddium turned to leave, but Timothy stopped him. "Dr. Maddium? Tell me the truth. Do you really think we have a chance?"

"It's an impossible task," Dr. Maddium said. "But I've seen the impossible done before."

* * *

Timothy replayed Dr. Maddium's words in his head over and over again as he walked back to his room to retrieve his armor.

It's going to take a miracle to get us out of this one alive.

His thoughts were interrupted by a hand on his shoulder. He turned around to see Jewel standing in the hallway behind him.

"Timothy! I've been looking all over for you."

"I was… helping Dr. Maddium with something," Timothy said. "What did you need?"

For a moment, neither of them spoke. Finally, Jewel said, "Look, about what Crystal said in the ruins… If the Orgwar win, I want you to know that-"

"The Orgwar won't win," Timothy said quickly. Hurt and confusion flickered across Jewel's face, and Timothy forced himself to pretend he hadn't noticed. "That's all there is to it."

Before Jewel could reply, Timothy slipped into his room, shutting the door behind him. He pressed himself against the door, trying to ignore the guilt in the pit of his stomach.

I can't know the answer, he thought. *I can't. There's too much at stake. Neither of us can afford to worry about that right now.* With trembling hands, he picked up his helmet and put it on. *Anyone else would have done the same thing,* he thought, trying to ignore the small, persistent voice that told him otherwise.

If we survive this, there will be plenty of time to make it up to her. And if we don't- His breath caught.

If we don't, it won't matter much, anyway.

Chapter 3

The banquet hall was a buzz of activity when Timothy arrived, having been transformed into a center of operations for the Guardians of Kawts' efforts. A large area had been cleared in the center of the room, where Howard was already standing knee-deep in scrap metal and tools. The tables bearing their lunch were pushed up against the wall, long forgotten.

Samuel stood near the entrance to the room, directing the chaos as best he could. When he saw Timothy, his eyes brightened. "Timothy! I have a job for you!" he said, coming over to him. "I need you to find Quill and pay a visit to the hospital. We need to let Idalbo and Adalbo know what's happening."

"Any ideas on where Quill might be?" Timothy asked, avoiding making eye contact with Jewel, who was standing near Howard's mess.

"My best guess is that he's still in his room," Samuel said. "No one's seen him since Gearwire dismissed everybody."

Timothy nodded. "Right. I'll go find him."

He slipped back into the hallway, making his way toward the room Draagetsew had given to Quill. Light shone out from the crack beneath the door, and Timothy eased the door open. Quill stood on the opposite side of the room, an open book in his hands.

"What could you possibly be reading at a time like this?" Timothy asked.

Quill started violently, looking slightly guilty. He closed the book and held it up, allowing Timothy to see the cross embossed on the cover.

"I see."

An awkward silence followed as Timothy tried to decide whether he should say anything further. Finally, Quill said, "Was there something you wanted to tell me?"

Timothy snapped back to the present. "Right. Samuel wants the two of us to go down to the hospital and let Idalbo and Adalbo know what's going on."

Quill nodded, grabbing the few bits of gear he had from the bed beside him. "Let's go."

The pair walked through the streets of Blancstadt in silence, Timothy being far too preoccupied trying to process everything that had happened in the last several minutes to carry on a conversation. Before long, they found themselves standing outside the hospital. The building bore a striking resemblance to the Kawts Hospital, causing Quill to hesitate at the doors.

"We'd better get inside," Timothy said at last, gently prodding his friend toward the building. "They're going to need time to prepare if they're coming with us."

Quill nodded, took a deep breath, and opened the door to the hospital. After consulting the directory and a nearby map of the building, they quickly located the room they were looking for. Timothy eased open the door, standing quietly off to the side while he surveyed the scene.

A big, tentacled mutant lay in the hospital bed in the middle of the room, his torso wrapped in blood-stained bandages from where he had been shot by one of Ethos' henchmen. He seemed to be asleep, though whether he was in imminent danger was more than Timothy could tell.

Around the bed stood three other mutants. Timothy immediately recognized Idalbo and Adalbo by their characteristic quills and beetle shell, respectively. The other mutant was Seililyad, a tentacled female mutant whom Timothy had met while planning for the final strike against the Council. The unconscious mutant in the bed was her father.

"Idalbo? Adalbo?" Quill said, interrupting the solemn scene. The mutants in question turned, noticing their visitors for the first time.

"I'm afraid we have some bad news," Timothy said, hoping his words didn't come across as insensitive. "It looks like Ethos managed to get a message out to the Orgwar before Aksell stopped him. They're on their way now."

Idalbo stared at him. "What do you mean, 'they're on their way?'"

"The Orgwar are bringing an army to invade Earth. Dr. Maddium estimates that we have about sixty hours before they arrive."

"We have a plan, though," Quill said. "We're going to reassemble the fail-safe devices and destroy their battleship before they can strike."

"You're asking us to come with you," Adalbo said. He glanced over at his brother, then at Seililyad. "I think there's some people I'm going to have to talk to first," he said at last.

Idalbo nodded. "Agreed." He turned toward Timothy and Quill. "You're still going to need some time to load up the ship," he said. "Adalbo and I will meet you at the castle once we've made our decision."

"I'll let Samuel know," Timothy said. "Come on, Quill."

He tugged Quill toward the door, ignoring his friend's puzzled frown. Once they were outside again, Quill turned toward him.

"Why didn't you insist they come with us?" Quill asked. "They're part of the Guardians of Kawts. If the Orgwar make it over here, we're going to need every fighter we have."

"They want to consult the rest of the Kriegerhelden before they make a decision," Timothy said. "You never really interacted with them before we came here. Last time Idalbo and Adalbo left—to join

Gearwire's crew—a lot of the Kriegerhelden felt betrayed. The group fragmented. If they hadn't, maybe the Council wouldn't have been able to take the castle." He shook his head. "Besides, Alpen is their home. They've been helping Kawts for years now. They deserve a break."

Quill nodded reluctantly. "I suppose you're right. They probably weren't planning on coming back to Kawts with us, anyway, were they?"

Timothy shook his head. "Probably not. There were actually quite a few of us who are planning on cutting down on how much Guardians of Kawts stuff we're doing once we get home."

If we get home, he added silently.

* * *

By the time Timothy and Quill got back to the castle, Gearwire and Dr. Maddium had already returned from the Weather Belt complex, detailed schematics in hand. Howard and Dr. Maddium were hard at work attaching the new rocket booster to the ship, and the others were beginning to load up their supplies. Timothy and Quill had just joined them when Timothy saw Gearwire coming their way.

"Timothy," Gearwire said. "May I speak to you for a moment?" He beckoned Timothy to follow him, and Timothy started after him, his head spinning.

This is the second time today. Did he somehow find out about what Dr. Maddium told me? he wondered as Gearwire led him to a secluded hallway. *Or is this about something else?*

Gearwire came to a stop and glanced around, making sure they were alone. For a long time, he was silent. Then he said, "Timothy, there's something you need to know. There is a very high chance I won't survive the next three days. If anything should happen to me, you need to take charge. Don't try to come back for me. The most important thing is that we stop the Orgwar from reaching Earth."

Timothy's eyes widened.

That's the same thing Dr. Maddium told me. Except Gearwire seems concerned for a completely different reason.

"What are you saying?" Timothy asked, a flutter of fear running through him. "What do you think is going to happen?"

"Just promise me you'll do whatever it takes," Gearwire said, his face grave. "Our mission must be successful. No matter what."

Timothy nodded slowly. "I promise."

Gearwire forced a smile. "Thank you. It's a great weight off my mind to know that the fate of the world is in good hands." Then, before Timothy could say anything, he turned and walked away.

Timothy stood frozen in the hallway, trying not to freak out over what Gearwire had said.

If the fate of the world falls into my hands, we're doomed, he thought. *But Gearwire seemed so sure that he wouldn't survive. What wasn't he telling me?*

Finally, his fears and questions swirling in his mind, Timothy made his way back to the others. He arrived just in time to witness Dr. Maddium's departure.

"I'll meet you back in Kawts before the sixty hours are up," Dr. Maddium said, taking the Weather Belt plans from Gearwire.

Gearwire nodded. "If you get there before we do, start preparing the cities for invasion. Just in case-" He swallowed, looking around at the rest of the Guardians of Kawts. "Just in case we fail."

"Will do," Dr. Maddium said. He walked a short distance away from the group, climbing to the top of a nearby hill. He removed a device from the pocket of his lab coat and adjusted the dials. A white light grew from the device, concealing Dr. Maddium from view. There was a blinding flash, and he vanished, racing backwards through time.

"Do you really think he'll be able to rebuild the Weather Belt in time?" Quill asked, staring at the spot where Dr. Maddium had stood.

"If anyone can pull it off, it's the people he's going to see now," Gearwire said. He stared off into space, seeming at once older and more resigned than Timothy had ever seen him.

"But do they really have a chance?"

Gearwire turned to face him. "I don't know. But we must pray that they're successful."

Timothy shuddered.

There's so much that could go wrong here. Even just one mistake could doom us all.

"Alright," Gearwire said, breaking Timothy out of his reflections. "We don't have much time before the Orgwar arrive. Let's get moving."

As the Guardians of Kawts made their way back to the ship, Draagetsew appeared to see them off, flanked by Idalbo and Adalbo.

"I wish I could come with you," Draagetsew said, thumping Gearwire on the back. "But Alpen needs me here right now. Especially if you don't make it back."

"I understand. Stay safe. And don't do anything reckless." Gearwire turned to Idalbo and Adalbo. "Are you going to be joining us on this mission?"

"We are," Idalbo said, staring resolutely ahead. His brother looked slightly less sure of his decision, but he nodded as well.

"Our best chance of ever living in Alpen again is if we help you defeat the Orgwar," Adalbo said.

"I'm glad to have you aboard," Gearwire said. He nodded to Penn, who had joined the little band. "You too, Penn. We could use a man like you on this mission."

"The fate of the world's at stake. How can I say no?"

Gearwire nodded approvingly. He turned to board the ship, but

Aksell stopped him.

"I'm coming with you."

Timothy watched Gearwire's face closely, remembering how reluctant he had been to allow Quill to join them to retrieve the Weather Belt. To his surprise, Gearwire nodded. "If you come with us, you will play by our rules and under my authority. If you can agree to that, I have no problem with you coming along."

"I won't let you down," Aksell said, his face settling into a look of grim determination.

"As long as we're on the subject, I should probably let you know that I'm coming, too," Samuel said.

Gearwire frowned. "Samuel, this is going to be a dangerous mission. And if we fail, someone needs to be there to help defend Kawts."

Samuel raised an eyebrow. "Gearwire, if we fail, Kawts is probably the least safe place for any of us to be, considering we're the ones in charge of it. I'm coming with you. And besides," he added, holding up his notepad. "Regardless of how this plays out, someone needs to record what happens. Future generations will need to know what happened here."

Gearwire was silent for a long moment, his eyes narrowing as he considered Samuel's words. "Alright," he said at last. "But I expect you to follow the same rules as Aksell. You may be the ruler of Kawts, but on this mission, I'm in charge."

Samuel nodded, a faint smile on his lips. "Of course. You are the one with experience in these matters. I will be merely an observer."

Gearwire stared at him for a moment longer, then turned and boarded the ship. The rest of the Guardians of Kawts slowly followed suit.

"Where are we going first?" Aksell asked as Adalbo boarded the ship, shutting the door behind him. "Ellada? Kawts?"

"We're going to Velikanov," Gearwire said, opening the door to the cockpit. "That's the last recorded location of the fail-safe device known as the Gravity Ray." He hesitated for a moment, looking around the cabin before settling on the team's robotic companion. "Jeff, you're with me. Someone needs to know how to fly this thing if something goes wrong." Then he disappeared into the cockpit, sealing the door shut behind him.

There it is again, Timothy thought as rumblings of the engine echoed through the ship. *Gearwire's convinced that something is going to happen to him. But what?*

Chapter 4

Velikanov, Severnaya
Fifty-Seven Hours Remaining

“So… How are you holding up?” Samuel asked, taking a seat beside Timothy.

“We just learned that an advanced race of aliens is on their way here to wipe us out,” Timothy said, a bit harsher than he’d intended. “Overall, not great.”

“Fair enough,” Samuel said with a hint of a smile.

“You don’t seem nearly concerned enough about this.”

Samuel chuckled. “I suppose maybe I’m not,” he admitted. “But I know that God is in control. Things will work out somehow.”

“That sounds a lot like what you told me the other day,” Timothy said. “After everyone got captured by the Council.”

“And we all survived,” Samuel said with a wink. His face grew more somber as he continued. “Where are you at with that, anyway?” he asked. “I feel like the two of us have hardly discussed spiritual matters since I got turned into a Blank.”

Timothy exhaled heavily. “I don’t know. I was finally ready to give it another shot, but now this happens… I don’t know what I believe anymore.”

“Well, you’d better figure it out soon,” Samuel said. “If Dr. Maddium’s calculations are right, we may all be dead by the end of the week."

"I thought you said that God would make things work out somehow."

"Things 'working out' doesn't necessarily mean we win," Samuel said. Then, before Timothy could say anything further, he turned and began talking to Aksell and Quill.

A short time passed before a robotic voice cut through the chatter.

"Captain Gearwire has requested that I notify you that we have almost reached our destination," Jeff said, staggering out of the cockpit as the ship rocked. Timothy turned to face the awkward robot, bracing himself for the inevitable bad news to come.

"Accordingly, Gearwire wishes me to tell you that because of the roughness of the terrain, he will be unable to land the ship in Velikanov."

"If we can't land, how is Gearwire planning on getting us down there?" Penn asked. "Unless some of you secretly have the ability to fly."

Jeff let out a low buzzing sound, followed by a sharp click. "Gearwire is looking for volunteers to parachute into the capital," he said. "Ideally, a team of five to six individuals."

"I'll do it," Aksell said at once. Timothy raised an eyebrow at him, slightly concerned by how quickly he had volunteered.

Why is Aksell so eager to come with us? Is he after the fail-safe devices for himself? Maybe he still is working for the Council-

No, he told himself, shaking his head. *Aksell knows the truth now. Now that he knows what the Council's really like, he wouldn't still be working for them.*

Still, he thought, *it wouldn't hurt for someone who knows him well to be there to keep an eye on him.*

"I'll go," Timothy said. He glanced over at Quill. "Quill? You want to join us?"

Quill grinned. "Why not? It'll be more fun than hanging out on the ship for hours."

Aksell smiled. "Perfect! It'll be just like old times!"

"Except for the fact that it will be almost nothing like old times," Crystal said, arching an eyebrow at him. "If you three are going, so are Jewel and I. Someone has to keep you out of trouble."

"We can take care of ourselves," Timothy protested, avoiding making eye contact with Jewel. For her part, Jewel didn't look particularly pleased with being volunteered, but she said nothing.

"I guess I'd better come along, too, then," Madison said, biting her lip as she glanced out the window at the mountains below.

"You don't have to come if you don't want to," Quill said quickly, but Madison shook her head.

"I'll be fine. Let's go."

"Wait," Timothy said. "Shouldn't Jeff or Gearwire or someone come with us? Someone who knows what to expect from this place?"

Jeff clicked. "My presence on this mission would be unadvisable. The inhabitants of Velikanov have been suspicious of strangers since the sacking of the city during the Robot War. They especially do not trust robotic strangers."

"Looks like we have our team, then," Samuel said, a knowing smile breaking out across his face. "Unless anyone else was planning on joining them?"

No one said anything, and Jeff turned to leave. Before he could get back to the cockpit, however, Quill asked, "What exactly is the device we're supposed to retrieve?"

Jeff's processors began to whir loudly as he answered. "The giants of Velikanov were the result of a government program to recreate the powers possessed by the heroes who died in the Great Heroes' War. After the end of the Robot War, they became the principal creators of the device known as the Gravity Ray. The exact location of the device is known only to select, high-ranking government officials, so the parachute team will need to meet with them and retrieve it."

His message delivered, Jeff turned and slowly walked back into the cockpit. After a few moments, Gearwire's voice came on over the intercom.

"I'll try to fly the ship as close to their capitol building as I can," he said. "You'll have a very narrow window to jump out of the ship before we're out of range again. Once you land, you'll need to find their leader and convince them to give you the Gravity Ray. It's not going to be easy. You'll have to overcome centuries of isolationism. And we have no idea how much they know about the situation in Kawts."

Gearwire paused for a moment before continuing. "Howard will give you a radio beacon in case anything goes wrong or you need an extraction. He'll also show you how to use the parachutes. I'll tell you when we're over the drop zone, but after that, you're on your own. The fate of the world depends on this."

The intercom clicked and then went dead. Timothy and Quill exchanged glances as Howard removed the parachutes from a compartment in the ceiling.

No pressure, he thought, his mouth suddenly dry. *It's only the fate of the world, after all.*

"You'll each need one of these," Howard said, handing Timothy a small device that looked like a wristwatch. "This will tell you how high up you are. You need to pull the cord to deploy your parachute when this reaches 6,000 feet."

"And what if we don't pull it in time?" Madison asked, her voice quavering.

"Then you are in for a particularly painful landing," the Mysterious Man replied, tossing her a parachute. She caught it awkwardly, a look of terror in her eyes.

"You do have a little bit of wiggle room," Howard said quickly, shooting a glare at the Mysterious Man. "Theoretically, you could open it as low as seven hundred feet, but that's extremely risky. The higher up you can deploy, the better."

"We'll be over the ideal drop location in sixty seconds," Gearwire announced. "Get ready to jump."

Penn made his way to the cabin door, sliding it open. The wind tugged at the occupants of the cabin, and they quickly sat down to avoid being sucked out. Penn stayed by the door, clinging to the ceiling with his gecko-like fingers. Through the open door, Timothy could see the mountains below, crowned with several large, boxy structures.

Gearwire's voice came on over the intercom again. "We're over the drop zone now. It's time to jump."

Timothy gulped as he looked out at the mountains below him, the Mysterious Man's grim warning suddenly seeming very real.

Why did I sign up for this? he wondered, suddenly reconsidering his decision. For a long moment, no one moved, none of them wanting to be the first to jump.

"Guess I'll get us started," Crystal said finally. Then, before anyone could reply, she ran toward the open door and jumped out. As if Crystal's words had broken a spell over them, Timothy shrugged off his reservations and charged toward the door, Jewel and Aksell close behind. His stomach flip-flopped as he began free-falling, plummeting toward the earth below. The air rushed up toward his face, and he felt like he could hardly breathe. The feeling soon passed, however, replaced by one of pure exhilaration.

The altimeter on his wrist emitted a warning beep, and Timothy snapped back to reality, yanking the cord to deploy his parachute. He continued to fall, and for a brief moment, he worried that the parachute had failed. Then the chute caught the wind, and his speed began to slow, dropping his momentum to what seemed like a crawl in comparison.

As he drifted to the ground, he tugged on the guidelines, steering himself toward a wide, open space in the middle of one of the buildings. The others saw the movement and followed suit. Before long, Timothy was landing in the courtyard, skidding a bit as he slowly came to a stop. As the others touched down around him, he unbuckled his harness, looking around at the place where they had landed.

The building seemed to be made of massive cubes of stone, some of them as wide as twenty feet. The walls were plain and unadorned, making it difficult to tell where the natural mountain had ended and the giants had begun.

"Does anyone know what we're supposed to do with these now?" Aksell asked, nudging his parachute with his foot.

"We can stow them in my chest plate for now. We'll have to ask Gearwire about it later," Timothy said, opening the Infini-case that was built into his armor. The remarkable device had been created by Dr. Maddium to store an infinite number of items. At Timothy's urging, the scientist had adapted it into a chest plate.

"Do we have everyone?" Jewel asked. "Did we all make it?"

Timothy glanced around the courtyard, doing a quick headcount. *Quill's not here.*

Trying to keep the panic from his voice, he called out, "Quill? Where are you?"

"I'm up here!" Quill shouted back. Timothy turned toward his voice to see Quill perched atop a high stone wall, waving his arms over his head. "I miscalculated my trajectory a little, I think."

"Hang on, Quill," Madison said. "We'll figure out a way to get you down." She turned to the others. "Does anyone have any ideas?"

"We might be able to rig something up with our parachutes," Timothy said. "But that might take more time than we really have."

"Crystal and I could build a crystal ladder for him to climb down," Jewel said. "But that runs into the same problem."

"I think we're about to have a much bigger problem," Crystal said, staring at a tall, square archway in the back of the courtyard. "We've got company. And they don't seem too happy to see us." She pointed toward the archway, and Timothy turned to look.

A small group of giants burst into the room, all heavily armed with a variety of guns and matching ceremonial spears. They all wore grey uniforms, with a small, dark grey square stitched over their hearts. It was their height, however, that struck Timothy most.

They're a lot... shorter than I thought they would be, he thought, staring up at them. *There's no way any of these guys are taller than fourteen feet.*

The giant barked something in a language Timothy couldn't understand, and Timothy slowly reached into his chest plate, pulling out a shuriken. The guard repeated his question, and his two companions tightened their grip on their weapons.

"Aksell? Do you happen to know how to speak… whatever language it is that they're speaking?"

Aksell shook his head. "I'm afraid not. We might have to fight them."

"We don't need to fight them," Jewel said. "They're just doing their jobs. Any one of us would do the same thing if a group of heavily armed strangers parachuted into the middle of Kawts. They think we're invaders."

Timothy hesitated for a moment.

She's got a point.

But what if she's wrong?

"How do you know they aren't just going to take our weapons and throw us in a dungeon somewhere?" Timothy said, keeping his gaze squarely on the soldiers in front of him.

"I don't," Jewel said, dropping her voice to a whisper. "But even if they do, Crystal and I still have our powers, we still have Marathon's rings, and we still have Gearwire's radio beacon."

For a long moment, Timothy didn't move. Then he slipped his shuriken back into his chest plate, holding up his hands to show that he was no longer armed. Slowly, the others followed suit.

"We have an urgent message for your leader," Aksell said, over-enunciating each syllable. "It's very important that we see him right away."

The giants exchanged glances. They murmured amongst themselves for a few seconds, then one of them stepped forward.

"What is the message?" the man asked, his heavy Slavic accent nearly obscuring his words.

"It's very important," Aksell said. "It's for your ruler only."

Again, the guards conferred amongst themselves. Finally, the guard who had spoken turned toward them again.

"Come," he said. "No weapons."

"You'll take us to see your king?" Aksell asked.

"We will see," the giant said. The head guard muttered something into his ear, and the giant nodded. "Stay there," he said, looking up at Quill. "We will get you."

Quill nodded. "Take your time," he said, looking around at the featureless strip of wall he stood on. "I'm not going anywhere."

The giant grunted in acknowledgement. He held out his hand, and Timothy realized he was waiting for them to surrender their weapons. He sighed and slid his chest plate off, passing it over to the guard. One by one, the others followed suit, surrendering their weapons and gear until they all stood in their ordinary street clothes.

Jewel had better be right about this, Timothy thought, instinctively reaching for a shuriken before he could stop himself. *If things go poorly here, we're going to be in a pretty tricky spot.*

His fingers brushed up against the radio beacon in his pocket, and he allowed himself to relax a little.

It's a good thing they haven't searched us fully. We still have a way to call for backup if we need it.

"Come," the giant said again. "We will take you to the..." A frown flickered across the man's face as he struggled to recall the word. "...the place of waiting," he said at last.

Timothy took a hesitant step forward, and the guards parted, giving him a passage to walk through. The others followed, and the giants closed in around them, surrounding them in a bubble as they marched deeper into the building and deeper below the surface of the mountain.

I hope the radio beacon will reach this far down, Timothy thought, glancing up at the shadowed stone ceiling above them. *Better yet, I hope we won't have to use it at all.*

While Timothy was still thinking over their situation, the guards came to a stop in a small stone room. They opened the doors, ushering the Guardians of Kawts inside.

"Wait here," the guard said. "We will get you." With that, he turned and left, closing the doors behind him.

"Well, that could have gone a lot better," Crystal said.

"It could have gone a lot worse, too," Jewel said. "We just need to give them time to figure out what they're going to do. They'll be back here sooner or later."

Crystal snorted. "Sure. And then, after that, Ethos will invite us over for a tea party. You do realize we're basically prisoners here, right?"

"Just because they confiscated our weapons doesn't mean we're prisoners," Timothy said. "Most diplomats don't even *have* weapons."

"Tim, I don't think they believe we *are* diplomats," Aksell said. "We parachuted into the middle of their capital wearing full battle armor. They think we're invaders. Or spies." He shook his head. "We should have fought them when we had the chance."

"I hope Quill's okay," Madison said. "If they put him somewhere different from the rest of us, we might never find him."

"He'll be fine," Jewel said. "We're not going to leave Quill behind. If it comes down to it, we'll break him out ourselves."

As if summoned by her words, the door swung open, and Quill was tossed inside. As he rolled to his feet, the doors slid shut once more, sealing them inside. Quill dusted himself off, his irritation plain on his face.

"So much for a diplomatic welcome," he muttered. "We're trying to save the world, and they toss us in their underground dungeon."

"It's not quite a dungeon…" Jewel said.

"Might as well be," Crystal muttered under her breath.

"So, what do we do now?" Quill asked, turning to Timothy.

Timothy sighed. "We wait. There's not a whole lot else we can do. Just wait and hope they decide to give us a hearing before it's too late."

Reluctantly, the group sat down on the benches that lined the walls of the room, waiting for the guards to return. Timothy glanced over at Jewel, who was sitting opposite from him. For a moment, he considered crossing the room to talk to her, but he quickly dismissed the idea.

She's still pretty upset with me, he thought. *Not that I don't deserve it.*
He sighed.
I screwed up. I should go apologize.
He stood, but Aksell interrupted him.

"This is ridiculous," he said, getting up and beginning to pace animatedly around the room. "We've been here for almost half an hour! They aren't planning on coming back. I say we get out of here and look for the throne room ourselves."

"We need to be patient," Quill said. "We're asking to borrow one of their greatest national treasures. We can't just barge in and start making demands. Besides—we don't even know where their throne room is. We couldn't get there even if we wanted to."

"It can't be that hard to find," Aksell said. He glanced over at the door, and Timothy realized a second too late what he was planning.

"Aksell, wait!" he shouted, jogging forward to block his friend's path. Aksell sidestepped him and charged through the doors, leaving a stunned pair of guards on the other side.

"He's going to get us all killed," Crystal growled.

"We have to catch up with him," Quill said, running out the door after him.

Timothy sighed and ran out as well, trying to catch up to Quill. He felt a sudden gust of wind and glanced over his shoulder to see Jewel running past him, the yellow ring on her arm glowing brightly as it increased her speed. They darted around a corner, and Timothy heard Aksell shouting something as Jewel caught up to him.

Timothy slowed to a stop as he rounded the corner, almost running into another pair of guards. The guards reacted quickly, thrusting a spear at him. Timothy swerved out of the way, the agility-boosting ring on his own arm glowing. The guard readied his spear again, but this time, Madison grabbed it from his hands, jamming it into the wall. His partner threw his spear at her, but at the last second, it swerved out of the way, two large shards of translucent blue crystal embedded in the shaft. Crystal stood at the end of the hall, her palms raised toward the weapon.

The guards looked at each other, then turned and fled, disappearing down one of the corridors.

"They're going to think we're enemies for sure now," Quill said, a look of horror on his face.

Timothy said nothing, the implications of Aksell's actions unfolding in his head. He locked eyes with Jewel, and he could tell she was thinking the same thing.

"They'll never bring us to their leader now," she said. "The only way we'll be able to make our case is if we find him ourselves."

"Then we'd better start looking," Crystal said. "It's only a matter of time before those guards come back. And this time, they'll be ready for us."

Chapter 5

Timothy ducked his head around the corner, looking back at the others.

"This has to be the place," he said. "Huge set of double doors and a pair of sentries standing guard."

"So, what's the plan?" Quill asked.

"We charge them before they figure out what hit them," Aksell said.

Timothy shook his head. "We have to be a little-" he cut off abruptly as Aksell sprinted around the corner, throwing himself at the giant guards.

Before the guards could react, Aksell had knocked one of them to the ground, winding him. The other guard whipped his gun around to face him, but Aksell ducked under it, sweeping the man's legs out from under him.

"We'd better catch up with Aksell before he does something even more rash than he already has," Crystal said. Timothy nodded and ran out after Aksell, reaching him just as he pushed open the doors and charged into the middle of the giants' throne room. Like the rest of the building, it was unadorned and utilitarian, the throne being nothing more than a simple armchair.

The giant seated on the throne looked up sharply as they entered, he and his advisors freezing in place at the unexpected interruption. The soldiers in the room, however, suffered no such shock, and they ran toward the little band, their weapons raised.

"Wait!" Timothy said, raising his hands in surrender. "We don't want to fight you. We just need to speak to your leader. It's a matter of life and death."

The guards paused, waiting for their leader's instructions. Timothy could feel the tension in the air as the giant's leader contemplated their request.

"Let them speak," he said at last. "I will hear what they have to say. But I will warn you that any lie you tell will be detrimental to your health."

Timothy nodded. "Of course." He hesitated, unsure of where to begin.

"A group of aliens called the Orgwar are coming to invade Earth," Jewel said. "We need to borrow the Gravity Ray to fight them off."

The ruler of the giants' eyes narrowed. "The Orgwar? No one's heard anything from the Orgwar in centuries. Why would they be coming now?"

"We come from a city called Kawts," Quill said. "Until recently, it was run by an evil oligarchy called the Council. After we chased them out of Kawts, they took over Alpen while they searched for the Weather Belt. We managed to stop them from getting it, but their leader sent a message to the Orgwar asking for backup. They made this deal earlier that-"

"Enough!" the giant interrupted. "Why should we believe you? Even if this story is true, how do we know that you yourselves are not this 'council?'" Or that the Council themselves are not the heroes of this story? Are we supposed to surrender one of the most powerful weapons ever invented to you on the word of a total stranger?"

"The Council is gone," Madison said. "They were arrested in Alpen earlier this morning. President Draagetsew will vouch for us."

"President Draagetsew isn't here right now," the giant said. "But this much I will do—I will send a messenger to him to confirm what you say. Until then, you will be kept in secure custody."

"No! We don't have time for that!" Quill said. "The Orgwar will be here in less than three days! If we can't stop them, we're all doomed."

"Proof!" the giant shouted. "Show me proof, then, that you are who you say you are!"

There was a long moment of silence as they tried to figure out how to respond. Timothy glanced up at the guards and saw them adjust their weapons.

They aren't going to give us much longer to think, he realized. *We'll have to come up with something soon-*

"I can verify it," Aksell said, stepping to the front of the group. "My name is Aksell Deogol. My father is Ethos Deogol, the head of the Council."

Timothy's eyes grew wide as Aksell spoke. "It's not what it sounds like!" he said quickly. "He turned against the Council. He helped us defeat-"

"Spies!" the giant bellowed. "Your own words condemn you! Guards! Lock them up!"

The guards began to advance once more, slowly backing the Guardians of Kawts into a corner.

"What now?" Quill whispered.

"Do we fight?" Crystal asked.

Timothy glanced around at his friends, then back to the guards. "No," he said at last. "We don't have our weapons. There's no way we could fight our way out without someone being seriously injured."

He raised his hands in surrender, and the giants pounced on him, pinning his arms behind his back. The others were soon similarly subdued, and the guards dragged them away, depositing them in a dark cell beneath the castle. The only light in the room came from one small window, which looked out from the side of the mountain.

The giants slammed the door shut, bolting it securely behind them. As the sounds of their footsteps died away, Quill turned toward Aksell.

"This is all your fault! If you had just waited for the giants to come get us, we wouldn't be in this mess right now!"

"My fault? They wouldn't have believed us anyway!"

"We still had a chance at getting the Gravity Ray until you went and told them you were a member of the Council!" Quill shouted back. "And you know what? I think you still are! Admit it—you came on this mission with us to prevent us from stopping the Council's master plan!"

Aksell didn't move, his face torn between hurt and rage. Then his expression hardened, and he threw a wild punch at Quill. It glanced off Quill's cheek, but Quill shrugged it off, the blue ring on his arm glowing. He threw a punch of his own at Aksell, nailing him in the jaw and forcing him to stagger back.

At the sound of the fighting, Timothy, who had mostly been ignoring the argument up to this point, realized he had to intervene. With the help of Madison and Jewel, he managed to pull Aksell and Quill apart. Timothy looked from one to the other, unsure of what to say.

Finally, Jewel broke the silence. "We need to call Gearwire."

Timothy nodded, retrieving the radio beacon from his pocket. He flipped it on, waiting for the connection to go through.

"What happened?" Gearwire asked.

"It didn't go so well," Timothy replied. "The giants think we're Council spies, and they threw us in their dungeon. We need a jailbreak."

"I was afraid something like that might happen," Gearwire said. "The giants haven't truly trusted outsiders since the Robot War." There was silence for a moment, then Gearwire's voice came back on the line.

"Can you give us a better idea of where you are?"

"We're under the main part of the castle," Timothy replied, looking around at the small cell. "I don't really know much more than that.

We got pretty turned around…"

"There's a window," Jewel said, walking over to it. "It leads directly out to the side of the mountain."

There was silence for a moment, then Gearwire's voice came back on. "I see them. Stick something outside so I know which one is yours."

Madison nodded and reached for the window, slipping her hand through the bars. "I'm waving to you," she said. "Can you see me?"

"Got it," Gearwire said. "Now stand back. Get as far away from the outside wall as you can."

Timothy hurried backwards, pressing himself against the side wall. "We're ready," he said as the others joined him.

"Incoming!"

Through the window, they could hear the whine of the engine as the ship drew closer. There was a loud thud, and the wall of their cell buckled, cracks spiderwebbing through the bricks. The wall stayed up for a moment longer, then began to crumble, revealing the nose of the ship. The ship slowly began to pull back, leaving a pile of rubble in the opening.

Timothy stared at the hole, his mouth hanging open. "That was risky," he stammered at last.

"The hull of this old ship is reinforced with invincium," Gearwire said. "It's a trick I picked up from an old pirate. Now let's see if we can get your gear back."

The ship pulled up alongside the hole, and the cabin door slid open. Samuel leaned out of the doorway, Gearwire's glue gun in his hand.

"Glad to see you're all right!" he called, a massive grin on his face. He let go of the doorway, holding the gun with both hands. He took aim and fired at the door of the cell, watching as the specially formulated, superheated glue ate through the metal.

The Golden Knight and Penn appeared in the doorway behind him, ready to jump across the gap. But before they could, something slammed into the ship, throwing them backwards into the cabin.

"Gearwire! What's going on?" Timothy shouted into the radio beacon.

"They're shooting at us," Gearwire said. "I think I can lose them-" He jerked the ship to one side, but he was too late to avoid the second missile. It crashed into the ship, sending it into a tailspin. The ship corkscrewed into the valley below, crashing to the ground with a massive explosion.

Timothy stood in the hole in the wall, staring in disbelief at the place where the ship had been seconds before. He felt numb, his feet rooted to the floor.

"Wha- What just happened?" Quill stammered.

"They're gone," Crystal said, her voice quiet.

"Maybe they survived the crash," Madison said, taking the radio beacon from Timothy's trembling hand. "Gearwire! Gearwire! Do you read me?"

Nothing but static came from the other end of the line. The color drained from Madison's face, and she fell to her knees, the radio beacon slipping from her fingers. Crystal knelt down beside her, trying to console her.

"No," Madison whispered. "No, it can't- not like this-"

"Just because the radio is down doesn't mean they didn't make it," Jewel said. "We need to go down to the crash site. We might still be able to help the survivors."

"No," Timothy said, tearing his gaze away from the crash at last.

"What do you mean, no?" Jewel demanded. The look in her eye made it plain that she thought Timothy had gone mad.

"We don't have time. Gearwire knew something like this might happen. He told me that if anything ever happened to him, we needed to continue on with the mission. No coming back for him." His voice caught in his throat. He turned to face Jewel, tears pooling in his eyes.

"There's nothing we can do for them. But we can still save the rest of the planet."

"How are we going to do that?" Aksell said. "Without the ship, we have no way of getting to the rest of the devices. And without Gearwire, we don't know where any of them are."

"I-I don't know," Timothy said, trying to compose his thoughts enough to think of a way forward. "I don't think Gearwire expected he'd be killed so quickly. But we have to try. And I'd rather die trying to save the world than trapped in this cell."

There was silence for a long moment as each of them tried to process what had happened.

"If we're really going to do this, we'll need to act fast," Crystal said at last. "And we all have to be in agreement."

"I suppose it's worth a shot," Aksell said. "Quill?"

"It's our *only* shot," Quill said, shaking his head.

Timothy looked at Jewel. For a long moment, she said nothing. "I still think we should go back to help whoever's left," she said, shaking her head. "Some of them might have survived the crash." She took a long, shuddering breath. "But either way, we're going to have to get out of this cell."

"When they were bringing me in, I saw where they were taking our gear," Quill said. "If we can get back to the original room we were in, I might be able to find it from there."

Timothy nodded. "That's better than nothing."

"Crystal and I will take the lead," Jewel said, glancing over at her sister. Crystal stood, helping Madison to her feet.

"Quill? You and Madison should hold up the rear," Crystal said. She made eye contact with Quill, who nodded and made his way to Madison's side.

Slowly and carefully, the little band filed out of their cell, making their way through the halls of the castle. None of them said a word.

I can't believe they're gone, Timothy thought as he followed Crystal and Jewel deeper into the labyrinthine corridors of the castle. The picture of Samuel standing in the doorway of Gearwire's ship came into his mind, and he shook his head.

They were all alive just a few minutes ago. And now they're gone, just like that. His mind drifted to memories of their deceased friends, recalling all that they had been through together.

It was bad enough when I thought the Council had killed Samuel, he thought. *But now he really is dead. And so is Gearwire. And the Mysterious Man. And Howard-*

Timothy almost stopped dead in his tracks as the realization hit him. *Howard was Madison's dad,* he remembered suddenly. He glanced over at Madison. She looked lost, staring blankly ahead as Quill did his best to pull her along.

Despite his own grief, Timothy felt a wave of sorrow for his friend. *This is not how the world is supposed to work.*

"We're almost there," Quill whispered from behind him. "I think it's the next door on the left."

The little group came to a stop in front of the door in question, and Timothy reached out and jiggled the handle.

"Locked."

He turned back toward the others to see Madison pushing her way to the front of the group. She took a step back, then threw herself at the door. Her foot smashed through the timbers, the red ring on her arm glowing brightly. She pulled her foot out of the hole she had created and reached inside, unlocking the door.

"That works," Timothy said, his concern for Madison only growing. He stepped inside the room, realizing at once that Quill had been correct.

At least one thing has gone according to plan today, he thought, picking up his chest plate and slipping it on. The others followed suit, and after only a few short minutes, they had retrieved all of their gear.

"Now what?" Aksell asked. "We might have our stuff back, but we still don't have a way to get the fail-safe devices. And in light of the present circumstances, I don't think the giants are going to tell us where the Gravity Ray is. We're stuck."

"All we need to worry about right now is getting out of this castle," Jewel said. "If we try to work out the whole thing at once, we'll never get anywhere. We have to trust that God will show us the way forward."

"Like how he's been helping us out this far?" Aksell retorted.

Timothy winced at his friend's tone. He had had the same thought himself, but it still felt jarring to hear someone say it aloud.

"Shut up, Aksell," Quill snapped, elbowing Aksell in the side.

A melancholy silence settled over the group.

There's got to be something we can do, Timothy thought. *It can't end like this.* A thought struck him, and his eyes widened.

"Aksell!"

"What? I haven't done anything!"

Timothy waved his friend's retort aside. "Do you remember back before we got involved in all this? You had a biography from Samuel…"

"… About the giants who lived in the north," Aksell finished, realization dawning on him. "You think this is the place they were talking about?"

"Do you know of any other giants?"

"You might be onto something."

"Would one of you care to explain to the rest of the class?" Crystal said.

Timothy nodded. "In this book, there were references to a powerful relic hidden by the first leader of the giants."

"Did it say where it was?" Quill asked.

Timothy exchanged glances with Aksell.

"It was somewhat vague about that," Aksell said after a moment's thought. "All I remember is it stressing how incredibly average the building was."

"So, we're looking for the most average building in town?" Crystal said. "That sounds like a wild goose chase if I've ever heard one."

"That wasn't the only thing it said, though," Timothy said. "The building was close to the city wall—I remember the author describing the sun rising over the wall from the vantage point of the device's hiding place."

"That'll still take hours to search," Crystal said. "Even if we knew where the city wall was a couple hundred years ago."

"It's still there," Madison said, speaking for the first time since her father's death. "I saw it… from the…"

Ship, Timothy finished silently. A heavy silence fell over the group as the reality of what they had lost struck home once again.

"If the wall is still there, I can do a reconnaissance run," Jewel said at last. "I've got the speed ring. I can figure out if there's still a building here that matches that description."

Timothy nodded slowly, trying to force himself not to think about the danger that Jewel would be running.

"Do it. We'll wait for you here."

* * *

"I think I found it," Jewel said, returning to the storage room once more. "This way." Before anyone could object, she started off again, leaving the startled remnant of the Guardians of Kawts to try to keep up with her.

Jewel maintained a rapid pace as she wound her way through the corridors of the castle, only coming to a stop when she reached the outer gate.

"We need to do something about those gate guards," she whispered as the others began to catch up.

Quill lifted his stun rifle. "I think I can handle that," he said. "Just tell me when."

Timothy glanced around the courtyard, scanning for any additional guards. He glanced over at Jewel, who nodded.

"Now!" he hissed. "Quickly!"

Quill popped out from behind the wall, firing his stun rifle as fast as he could. His blasts hit the gatekeepers, causing them to spasm and fall to the ground.

As soon as they hit the ground, Jewel sprinted toward the gate, throwing it open. The hinges let out an ear-piercing shriek, and Timothy winced. Moving quickly to avoid being spotted, the group took off down the cobbled street, Jewel in the lead.

They took a roundabout route through the city, meandering down a network of narrow side streets to avoid being detected by the castle guards. Though they kept clear of the main roads, they still ran into giant civilians fairly frequently. The simply clad giants stared in disapproving puzzlement at their colorful clothing, but for the most part, they kept to themselves.

Before long, Timothy emerged into a much wider space, watching a guard enter an ordinary-looking house. As he watched, the guard reappeared, taking off at a brisk walk back toward the castle. Timothy hesitated, part of him wanting to follow the man who was leaving. But a momentary flash of color from the closing door made up his mind for him.

Whoever's in there looks like they're wearing the same kind of uniform as the other guards. This has to be it.

"Are you sure this is the place?" Aksell asked, studying the building skeptically. "It just looks like an ordinary house to me.

"This 'ordinary house' is being manned by Velikanovi soldiers," Jewel said. "If this isn't the place, I doubt we're going to find it."

"If you're really sure about this, I guess we'll just have to go up there ourselves," Quill said. "Let's go."

Timothy nodded, crossing the street and climbing up the front steps of the house. He stood in front of the door, about to push it open, but he hesitated.

What if we're wrong? If someone's really living here, they'll call the police, and we'll be back in the dungeon before the end of the day.

Before he could gather the courage to commit, Quill pushed past him and swung open the door, his stun rifle in his hand. The instant the door opened, Timothy knew immediately that his suspicion had been correct.

Chapter 6

Four giants sat around a table, eating some kind of bright red soup. All four of them wore the uniform of the royal guards. Through an open door, Timothy caught a glimpse of two others asleep in a bunk room.

The giants leapt to their feet at the disturbance, reaching for their weapons. But Quill was already firing, taking out the first of the giants before he could even get his gun out of his holster. The giant's partner reached for a radio at his waist, but Timothy lunged for him, knocking the radio from his hand with one end of his staff and rendering the giant unconscious with the other.

In the neighboring room, the other two guards scrambled to their feet, but Crystal and Jewel were already on their way to meet them. Timothy scanned the room for another opponent, but the other guards seemed to have already been handled by the rest of his team. A flash of red caught his eye, and Timothy turned to see Madison punch one of the guards in the face, the full force of the red ring behind it. The giant's head snapped back, and he fell to the floor, unconscious.

Timothy frowned.

A hit like that could easily cause permanent damage, he realized. As Madison continued to punch the fallen giant, Timothy detached a shuriken from the holster on the side of his leg and threw it toward her, the weapon whizzing by a few inches in front of her face.

Madison jerked back, and Timothy shook his head. "That's enough, Madison," he said, hoping she couldn't hear the tremor in his voice. "He's already unconscious."

Madison's eyes widened, and she slowly leaned back, her hands shaking. She looked at the giant's face and quickly stood up.

"I didn't mean to-" She shook her head. "I almost killed that man."

"The giants just killed your father," Aksell said. "It makes sense that you're upset."

Madison shook her head. "No. That was… more than upset." The glow from the red ring on her arm began to fade, catching her attention for the first time. "I don't think I can be trusted with this right now," she said, sliding the ring from her arm and handing it to Quill.

"The rest of the guards are taken care of," Jewel said, emerging from the bunkroom, where the remaining giants were now encased in blue crystal. She looked over at the rest of the group, her eyes narrowed. "What's going on here?"

"Nothing," Quill said quickly. "Everything's fine."

"We don't know how long we have until someone comes looking for these guys," Timothy said, trying to take control of the situation. "We'd better keep moving."

"Help me drag the rest of them into the bunk room," Crystal said. "That should keep them contained for a while." The others quickly complied, leaving the unconscious giants in a heap on the bunkroom floor. Crystal shut and locked the door, and she and Jewel sealed it shut with a layer of crystal.

"Where to now?" Crystal asked, looking over at Timothy. "You didn't happen to discover where in this building the Gravity Ray is, did you?"

Timothy shook his head. "This is as far as I've gotten. But my best guess would be that we're looking for the basement."

"Sounds good to me," Crystal said. "Lead the way."

The group wandered through the house, searching for the stairs to the basement. The building wasn't terribly large, and it only took them a few minutes to find what they were looking for. But as they emerged into the basement of the house, Timothy's heart sank.

There's nothing down here but a pair of water heaters, he realized, looking around the large empty space.

"Maybe they're storing it upstairs," Jewel said. "I'll go check."

Before Timothy could object, she took off back in the direction they had come, the yellow ring on her arm drastically increasing her speed.

"It might still be down here," Quill said. "Maybe it's in a hidden compartment somewhere."

Aksell took a slow look around the room. "If there's a secret door here, it's very well hidden," he said. "I don't see any obvious cracks in the walls. Or the floor, for that matter."

"Maybe it's just hidden really well," Quill said. "I mean, without that book you and Timothy read, we never would have guessed it was in this building."

"It's worth a shot," Crystal said.

"Spread out," Timothy said. "Start tapping the walls and floor. Keep an eye out for anything that seems out of the ordinary. A hollow spot, or a loose tile or something."

The remaining Guardians of Kawts fanned out across the room, searching for any clue on where to go next. After a few minutes, Jewel returned, confirming that the device they were seeking wasn't on the upper floors of the house.

They had been searching for several minutes more when Quill called out, "Guys? I think I found something."

Timothy turned toward the sound of his friend's voice. Quill stood beside one of the water heaters, staring at it intently.

"What is it?"

"This heater's fake," Quill said. He rapped on it with his knuckles. "See? It's hollow. And there's a hinge that runs all the way down the side."

"Can you get it open?" Jewel asked, jogging over to him.

Quill tugged at a crack in the seam of the heater. "Locked." He stared at the false heater for a moment, then slid Madison's ring onto his arm. He tried once more to pull the door open, this time meeting with considerably more success. Slowly, he began to peel it open, the metal making a painful grating sound as he did.

Once he had made an opening large enough for a person to fit through, he stopped, listening intently. They stood in silence for a moment, waiting to see if anyone had heard. When several seconds passed without any signs of an alarm, the group turned their attention to the interior of the false water heater. Back behind where the door had once been, there was now a ladder, extending into the darkened catacombs below.

Aksell let out a low whistle. "I think we've found it," he said. "If this isn't the entrance to some kind of treasury, I don't know what is."

"Then we'd better get down there before someone comes to investigate," Crystal said, climbing into the tube. She vanished from sight, and a few minutes later, they heard her voice call up from the bottom.

"The coast is clear," she called up. "For now, anyway."

Timothy nodded and climbed into the water heater, his boots clanging off the metal rungs. He dropped down the last few feet, landing silently beside Crystal. He heard the echoes of footsteps approaching, and he whirled around. The hallway was empty. Before long, the footsteps began to recede.

"Did you hear that too, or was that just me?" Timothy whispered.

"I thought the guards were right around the corner when I first got down here," Crystal said. "But it's just echoes. This place seems like it was designed to carry sound."

"If we can hear them, they can probably hear us," Jewel said, landing beside the pair. "They probably already know we're here."

"Then we'll just have to move fast," Timothy said. "And stay as quiet as possible. No talking unless it's absolutely necessary."

Timothy turned toward the twisting labyrinth, taking a deep breath to calm himself before stepping off into the maze. As he walked, he let one hand drag along the wall, trying to avoid getting lost inside. The footsteps of his friends behind him sounded painfully loud, causing him to wince.

Hopefully, the guards are just as confused about where the sound is coming from as we are, he thought, hearing the echo of the guards' footsteps coming from somewhere down the passage.

On the other hand, they might already know where we are. If they have security cameras, they might already be-

"I think I found something," Aksell hissed behind him, forcing Timothy to put his concerns aside. Aksell pointed up to a small carving on the wall above their heads.

Above our *heads, but right at eye level for the giants,* Timothy realized.

"What is it?" Jewel asked.

"It looks like a coin," Timothy said.

"Do you think it could help us find the treasury?" Quill asked.

"There aren't any arrows or directions or anything like that," Timothy said. "It's definitely a clue, but I don't know what-"

"It's a button," Madison interrupted. "See the gap that runs along the outside?"

"She's right," Crystal said, inspecting the coin for herself. She lifted her hands toward the carving, and a sliver of crystal shot out from her palm, stabbing into the coin. The coin slid out of sight, and a nearby section of the wall slid open, revealing a large room, filled with shelves of sturdy square boxes.

This is it, Timothy thought. *It has to be.*

He took a deep breath and followed the others into the treasury. As soon as he stepped inside, the door slid shut behind them, leaving them in darkness for a moment before the lights flickered on.

"We don't have much time before they find us here," Jewel said, pointing up to a security camera. "We have to move fast."

Timothy moved over to one of the boxes. A neat label was mounted on the front of the box, written in the giant's language. He pulled off the lid and peered inside. A pile of ancient coins greeted him, and he frowned.

This is going to be like searching for a needle in a haystack.

"Jewel? Can you and Crystal try to barricade the door? We're going to need as much time as you can give us."

"On it," Jewel said, already beginning to seal the door shut with her powers.

Timothy moved on to the next box, tossing the lid to the floor beside him. Even before he saw what was inside, he was already reaching for the lid of the next box. On the other walls, the others were already doing the same.

They had been searching for ten minutes when a loud creaking sound suddenly echoed through the chamber. Timothy turned toward the door to see the gears turning, straining to overcome the crystal that bound it shut.

Jewel abandoned the box she was searching and ran over to the door, hurrying to reinforce the crystal.

Timothy glanced over at her.

Jewel's powers alone won't keep them out for long, he realized.

"Quill!" he shouted, running toward the door. "I need the red ring!" Quill nodded and tossed the ring to Timothy. "Everyone else, keep searching! Jewel and I will hold the door!"

Timothy slid the ring onto his arm, bracing himself up against the door. The door stopped for a moment, held in check by their efforts. Then the pressure on the door redoubled, sending cracks snaking through the crystal. The door creaked, and Timothy could tell it was on the verge of opening. He gritted his teeth and shoved back, the red ring glowing like a tiny star.

"Have you found the Gravity Ray yet?" Timothy shouted.

"Not yet," Quill said. "But we're getting close!"

"No, we aren't!" Crystal shouted back. "We need more time!"

Timothy exchanged glances with Jewel. Blue light continued to stream from her palms, reinforcing the crystal seal. But already, the color had begun to drain from her face. It was only a matter of time before the strain of using her powers in this way became too much.

"We'll never make it if we keep trying to hold the door shut," Timothy said.

"What do you suggest, then?" Jewel snapped, gritting her teeth as she redoubled her efforts.

"We let them get in," Timothy said. "And then we trap them in the doorway."

Jewel glanced up at the door, then back at Timothy. Underneath the sound of the giants trying to force their way into the room, they could just barely hear the commotion behind them as the others frantically tried to find the Gravity Ray.

"Okay," Jewel said, lowering her hands. "What's the plan?"

"When they get into the room, encase them in crystal. That should keep the doorway blocked," Timothy said, popping a pair of shurikens off into his hands. "I'll take care of anyone who gets past you." He stood back beside Jewel, waiting as the cracks spread and the door began to inch open.

"I'm going to dissolve the crystal," Jewel said, her eyes fixed on the door. "Ready?"

Timothy nodded. "Ready."

"Opening the door in three… two… ONE!"

Before Timothy's eyes, the crystal began to melt, leaving behind a bluish residue. The door swung open, and he threw a shuriken toward the opening, sending the first of the guards staggering back into his comrades. Before they could react, the first row of giants was encased in crystal. The remaining guards fell back, trying to figure out how to proceed.

"How's the Gravity Ray coming?" Timothy shouted back, keeping his eyes on the guards in front of him.

"Still looking!" Aksell shouted. "They really need to label these boxes better!"

Suddenly, Timothy heard a shout from Madison. In spite of himself, he turned around to see what had happened. Madison held a ray gun in her hand, waving it above her head.

"I think I found it!" she shouted. She twirled a dial on the side of the gun and fired it at a pile of boxes. The boxes floated up into the air, coming to rest on the ceiling.

"This is great!" Quill shouted, hugging her.

"We're still stuck in here," Crystal said.

"Not for long," Madison said, unclipping one of her ravioli-shaped grenades from her belt and attaching it to the wall. Even from where he stood, Timothy could feel the heat emanating from the blast. The smoke dissipated quickly, revealing a gaping hole in the treasury wall that led into an adjacent passage.

A harsh grating sound brought Timothy's attention back to the situation at the door. The chunk of crystal that encased the guards was slowly inching forward into the treasury. Timothy glanced over at Jewel. "Go with the others," he said. "I'll hold them off until you get out."

Jewel shook her head. "We leave together or not at all."

Timothy hesitated a moment, then nodded.

"On three."

"One!" Timothy shouted. "Two!"

"Three!" they both shouted at the same time. The guards burst into the room, and they turned and ran for the exit. Timothy looked over his shoulder at their pursuers and threw several shurikens at them. Most of them went wide of their targets, but the giants slowed down a little, regardless.

"The guards are right behind us!" Jewel shouted as they emerged into the passageway.

"See if you can find another way out!" Timothy shouted.

Jewel nodded and increased her speed, quickly outpacing the others. They continued to run in the direction Jewel had disappeared in, hoping desperately that they weren't running toward a dead end.

Timothy heard an echo of gunfire from somewhere in the maze, and he felt his blood run cold.

Not Jewel, he thought. *Not now. I—WE need her.*

He breathed a sigh of relief when Jewel reappeared a few moments later, looking disheveled but alive. He almost ran over to her, but at the last moment, he stopped himself, wiping the emotion from his face.

"There's a way out straight ahead," Jewel said. "But it's guarded. And they have guns."

"With a little luck, we should be fine," Crystal said, pulling a smoke bomb from her pocket. "As long as we move fast. As soon as this thing goes off, sprint for the exit."

Aksell glanced at the device nervously. "Are you sure that will work? They're still heavily armed and we'll be completely unprotected..."

"These smoke grenades did a pretty good job covering our escapes from the Council," Crystal said. "For a number of years."

Aksell shifted uncomfortably. "Fair enough."

Timothy glanced over at his friend, his eyes narrowed.

I can't tell if he's nervous about the giants or about the Council, he thought. The memory of Quill and Aksell's fight in the giants' dungeon came back to him, and he frowned. *I hope Aksell is ready for this.*

"Enough talk," Crystal said. "The longer we wait, the more time they have to prepare for us." She set off at a jog toward the entrance, the others following close behind. As she neared the last turn, she rolled the device toward the giants. A thick smoke filled the area, and they charged past the giants. As Quill started up the ladder, Timothy realized with growing dread that the smoke was beginning to dissipate.

"Climb faster," he hissed. "I'll hold them off until you guys get out."

No one responded, all their energies focused on climbing the ladder. Timothy ducked into the space just as the guards opened fire, bullets pinging off the walls around him. A few of the bullets found their mark, but they ricocheted off his armor, leaving him unscathed. Timothy scrambled up the ladder, almost running into Jewel. They tumbled out into the basement just as the giants started shooting up the tube after them. They sprinted through the empty house and out into the street, escaping into the city.

Only when the city had shrunk into the distance behind them did Timothy finally dare to slow down. He flopped down on the ground, breathing heavily. The others joined him, trying to catch their breath. Only Quill seemed to still be ready to go, although Timothy noticed that the ring on his arm was glowing brightly.

As Timothy began to catch his breath, the thrill of victory ebbed away, replaced by the reminder of what had happened to the rest of their team. One by one, the others fell silent as well, their grief returning in full force.

What do we do now? Timothy wondered, looking around at what remained of the Guardians of Kawts. *We've already lost all but five of us, and we've only managed to retrieve the first fail-safe device. We don't stand a chance.*

For a long time, no one spoke.

Finally, Aksell started, "I know you are all sad over what happened to your friends-"

"I watched my father get blown out of the sky," Madison interrupted, her tone sharp.

"You're not the only one who lost their father today," Aksell shot back. "My father might still technically be alive, but today I learned just how much of a monster he is. And then when I tried to do the right thing and stop him-"

His voice broke, and Timothy realized that his friend was on the verge of tears.

"I even went to visit him after the dust settled. And he told me that I was a disgrace to the family name and that he never wanted to see me again." He turned to look at Madison, pain etched across his face. "This has been a pretty awful day for all of us. But we have to put that aside for right now. We might have lost people we care about today. But if we don't figure out how we're going to stop the Orgwar, we're going to lose everyone else, too."

"Aksell's right," Timothy said at last. "As callous as it might seem, right now, the most important thing is stopping the Orgwar. We can properly mourn the others after we do that."

Timothy glanced over at Jewel, hoping that she would back him up. To his relief, she nodded slowly.

"So, what now?" Crystal asked. "We have the Gravity Ray, but we're stuck. We have no idea where the rest of the devices are, let alone how on earth we're going to get there in time."

"I think we need to go to the crash site," Jewel said. "Some of the others might have survived. And if Gearwire or Jeff is among them, we might still be able to find the locations of the other devices."

Timothy shook his head. "We don't have time for that. It could take us hours just to get to the crash site." He glanced at the others before continuing. "Before we left Alpen, Gearwire told me that if anything happened to him, I was to make sure that we completed the mission. He explicitly told me not to go back for him, no matter what happened."

He looked up at his companions. "Gearwire has been our leader for a long time," he said. "We owe it to him to honor his last command."

"We still don't know where the other devices are," Crystal said. "Either way, I don't see a way forward here."

"I think I might know where one of them is," Aksell said. "The scientist who built the attack drones and the evaporation cannon for the Council—his country has one of them. Not sure how much good that will do us, though."

Timothy and Jewel locked eyes, both of them coming to the same conclusion.

We don't have a chance, Timothy realized. *But we can't let them know that.*

Slowly, he got to his feet. He stared up at the sun, gauging its position in the sky. He turned toward the south, his face settling into the same look of grim determination he had come to associate with Gearwire.

"We'd better start walking," he said. "We have a long journey ahead of us."

Chapter 7

Orgwarian Flagship
Orbiting the Planet Threye

The Orgwarian High Command piloted his small ship toward the Orgwarian flagship, seething. He glowered back at the landing pad where the Defender stood, watching helplessly as High Command escaped.

I've had entire planets bend to my commands, destroyed anyone who got in my way. And now this insolent earth-man has forced me to retreat. The Orgwar have not fled in battle since the days of disgraced Admiral Groor!

The escape pod hissed as it docked with the flagship, and High Command waited only a moment before storming onto the ship.

"Get the men ready for battle!" he shouted. "And set a course for Earth! The Defender will pay dearly for what he has done!"

* * *

Timothy trudged through the snow, glancing up at the sun overhead. It had been well over an hour since they had started off over the mountains, and his legs ached.

We're never going to make it, he thought. *We'll be lucky just to get two fail-safe devices before the Orgwar arrive.* Despair threatened to overwhelm him, and he quickly turned his thoughts elsewhere. His mind drifted to the events that had led up to their mission, and before long, he found himself thinking about Quill and Aksell's fight in the dungeon.

Even after everything that had happened, the memory still brought a frown to his face.

Quill isn't normally the sort to pick a fight, he thought. *Something must have been bothering him even before-* He broke off, not willing to finish the thought.

I need to talk to him.

Timothy pushed his way to where Quill was, several meters in front of everyone else. He spotted the blue ring glowing faintly on his friend's arm and knew immediately how Quill still seemed to have so much energy.

Brushing such thoughts aside, he said, "Quill? We need to talk."

Quill turned back to face him. "About what?"

"You started a fistfight with Aksell in the dungeon. Even before things went sideways."

Quill flinched, biting his lip. "I shouldn't have done that," he said. "It was uncalled for. Aksell's been through just as much crap as the rest of us. Maybe more, considering that Ethos is his dad." He paused. "I guess-"

He sighed, falling silent for a moment before continuing. "I guess a part of me just blamed Aksell for everything that happened. And I don't mean the mission. Me getting turned into a Blank, all the murders that the Council has done—and I know it's not really Aksell's fault. He wasn't even a part-time Council member yet when most of that stuff happened." He looked up at Timothy. "I guess I resented the Council a lot more than I thought I did. And I took it out on Aksell."

"You have every right to hate the Council," Timothy said. "They turned you into a brainwashed slave for years!"

Quill was silent for a long time before responding. "I'm not so sure about that, Tim," he said at last.

"Quill, they're the Council. If there was ever someone it's okay to hate, it would be them. After everything they've done? All the people they've killed?"

"You don't have to agree with me, Tim," Quill said. "But the more I think about everything that's happened recently, the more convinced I am that God would want me to show mercy to the Council if the situation arises. Just like the bridge trap back in the Weather Belt complex."

Timothy was silent, and Quill added, "I should go apologize to Aksell."

He dropped back toward the middle of the pack, leaving Timothy alone in front.

And I should apologize to Jewel, he realized. *I hurt her, and now we're hardly speaking to each other. If we don't address it, it's going to tear us apart.*

Timothy glanced up at the mountainous terrain ahead of them, gauging what was to come. He sighed.

"We might as well take a break here for now," he said, sitting down on a nearby rock. The others followed his example, too exhausted and shell-shocked to speak.

As he looked out at the faces of his friends, a feeling of hopelessness washed over him. Madison had hardly said a word since the ship exploded, slowly but surely distancing herself from the rest of the group. Aksell had been strangely quiet too, although Timothy had some hope that Quill's apology would help.

Timothy looked at the snow glistening on the peaks of the mountains and realized with sudden clarity that unless something changed soon, they would be lucky to survive even until the Orgwar arrived.

"Why does it matter, anyway?" he whispered. "Is there really that much of a difference between dying now and dying during the invasion?"

I suppose I'll finally know for sure whether Gearwire and Henry were right about this heaven stuff.

"Do you hear that?" Crystal asked suddenly, interrupting Timothy's thoughts.

Timothy looked up, straining to figure out what she was talking about. He started to shake his head, but the sound stopped him—the soft crunching of footsteps on the snow. Timothy was back on his feet in an instant, slipping one of his shurikens into his hand. A giant dressed in a simple robe stepped around the pile of rocks, a look of astonishment on his face. He said something in what Timothy took to be the giants' native tongue, then, seeing their confusion, switched to English.

"What are you doing way out here?" the giant asked. "You all look exhausted! Come! My cell is just a short distance up the mountain. You can rest there."

"We've seen quite enough cells for one day, I think," Aksell said.

The giant looked puzzled for a moment, then realization dawned on him. "You misunderstand me. I am a hermit. My quarters are called a cell."

Timothy looked around at the others, but they offered no indication of their opinions of the strange giant. "We're only passing through," he said. "We're on an urgent mission."

"We could use a place to rest for a while," Jewel said, staring intensely at Timothy.

Timothy sighed, clipping his shuriken back into place. "If you have somewhere we could warm up for a bit, that would be... great."

The hermit nodded and began to walk among the group, helping them to their feet and picking up their gear that they had let fall when they stopped. Timothy watched him from a distance, finding himself less and less apprehensive about the giant's arrival.

Maybe we can just live out the rest of our lives here, he thought. *Surely the Orgwar wouldn't bother attacking an isolated monastery.*

Once they were all standing, the giant led them up around the rocks. True to his word, the hermit's dwelling was only a short distance away from where they had been resting, taking them a little under fifteen minutes to arrive.

The monastery was an impressive building, towering over the travelers. The walls were white, but the roofs were covered in teal tiles, matching the color of the tops of the garlic-shaped towers. Yet despite the grandeur, it was clear that the monastery had seen better days. In many places, the paint had peeled away, and one or two of the magnificent spires seemed about ready to collapse.

The giant noticed Timothy inspecting the building and gave a wry smile. "The Monastery of St. Sandoval isn't quite as sound as it used to be," he said. "There used to be an entire regiment of monks living here. They kept the building in remarkable shape. But now that it's just me, some of the maintenance has been lacking."

"As long as it's still structurally sound," Timothy said, glancing nervously at the leaning tower. To this, the monk made no reply, ushering them into the building.

"Let me show you to the bedrooms," he said, starting off down one of the corridors. "They're a little dusty, but they'll have to do, I'm afraid."

Timothy shook his head. "We can't stay," he said, reassuring himself as much as the hermit. "Just give us somewhere warm to sit down for a few minutes, and then we'll get out of your hair."

"At least allow me to make you a meal before you leave," the monk said.

Timothy opened his mouth to disagree, but the nearly forgotten pangs of hunger chose that moment to return in full force.

When was *the last time we had a meal, anyway?* he wondered. His mind drifted back to the feast they had begun in Alpen before Dr. Maddium brought the news of the invasion.

It's hard to believe that was this morning.

"Well, if you won't go to the cells, then wait here while I go make up some soup," the giant said, apparently taking Timothy's lack of protest for agreement. The others had already taken him up on his offer, sitting down at random across the floor. Timothy nodded wearily and sat down with his back to the wall. Despite his vigilance, the events of the day caught up with him, and he dropped off to sleep.

* * *

Timothy woke up with a start, looking around the room in terror. As he realized where he was, his fear subsided somewhat, although a glance out the window told him he had been asleep for far too long. He slowly got to his feet, checking to see whether any of the others were awake. His stomach growled, and he remembered the giant's promise of food. He hesitated for a moment, then started off down the hallway he had seen the hermit disappear into.

"Ah! You're awake!" he heard a voice call from an adjacent passage. "I was just about to come check on you."

"How long have I been out?" Timothy asked.

"Not more than a few hours," the hermit said. "Though I think you would have slept better in a real bed."

Timothy shook his head in frustration. "We weren't supposed to fall asleep," he said. "We're on a very time-sensitive mission. We don't have the time to waste."

The hermit frowned. "Considering that I found you wandering in the mountains, it seems safe to say that your mission has gone awry."

Timothy hesitated for a moment, then nodded.

"I'll tell you what," the hermit said. "You go wake up your friends and meet me in the room at the end of this hallway. I'll go warm up the soup. Then you can tell me all about this mission of yours."

Timothy did as the giant instructed, and soon, what remained of the Guardians of Kawts stood clustered near the stone benches around a table in what had evidently once been the refectory.

"I'm glad to see you're all awake," the hermit said, setting the steaming bowls of broth in front of them. He took a seat near the middle of the table and gestured for the others to do likewise. "Now, if you would explain to me this 'urgent mission' of yours, you may find that I can provide you with useful counsel."

Timothy hesitated for a moment, but before he could consult the others, Jewel began to speak, telling the giant everything that had happened to them since their departure from Kawts a month earlier. Timothy winced as she got to the part about their theft of the Gravity Ray, wondering how the giant would respond.

To his surprise, the giant seemed almost mournful. "You have all been through a lot more than people your age should have to go through," he said at last, shaking his head slightly. "And to lose the rest of your team right after something like that… you must have been close to them, weren't you?"

Timothy nodded slowly, memories of all that he and the Guardians of Kawts had been through rising to the surface. "They've all saved our lives on multiple occasions," he said at last. "In more ways than one," he added, remembering how instrumental Gearwire and Samuel had been in his personal battle against the Council. Tears pooled in his eyes, and he turned away from the giant, swallowing the lump in his throat.

"Gearwire and his team saved Jewel and I from being turned into the Council's weapons," Crystal said. "And they saved Quill and Madison from being brainwashed puppets."

"And one of them was my dad," Madison choked out, tears streaming down her face.

Timothy turned back toward the table to see that each of the others was also crying. He put aside his reservations and let his own tears fall. For the first time since the crash, he allowed himself to feel the full force of his grief.

The giant listened in silence as the little group remembered their fallen friends. Finally, he said, "If you'd like, I could officiate a funeral service for them before you continue with your mission."

For a moment, Timothy was tempted to refuse. But as his own tears continued to trickle down his face, he knew that they needed to accept the giant's offer.

"That would... be great," Timothy managed. "We've... already failed the mission, anyway."

At this, the giant frowned, suddenly puzzled. "Why are you so sure that your mission has failed? You've made it here. That was your plan, wasn't it?"

Even amidst his grief, something in the giant's tone made Timothy pause. "What do you mean this was our plan? We didn't even know this place existed."

The giant looked at them with bewilderment. "But you must have. Why else would you have come to the Monastery of St. Sandoval on a mission like yours?"

"I've never even heard of St. Sandoval," Timothy said. He glanced back at Jewel, but she only shrugged.

"Surely God has been guiding your footsteps!" the monk said. "If you'll follow me, I think I have just what you need."

He started out the door, and Timothy hesitated, wary of a trap. Then he brushed the thought aside.

He has no reason to attack us, he told himself. *He's been nothing but helpful so far.*

"There's a lot to be said about St. Sandoval," the hermit said as he led the group through a maze of stone passageways. "Most people are most familiar with his work as the Learner. He did a lot of good—he even fought in the Heroes' War." He turned the corner and began walking down a flight of stone stairs into an underground catacomb. "What most people don't know is that he is also the patron saint of extraterrestrials. After the war, he became one of the first missionaries to outer space. He was eventually martyred while ministering to the Orgwar."

The hermit came to a stop in front of a sliding metal grate. He withdrew a key from his pocket and inserted it into the rusty lock, pulling the gate open. Timothy shuffled to the side, trying to catch a glimpse of what was inside the cage. The hermit turned around, holding an ancient, teardrop-shaped medallion in his hands.

"It is said that after the Heroes' War, Sandoval put some of his power into this medallion. Having made a careful study of the relic myself, I can confirm this to be the case."

"What are you saying?" Aksell asked.

The hermit held the medallion out toward Timothy. "Take it. Use it to complete your mission."

Timothy accepted the medallion awkwardly, not sure how to respond.

"We can't take this from you," Jewel said.

"Of course you can," the hermit replied. "In fact, I believe that's the very reason God brought you here. The story of St. Sandoval comes back to the Orgwar again and again. What are the odds that you should arrive at the monastery built in his name on a mission involving the same aliens?"

"No offense, but how does this help us?" Crystal asked. "I get that it has powers, but unless it's strong enough to defeat the Orgwar, I'm not sure how useful this is going to be."

"St. Sandoval had many abilities," the hermit said. "I don't know if anyone knew the full extent of his powers. But one of them enabled him to travel large distances remarkably fast. His letters describe it as 'slipping into the outer layers of our reality.' A sort of in-between place."

"And by going into this 'in-between place,' he was able to travel quickly?" Timothy asked, turning the medallion over in his hands. "Would it be enough to make a several-month journey in a few hours?"

"That I can't say," the giant said. "But I'm persuaded that it might be."

"It's worth a try," Timothy said, his hope returning. He looked up at the hermit. "Thank you."

The hermit nodded solemnly. After a long pause, he said, "If you all would go back upstairs to the chapel, I can begin the funeral service."

We don't have time for that anymore, Timothy thought. *Not now that we have a chance of completing our mission.* He opened his mouth to say as much, but a quick glance at the others changed his mind. They seemed extremely grateful for the giant's words, and Timothy could tell that they intended to take the hermit up on his offer.

I guess we could afford to stay one more hour, he thought, glancing at his watch. *If only we weren't in such a hurry...*

Slowly, he nodded. The others turned to go back up the stairs, but the hermit pulled Timothy aside.

"Timothy. May I have a word with you?"

Timothy tensed, watching the giant closely for any signs of hostility. The giant seemed not to notice, and Timothy hesitantly allowed himself to relax.

"What is it? Is there something more we need to know about the medallion?"

The hermit shook his head. "The medallion is not my concern right now. I'm more concerned about you and your friends." He smiled kindly. "A great burden has been placed upon your shoulders. A burden that no one should have to bear. But you don't have to bear it alone. This Gearwire may have appointed you to take his place, but from what you've told me, even he did not lead alone."

He looked Timothy directly in the eyes. "Allow your friends to help you. Trust their insight. And trust that God will see you through even this."

"I'm not even sure if God exists," Timothy said.

"Whether you believe it or not, God is willing to help all the same," the monk said with a faint smile. "This week may not turn out the way we all hope it will. It may be that the Orgwar invasion will be successful. It may be that this drama will end in a way no one expected. But God will still be faithful, nonetheless."

Timothy remained silent, the giant's words reminding him of what Samuel had said to him on their way to Velikanov.

Finally, he shook his head. "I hope you're right," Timothy said. "I really do."

There was silence for a moment, then the giant said, "I had better prepare the service. You should rejoin your companions."

Timothy hesitated, then turned and went back up the stairs after the others.

After a few minutes of waiting, the giant returned, wearing a black robe and holding a book in his hand. Then he began to chant in a language Timothy didn't recognize, the monotone song echoing throughout the chapel. As the chant continued, the monk picked up a small golden object from the table in front of him, swinging it gently by its chain. A strange-smelling smoke emanated from the object, filling the air. The monk set the smoking object down once more and began to read from the book he had carried in with him. Overwhelmed by the unfamiliarity of the situation, it took Timothy a moment to realize that the monk had switched to English.

"We do not want you to be uninformed, brothers and sisters, about those who have died, so that you may not grieve as others do who have no hope. For since we believe that Jesus died and rose again, even so, through Jesus, God will bring with him those who have died. For this we declare to you by the word of the Lord, that we, who are alive, who are left until the coming of the Lord, will by no means precede those who have died. For the Lord himself, with a cry of command, with the archangel's call and with the sound of God's trumpet, will descend from heaven, and the dead in Christ shall rise first. Then we who are alive, who are left, will be caught up to meet the Lord in the air, and so we will be with the Lord forever."

He's reading from the Bible, Timothy realized, recognizing the words from his time with Gearwire's crew. The giant read a second passage, but Timothy hardly noticed, his thoughts on the fates of his fallen friends.

A sad smile crossed his face as he remembered what Samuel had said to him as they left Alpen.

'If Dr. Maddium's calculations are right, we may all be dead by the end of the week.'

Timothy sighed. *He was right about that much, at any rate.* His smile faded. *First Maurice, then Henry, and now everybody else,* he thought, tears pooling in his eyes.

The giant resumed his chant once more, and a thought suddenly rose to the surface of Timothy's mind.

I need to figure out what exactly I believe about God and an afterlife. I owe them that much.

As the ancient melody of the giant's chant washed over him, Timothy's mind drifted back to the early days of his involvement with Gearwire and his crew. He was so wrapped up in his reflections that he hardly noticed that the giant had left his place at the front of the chapel and had made his way over to where the surviving Guardians of Kawts sat.

"I understand that you will be wanting to get on your way as soon as possible," the monk said. "But if I might detain you a little longer, I have some extra food that I can give you for your journey. I just have to find something to pack it in."

"Don't worry about packing it," Timothy said. He knocked on his chest plate. "I have a compartment in here that will hold anything you need."

"Good," the hermit said. "I'll show you back to the kitchen."

They followed the hermit back through the winding corridors to the place where they had first entered. At the door to the kitchen, Timothy turned around and faced the others. "You guys wait for us by the exit," he said. "Jewel and I can handle this."

The others hesitated a moment, but at the hermit's example, they did as Timothy requested.

For a long moment, neither of them spoke.

Finally, Timothy sighed.

"I'm sorry about what I said back in Alpen," he said. "I just... I wasn't ready to discuss what happened in the Weather Belt complex. I'm still not. There's too much at stake right now for us to be worrying about that."

Jewel didn't respond, so Timothy continued. "The truth is, I need you. I can't lead us through this by myself. We're the only hope Earth has right now, and that's terrifying." He hesitated a moment, then added, "And I don't want to spend what might be my last few days knowing you're mad at me."

"I'm not mad at you," Jewel said finally. "Not right now. Maybe when all this is over, I will be. But you're right—we're the best chance Earth has right now. We can't afford to be fighting with each other."

Timothy breathed a sigh of relief. "And we can agree not to discuss the machine gun room…?"

"Not until this is all over."

Timothy nodded, feeling like a great weight had been lifted off his shoulders. "Thank you."

"We should probably get these supplies packed before everyone else gets worried," Jewel said, a soft smile crossing her face.

Timothy nodded, and the pair quickly loaded the food the giant had given them into the Infini-Case compartment in Timothy's chest plate. Once their provisions had been secured, they hurried back to the entrance of the monastery.

The others were already waiting for them in the courtyard when Timothy and Jewel arrived. Quill held the medallion in his hand, scrutinizing it.

"How do you work this thing?" he asked the giant as Timothy reached them.

"I've never used the device myself," the hermit said. "But if St. Sandoval's letters describe it adequately, you need to focus on phasing out of reality. Like slipping between layers of paper."

"Just try using it like you use Marathon's ring," Madison whispered.

Timothy nodded. "Everyone, huddle up."

As the others gathered around him, Timothy looked up at the hermit. "Thank you," he said. "We couldn't have done this without you."

"Don't thank me," the hermit said, leaning up against the doorway. "Thank God." He opened his mouth as if about to say more, but the sound of someone pounding on the outer door of the monastery interrupted him.

The guards, Timothy thought, his heart sinking. *They must have tracked us here.*

"Don't worry," the hermit said, noticing the look on Timothy's face. He stood and started toward the door. "Go. I can stall them long enough for you to get out of here." Then he was gone, leaving Timothy and the others alone in the courtyard.

"Alright," Quill said, looking down at the medallion in his fist. "Looks like we'd better hurry."

Timothy glanced nervously toward the door as Quill tried to activate the medallion. He could hear the distant sounds of voices as the hermit spoke to the guards.

"Quill? Are you almost done?" he asked. "I'm not sure how long-"

He cut off abruptly, flinching as an odd twang ran up his spine.

Chapter 8

High Command paced the bridge of the flagship, studying a holographic map of Earth.

"We'll annihilate their largest cities first," he said. "A cannon blast before they can react. Then we'll move in with the infantry. Kill half the population and take the rest."

"Sir—isn't that a little extreme?" one of the pilots objected from his place at the control panel. "It… well, it isn't the usual procedure." Beside him, his partner nodded in agreement.

"They don't have anything to do with the Defender," he said.

High Command turned slowly to face them. "We must make an example of them," he said. "And if you insist on questioning your emperor, you may join them."

"Right. Of course, sir," the pilot said, sitting down quickly. But the glance that he shared with his partner made it clear he was still uncomfortable with High Command's order.

I'll deal with their treachery later, High Command thought, giving them one last glare before turning back toward the screen. *Right now, I have bigger problems to deal with.*

* * *

Timothy looked up as the others staggered backwards. Everything seemed to be just as it was before, only warped and slanted—as if the entire world was suddenly in italics. The sounds of the hermit and the guards had vanished altogether.

"This is definitely in the top five weirdest things I've ever seen," Crystal said, turning in a slow circle. "And I've seen a lot of weird stuff the last few years."

"This place is definitely a little unsettling. But how did St. Sandoval use this place to travel so fast?" Jewel said. "It doesn't look like anything major has changed."

"I don't know," Quill said. "Maybe there's some sort of-" He started to take a step away from the monastery, and his body began to stretch. His foot touched down on a neighboring mountaintop, and Quill jerked back in surprise. He snapped back into focus, and he froze, staring at his foot.

"I'm going to guess that's it," Crystal said. "You could walk a mile a minute with steps like that."

"Even so, we'd better get going," Timothy said. "We've got a long way to go and not much time to do it." Glancing up at the sun, he oriented himself toward Ellada and began to walk.

* * *

Timothy glanced up at the starry sky, stifling a yawn. They had been walking for several hours, but despite the help of St. Sandoval's medallion, the chaos of the day was catching up with him.

Definitely one of the worst days of my life, Timothy thought, remembering all that had happened. *First, we almost got executed by the Council, then we learned that an alien invasion is imminent, and then-* He broke off, still hardly daring to think it.

"We might as well take a break here," Jewel said. "We can afford to rest for a few minutes, at least."

Timothy nodded. When they had first set out, he and Jewel had discussed whether they should stop somewhere to sleep before reaching Ellada. In the end, they had decided against it, aware of how precious every minute was.

When was the last time any of us got a good night's sleep? Timothy wondered as everyone sank gratefully to the ground. He shook his head. *I suppose it doesn't really matter. We're all in at this point. We can sleep after we save the world.*

"So… would anyone mind filling me in on what that was all about?" Aksell asked, breaking the silence.

Timothy looked up at him. "What was what all about?"

"Back in Velikanov. At the funeral. He said something about someone coming back to life?"

Timothy glanced over at Jewel. *How do I answer that? That people live on after death? I'm not even sure whether I believe that. Do I just tell him that-*

"Because someone did come back to life," Quill said, coming to Timothy's rescue. "He sacrificed himself for humanity, and then he came back to life three days later."

Aksell raised an eyebrow. "If a member of the resistance came back to life, I'm pretty sure the Council would know."

"Not… not a member of the resistance," Timothy said. "This was like… maybe 2500 years ago or something."

Aksell let out a bark of laughter. "You're joking, right?" His smile was replaced by puzzlement when he saw the looks on the others' faces.

"You're not joking, are you?"

Timothy shook his head. Aksell fell silent for a moment, trying to wrap his head around what he was hearing.

"And you guys believe that?" he said at last, a bewildered look on his face.

"For the record, I'm not really sure what I think," Timothy said. "But Gearwire and the rest of the team did. And so did Maurice."

Aksell fell silent once more, staring off into space. For a moment, it seemed like he was going to ask another question, but instead, he just nodded.

"Interesting." He glanced up at the sun and slowly got to his feet. "We'd better keep moving," he said. "We don't have much time left."

* * *

Oria, Ellada
Forty-Eight Hours Remaining

"Okay, Aksell. Where's this fail-safe device hidden?"

Aksell made his way to the bluff overlooking Oria, the capital city of Ellada. Far below them, hovercars zipped past each other in the air, their headlights creating a cacophony of scattered colors on the bronze-colored skyscrapers that surrounded them. Even though the sun had long set, the city resembled a beehive in its ceaseless activity. He stared at the city for a long time before responding.

"I'm not completely sure," he said at last. "But I know a guy who has some connections. He'll be able to tell us for sure. He might even be able to help us break into the building."

"Break in?" Madison interrupted. "You mean you want us to steal it?"

"Technically, we stole the last one too," Aksell said. "Besides, they're never going to believe us if we tell them the truth. I don't intend to make the same mistake twice."

"I feel like there's a difference between what happened in Velikanov and jumping straight to armed robbery," Jewel said.

Aksell opened his mouth to reply, but Timothy cut him off. "We can worry about how we're going to get the device later. For now, we just need to focus on figuring out where it is."

Aksell nodded. "Right. Well, as I said—I know a guy who might be able to help us."

"When you say you know a guy, do you mean *the Council* knows a guy?" Crystal said.

Aksell hesitated for a moment, then nodded. "He is one of our Council contacts," he admitted. He glanced over at the others, as if suddenly remembering something. "You guys might want to change into your street clothes," he said. "The only way this is going to work is if he thinks I'm here on official Council business. And if he sees you guys in your suits, he might recognize you. I don't know how much my dad told him."

The others still looked hesitant at this, but Timothy came to Aksell's rescue. "I know that working with a Council contact isn't ideal. But we need information, and this is the quickest way to get it. Remember the bridge trap in the Weather Belt complex? We were all ready to work with Ethos if that's what it took to save Alpen, remember?" He paused for a moment, then added, "Just because we're using their information doesn't mean we have to use their methods."

Aksell glanced up at Timothy, puzzled, but the others hesitantly nodded in agreement.

"I guess that settles it," Quill said. "Aksell? Lead the way."

Timothy followed Aksell down from the bluff and into Ellada, picking his way over the debris and potholes that filled the streets. On either side of the street, towering buildings stretched up toward the sky, made of a brownish, bronzelike metal decorated with ornate patterns.

"They really need to fix their roads," Crystal said, walking around a pothole almost as long as Gearwire's ship.

"They don't have a need to," Jewel said, pointing up toward the sky.

Timothy followed her gaze to see a car flying overhead, vanishing deeper into the city.

That would explain the state of the roads, he thought. *Let's hope Aksell's contact is close by.*

"Aksell? How much farther?"

"It's going to be a bit," Aksell said. "I've only been here a couple times before."

Timothy frowned, but didn't say anything. He turned his attention back to the road in front of him, swerving to avoid the burnt-out husk of a vehicle in front of him.

He heard a dull clang, and turned around just in time to see Quill jump down from on top of the vehicle, landing right beside Timothy.

"So. How did it go?" Quill asked.

Timothy looked at him quizzically. "How did what go?"

"Your talk with Jewel. What did she say?"

"I don't know what you're talking about," Timothy said.

"You know exactly what I mean," Quill said. "You and Jewel had a private conversation back in the monastery. And since then, you've actually been interacting with each other. So, what did she say? Does she feel the same way you do?"

"We didn't talk about it," Timothy said, finally turning to face his friend. "I apologized for what I said to her back in Alpen, and we agreed not to discuss it until after we stopped the Orgwar."

"Why? Don't you want to know?"

"Of course I do," Timothy whispered back. "But... not right now. There's too much at stake."

"When *isn't* there too much at stake?" Quill asked, a smirk spreading across his face. "You know what I think? I think you're just scared of what she's going to say."

"There's more to it than that," Timothy started.

"Suuuure there is," Quill said. Then he grew solemn once more. "But seriously, you need to talk to her. Either one of you might be killed before this is over. And then you'll regret not discussing it."

"Quill, I can't-"

Before he could finish, Quill was gone, hurrying off toward Madison.

We just agreed not *to discuss it,* he finished silently, glancing back at Jewel. In spite of that, however, he couldn't get Quill's words out of his head.

Maybe Quill's right, he thought, glancing back at Jewel again. He was on the verge of going over to her when Aksell slowed to a stop in front of him.

"What is it?" Timothy asked, suddenly alert. He glanced around the alleyway, but saw nothing out of the ordinary.

"We're here," Aksell said. He turned back to look at the group. "Let me do the talking, okay?"

After a second's hesitation, Timothy nodded. "We'll try."

Aksell took a deep breath and exhaled heavily. "Alright. Here goes nothing."

He walked across the street to a little wooden door at the base of one of the towering buildings. He rapped on the door with a short series of knocks. After a moment, the door swung open, revealing a tall, thin man with a slightly crooked nose. He blinked tiredly for a moment before realizing who stood before him.

"Aksell," the man said, his voice barely audible from where Timothy stood. "This is unexpected. What brings you to Ellada all by yourself?"

"It's a long story," Aksell said. "But I'm not actually alone. My traveling companions are over there," he added, pointing to where Timothy and the others stood.

The other man looked up at them, noticing their presence for the first time. For a long moment, he stared at them, his eyes narrowed. Finally, he nodded. "Come in. We'd better discuss this inside."

Aksell nodded, waving what remained of the Guardians of Kawts over.

Right into the belly of the beast, Timothy thought as he followed Aksell inside. *If this guy suspects we're lying, we're done.*

He glanced over at Crystal and Jewel, but they seemed oblivious to the danger.

Of course, they have plenty of experience being undercover, Timothy recalled. *And they're still armed.*

"Now then," their guide said, emerging into a dimly lit coffee kitchen. "What's the situation here? Is the Council in trouble?"

Aksell nodded. "Our situation has become… very precarious," he said. "The anarchists actually managed to gain the upper hand. But before they captured him, Ethos initiated our backup plan. Unfortunately, the anarchists discovered this, and now they're trying to collect the fail-safe devices in order to put a stop to it. That's why we're here. We need to get to them first."

Timothy shifted uncomfortably as Aksell finished telling his story.

I don't like this. It's too close to the truth. What if it really is? How confident am I that Aksell hasn't been using us this whole time?

He shook his head, dismissing the thought. Even so, a tiny worm of doubt remained.

"What's that?" the man asked, turning to Timothy.

"What's what?" Timothy asked, hoping the man couldn't see how startled he was.

"Just now. You were shaking your head. Why?"

For a moment, Timothy froze, unable to think of a good excuse. "It's disgraceful," he said at last. "How those… hooligans keep trying to overthrow the Council."

To Timothy's relief, the man nodded. "My thoughts exactly." He turned back to Aksell. "It sounds like the Council is in serious trouble. But what have you come to me for?"

"We need information," Aksell said. "Ethos wasn't able to tell me much about the device we're looking for. We don't have any idea where it is or how to get to it."

"I may be able to help you on both counts," the man said. "As to the location, it's in a vault beneath the capitol building. And in terms of getting in… I might have just the thing. Wait here."

The man stood and left the room, leaving the Guardians of Kawts alone. Once he was out of earshot, Timothy breathed a sigh of relief.

"That was a close one," Aksell whispered, turning back to look at Timothy. "For a second there, I thought he was onto us." He paused for a moment, then added, "What were you really thinking about, anyway?"

Timothy shook his head, his face flushing. "Nothing. Nothing important, at least."

Aksell looked skeptical, but before he could say anything further, the man returned, holding a roll of papers.

"I've been holding onto these for a long time," he said. "I knew they'd be useful one day."

"What are they?" Crystal asked, earning her a sharp glance from Aksell.

"They're the floor plans for the capitol building," the man said, unrolling them onto the table. "You don't want to know what I had to do to get these."

"So, what's the move?" Aksell asked.

"You'll have to break in," the man said. "That idiot of a High Baron we have would never give the device to you willingly. He's an anarchist sympathizer." He glanced down at the map, stabbing it with his finger. "The easiest place to make entry would be here, but you'd need a hefty amount of explosives to blast through that wall, which I don't happen to have."

"We've got plenty of those ourselves," Madison said.

The man nodded. "Perfect. Here's what you're going to do."

Chapter 9

Velikanov, Severnaya
Several hours earlier

Gearwire staggered out of the ship, blood trickling down his forehead from where he had smacked it on the control panel in the collision. He took a moment to reorient himself, trying to ignore his splitting headache. The smell of burning fuel filled the air, accompanied by the intense heat of fire.

A few of the others had already made it out of the downed ship, but a quick glance was enough to tell him that there were still a few that were unaccounted for. Pulling his shirt up over his mouth and nose, he charged back into the ship.

Dense smoke filled the cabin, making it difficult to see. As he stumbled forwards, he almost ran into Howard. The scientist seemed dazed, but otherwise unharmed.

"Have you seen Samuel?" Gearwire shouted, straining to be heard over the roar of the fire.

Howard shook his head. "I thought he was already out!"

Gearwire nodded grimly and pushed on deeper into the ship. He found Samuel lying face down on the floor near the cargo hold, a large bruise already forming on his forehead. Gearwire rolled him over and felt for a pulse. He was still breathing, but the smoke was making even that difficult.

Gearwire crouched down beside him and heaved him up over his shoulders. He turned and lurched back toward the door, struggling under the weight of the unconscious librarian. Once, he nearly fell, and he was forced to put his hand against the wall to steady himself. He bit down a cry of pain as the heat began to sear his palm. He pushed off from the wall and slid outside, lowering Samuel to the ground.

He scanned the waiting crowd once more, double-checking to make sure they had all made it out. To his great relief, no one was missing, and he turned his attention toward his ship. He walked in a slow circle around it, trying to find the source of the fire. The mangled remains of Howard's experimental rocket booster quickly answered his question. The booster had exploded when they hit the ground, spreading the fire to the other two engines and spraying burning jet fuel all over the valley.

Gearwire squinted through the flames, inspecting the body of the ship.

If we can put the fire out and repair the engines, we still might be able to get her flight-worthy again, he thought. A loud pop suddenly interrupted his thoughts, and he looked over to see one of the engines collapse.

On second thought, we're going to need completely new engines.

"How bad is it?" Howard asked. "Can we fix her?"

"The main body of the ship is still intact," Gearwire said. "But the engines are completely shot. And by the time we get this fire out, I don't think we'll have much left in terms of fuel and supplies."

If not for the invincium lining on the hull, we'd all be dead right now, he realized, but he kept the thought to himself.

"So, what do we do?" Penn asked, limping over to them.

Gearwire looked up at the city looming overhead. "We're going to have to go into Velikanov to pick up parts."

"The Council will be waiting for you," the Golden Knight said. "It's suicide." A flicker of confusion crossed his face. "The giants, I mean. Not the Council."

"It's the only chance we've got," Gearwire said. Something moving on the slope caught his attention, and he pulled out his field binoculars. "It looks like we aren't going to have much of a choice, anyway. There's a whole squadron of armed guards on their way down here as we speak. The only way we're going to get out of this is to cooperate with them."

"And if they try to take our weapons?" the Mysterious Man asked. "We'll be completely defenseless."

"We won't be completely defenseless," Gearwire said. "We'll still have Idalbo and Adalbo and Penn. And me."

"Let's hope you're right," the Mysterious Man muttered as the guards came into earshot. "Otherwise, we're toast."

* * *

Timothy stood outside the wall that the man had indicated, watching as Madison attached several of her ravioli-shaped grenades to the surface. He glanced down at the copy of the floor plans in his hand, their route marked out in red ink.

"We're all set," Madison said, stepping away from the wall. "Whenever you guys are ready."

Timothy nodded, folding up the plans and slipping them into his chest plate. "Our main goal is to get the device and get out as fast as possible," he said. "We don't want to get into a prolonged fight with any guards we run into."

"I don't think that will be a problem," Aksell said, unholstering the pistol that his contact had given him.

Timothy shook his head. "No killing."

Aksell raised an eyebrow. "The fate of the world is at stake, and you're worried about the lives of a few guards?"

"They're just doing their jobs," Timothy said. "We're the ones breaking the law."

"I'll make sure to tell the Orgwar that when they get here and we're not ready for them," Aksell said. "Wait a second, Mr. Alien! I wanted to fight you, but the guards were just doing their jobs, so I can't."

"We're not killing anybody," Timothy said. "Gearwire was very adamant about that."

"Gearwire's dead. And if he had fought back against the giants that were shooting at him, maybe he wouldn't be!"

Timothy heard Madison's sharp intake of breath behind him, and he grabbed Aksell's arm. "That was uncalled for," he whispered forcefully. "Killing people who get in your way may be how you do things in the Council, but that isn't how we do things here." Hurt flashed across Aksell's face, and Timothy knew he had gone too far.

"No lethal force," he repeated.

Aksell stared at Timothy for a long time, then slowly put his pistol away. "Whatever you say, *commander*."

"If you two are done, we need to keep moving," Crystal said. "It won't take long before someone comes over to investigate what we're doing down here."

Timothy nodded. "Right. Madison?"

"Everyone stand back," Madison said, pulling a detonator from her belt. She waited until everyone was safely out of the way, then activated the device, blowing a hole in the side of the building.

Immediately, alarms began to blare, and Timothy cursed under his breath. "Well, they certainly know what we're up to now. Let's go."

Readying a shuriken, Timothy scrambled over the rubble and into the building. He rounded the first corner and came face-to-face with a man dressed in shining bronze-like armor. Timothy threw the shuriken at the man's head, but the man sidestepped it, lashing out at Timothy with the butt of his weapon as he did.

Timothy quickly pulled his staff from his chest plate and moved to block the blow, knocking the weapon aside. Before the startled guard could react, Timothy swept his legs out from under him and knocked him unconscious with a swift punch. The man fell to the ground, his armor and raygun clattering loudly on the floor. As the others ran into the hallway behind him, he kicked the weapon across the room, unwilling to take the chance that the man was faking it.

Going off the map from Aksell's contact, Timothy led the group deeper into the capitol building, making his way to the vault where the fail-safe device was kept. Occasionally, they encountered other guards, but they were swiftly dispatched.

Timothy was just beginning to feel like they had a chance when he rounded the last corner between them and the vault. A large force of over twenty guards stood in the way, their weapons raised. Before Timothy could decide how to react, another force of guards closed in from behind them.

"Drop your weapons," one of the guards shouted. Timothy hesitated, and the guard repeated his command. "I'm not going to ask again."

Out of the corner of his eye, Timothy noticed a guard holding a rifle, which was trained on Jewel.

For a moment, he debated throwing a shuriken at the man, but then he spotted the other guards scattered around the room with similar weapons.

If I make a wrong move, Jewel's going to die, he realized. *And so will everyone else.*

Reluctantly, he lifted his hands in the air, allowing his staff to fall to the ground. One by one, the others did the same. The guards came forward and tied their hands behind their backs, marching them off to another part of the building.

"Where are you taking us?" Quill asked as the guards bundled them together.

"You're going to have a little meeting with the Baron of Information and the High Baron," one of the guards said. "They're very interested to learn who sent a bunch of teenagers to attack the capital of Ellada."

"Okay, Aksell. Talk to us," Crystal whispered as the guards hurried them along. "What do you know about this High Baron guy?"

"I don't know much more than you do," Aksell said. "Ellada is ruled by a group of ten barons, each of whom is responsible for a different aspect of government. The guy who built the attack drones and the evaporation cannon for us was the Baron of Technology, for instance. The guy in charge is the High Baron. Beyond that, I can't tell you much."

"If that's true, we still have a chance to get that device," Jewel said. "If we explain the situation to the High Baron, he might be willing to help us."

"And why would he do that?" Aksell asked.

"Because Gearwire's been here a couple times before," Timothy said, picking up on what Jewel was implying. "Henry told me that he and Gearwire and Dr. Maddium visited here to investigate the source of the attack drones in the early days of the rebellion."

Jewel nodded. "Exactly. He's been back a few times since then, too."

"We just need to figure out how to convince them that we really *are* working with Gearwire," Crystal said. "Which is easier said than done now that he's… well, you know."

"We'll come up with something," Quill said. "We have to."

"Whatever you're planning on saying, you'd better figure it out soon," Aksell said. "I think we're stopping."

Just as Aksell had said, the guards soon came to a stop in front of a large door, guarded by a pair of knights dressed in armor made from the same bronze-like metal as the buildings. Each carried a raygun, larger than the ones the other guards had been using.

The guards stepped aside as the Guardians of Kawts approached, ushering them inside. As the heavy doors swung shut behind them, Timothy had the fleeting thought that he should have listened to Madison and found another way to get the device.

Chapter 10

The Defender's Starship
Forty-Five Hours from Earth

"Any luck on getting a message through?" the Defender asked, peering into the doorway.

Ally shook her head. "Nothing. If there's anyone on Earth listening, they haven't tried to reply."

"What about the other defenders?"

"They're on their way, but their ship was damaged in the fight. They won't reach Earth before we do."

"Keep trying," the Defender said. "We're their only hope."

He stared off into the starry sky.

I hope Timothy's okay.

* * *

Timothy looked toward the front of the room and saw a man sitting on a throne, wearing a ceremonial suit of armor similar to the others.

The High Baron, he thought, trying to ignore the nervousness he felt.

"The Baron of Security tells me you were trying to break into our vault," the High Baron said. "What were you after? Who do you work for?"

"We work for Gearwire," Timothy said. "Or, we did until he and the rest of our team were killed yesterday in Velikanov."

The High Baron narrowed his eyes. "Lying will get you nowhere. There's no way you could make it all the way here from Velikanov so fast."

"It's true," Quill said. "We got a magic medallion from this monk, and…" he trailed off, realizing how ridiculous he sounded.

"The important thing is, Ethos is in custody," Jewel said. "But before we captured him, he invited the Orgwar over here to avenge him."

"You're after the Anti-Friction Ray," another voice said. Timothy turned to see another man standing in the corner, mostly concealed by the shadows of the room. "That's why you're here. You want our fail-safe device."

Timothy nodded. "We should have just come up here and asked you for it, but that strategy didn't work so well in Velikanov. It's what caused Gearwire's ship to be shot down."

The High Baron was silent for a long time, scrutinizing the travelers. Finally, he said, "Your story is plausible. You know too much about these matters not to be connected to Gearwire in some way." His frown deepened. "But I have no way of knowing that said connection was an alliance. You have yet to tell me a single thing that the Council could not have said themselves. Tell me something that only one of Gearwire's crewmembers would know."

The Guardians of Kawts fell silent for a moment, thinking over the High Baron's challenge.

"I can tell you the names of every member of his team," Madison said. "And our respective specialties."

The High Baron shook his head. "I wouldn't put it past the Council to have figured that out," he said. "Especially if they were trying to masquerade as his crew members."

"I know that Gearwire's real name is Milkop Quawz," Aksell said. "And that he's come here from the past to defeat the Council."

"A clever Council agent could divine that as well," the Baron of Information countered. "Our own archives might reveal that much."

Evidently, they are, Timothy thought, suspecting that was exactly how Aksell had come across this information. The silence returned, and the High Baron seemed to grow impatient.

"If you can't come up with something, I'm going to have no choice but to see you locked up." He motioned to the guards, but Timothy was suddenly struck by an idea.

"Wait! I know how Gearwire and Henry first met."

The High Baron hesitated. "That would be a story unlikely to be discovered by an enemy," he said. "You may proceed."

"It was after the death of Gearwire's old commander," Timothy said, trying to remember what Henry had told him all those months before. "Gearwire got promoted to take his place, and Henry didn't like it. They got into a fistfight."

The High Baron nodded slowly. "That's the same story Henry told us when he was last here." He motioned to the guards, and they moved to untie the Guardians of Kawts. "How is Henry these days?"

"He's dead," Timothy said quickly, before the thought could dredge up the overwhelming grief from the days after Henry's death. "He died fighting Ethos a few months before we liberated Kawts."

The High Baron frowned. "I'm sorry to hear that. Tell me your story again. How did you come to be here?"

Taking a deep breath, Timothy recounted their adventures thus far, this time omitting nothing.

When he had finished, the High Baron was silent, mulling over what he had heard. Finally, he spoke.

"Baron Drakos, bring in the Anti-Friction Ray."

"You're just going to *give* it to us?" Aksell said, his eyes narrowed. "Why?"

"You need it to save the world," the High Baron said. "Besides, we don't need it anymore. We have low-powered copies in every factory from here to Crete!"

"That's how you've managed to reach such a high level of technology," Crystal said. "Impressive."

The High Baron smiled. "It's amazing the things you can do when you don't have to worry about friction. All the discoveries you can make."

Crystal and the High Baron went back and forth for several minutes, discussing the implications of the Anti-Friction Ray on technology. Timothy listened in bemused silence, understanding only a fraction of what was being said.

After a while, the Baron of Information returned, carrying a raygun like the ones carried by the guards outside. He handed it to Timothy, who slipped it into the compartment in his chest plate.

"If you need anything else, please let us know," the High Baron said. "We'll help you as best we can."

"I don't think there's a lot you *can* do," Aksell said. "Unless you know where the rest of the fail-safe devices are."

"Actually, we might be able to help with that, too," the Baron of Information said. "Follow me."

He turned and left the throne room, the remaining Guardians of Kawts trailing behind him. He led them through the capitol building, stopping in front of a windowless door.

"I have a map in my office," he said, inserting a key into the lock. "It'll tell you where they're supposed to be." The lock clicked, and he turned back to face the others. "Stay here," he said, easing the door open just wide enough to sneak through. "I'll be right back." Then he vanished into the room.

Timothy glanced around at the others, his hope returning.

We just might be able to pull this off after all, he thought. *Between the map and the medallion, we have everything we need to track down the rest of the devices.*

Before Timothy could contemplate the matter further, the Baron reappeared, holding a worn map in his hand. "This should get you the last known locations of all the fail-safe devices," he said, passing the map to Quill. "If you ask me, the best place for you to go next is the South Floridian Republic."

"Where's that?" Jewel asked.

"Across the ocean," the baron said. "And under it, too. I'll send for some diving suits."

"If the city's underwater, there's no way the device is still there," Aksell said. "And even if it is, there's no way it's still functional."

"The city may be underwater," the Baron said. "But that doesn't mean it's flooded. It was built on the seafloor several centuries ago. If I'm not mistaken, their current Governor is a man named Durgan. I'll get you a letter for him officially authorizing you as emissaries from Ellada. We can't take the chance that he doubts your story."

"Thank you so much," Jewel said. "We needed this."

"Just don't get us all killed. That's all the thanks we need." The Baron glanced at his watch. "You'd better hurry. I'll have someone bring the gear you need up to you. Go save the world."

Before any of them could say a word, the baron was gone, vanishing down the nearest hallway.

* * *

Timothy glanced up at the sky, trying to gauge how long it had been since their last break.

Not since we first stepped onto the ocean about an hour back, he realized. He remembered everyone's shock at being able to walk on the surface of the water, and added, *I don't know what we'd do if the ocean wasn't frozen in time.*

"We can rest here for a bit," Timothy said at last, satisfied that they were making good time. The others breathed a sigh of relief, setting down their gear. Timothy couldn't help but smile at the sight of his friends sitting on the surface of the water, the world slanting drunkenly around them.

Slowly, he eased himself to the ground, his aching muscles screaming in protest.

When this is all over, I'm not going to walk anywhere for a week! he thought, settling into a sitting position.

"I know this probably isn't something you all want to discuss," Aksell said, interrupting Timothy's reflections. "But at some point, we need to think about what we're going to do if we can't pull this off. If the Orgwar win."

"You're right," Crystal said. "I don't want to discuss it."

"I think Aksell has a point," Madison said, with an amount of conviction that surprised Timothy. "This mission was always kind of a long shot. Even before-" She cut off abruptly, and for several seconds, she didn't say anything. "It's pretty likely that we're not going to be successful," she said at last.

"I'm not sure how much planning we really can do at this point," Jewel said. "Part of that will depend on *why* we weren't able to complete the mission." She looked around at the others, her eyes finally coming to rest on Timothy. "But if we can't stop the Orgwar from invading, I'm going to do everything in my power to save as many people as I can before they kill me."

Timothy nodded slowly, his thoughts once more on his fallen friends.

"Okay…" Aksell said. "But I still think we need a concrete backup plan. If there's one thing I learned with the Council is that it's always good to have a contingency plan. My dad even had backup plans for his backup plans. And I'd prefer not to be killed."

"Gearwire had plenty of backup plans of his own," Timothy said. "But I don't think even he really knew what he would do if we failed."

The image of Gearwire's reckless abandon in the Battle of Kawts flashed into his mind, and Timothy realized that he knew exactly what Gearwire would have done.

"Gearwire would have kamikazed the Orgwar ship," Crystal said. "He would have just thrown himself at the Orgwar until they took him down in a blaze of glory."

"That doesn't seem like it would be very effective," Aksell said. "Wouldn't it be smarter to find someplace to build a new rebellion from?"

"I didn't say that it would be effective," Crystal said. "I just don't think Gearwire would have been able to live with himself if he did anything else. He blamed himself for all of this."

Timothy nodded. "I can vouch for that much. Gearwire wasn't the only person who asked me to take over if anything happened to him. Dr. Maddium wanted me to take charge if Gearwire was no longer in the right mind to lead. He was saying the same kind of thing."

"You guys are something else," Aksell said, shaking his head in disbelief. "If one of the Council members suggested something like that, they'd probably get banished."

"You're not on the Council anymore," Quill said with a smile. "We do things a little differently here."

"I can see that."

In spite of everything that had happened, Timothy couldn't help but smile. For a moment, he could almost believe that everything was normal. The moment quickly faded, however, when Crystal spoke.

"On that note, we should probably keep going. We still have a long way to go."

Begrudgingly, Timothy got to his feet.

Someday, he thought, *I'm going to be able to hang out with my friends without worrying about a major disaster looming on the horizon.* His mind flitted to Jewel, and for a moment, he found himself wondering where they would be if not for the impending invasion.

There's no use in speculating about it, he thought at last. *Maybe when this is all over...*

Chapter 11

Velikanov, Severnaya

Gearwire drummed his fingers against his robotic leg, waiting for the giant's messengers to return.

They can't have gotten very far, he thought, staring out into the snowy peaks. *Not without better gear.*

"I still can't believe they managed to break out of the dungeon and make off with the Gravity Ray," Penn said, shaking his head. "They're much more formidable than I gave them credit for."

"I'm not surprised," the Mysterious Man said. "They have skill. And having the Orgwarian rings should make them even more powerful."

The rings won't help them survive in these mountains, Gearwire thought. But he said nothing, keeping his concerns to himself.

A knock at the door interrupted their conversation. Gearwire turned to see a guard standing in the doorway.

"The scouts have returned," he said. "Come."

Gearwire followed the giant back through the castle to the throne room, the rest of the Guardians of Kawts close behind him. The giant's ruler nodded respectfully to him as he entered, although Gearwire thought he still detected a hint of skepticism in the man's expression. The only way he'd been able to convince the giant of their intentions was to reveal his true identity, but the giant had been hesitant at first.

It was only after Gearwire had shown that he knew every detail of the Battle of Velikanov that the giant had reluctantly decided to trust him.

The double doors slammed shut behind the group, and one of the scouts began to speak. The king waited until he was finished, then repeated his words, acting as a translator.

"He says that they couldn't find them. They found a trail that seemed promising, but it disappeared outside the monastery of St. Sandoval. They spoke to the hermit who lives there, but he wasn't able to tell us anything."

Gearwire frowned. "How much longer until the ship is repaired?"

"It will still be another hour or two. We had to build most of the parts from scratch."

"What are you thinking, Gearwire?" Samuel asked.

"I'm going to follow their trail myself. They can't have just disappeared."

"You won't be able to find them," the giant's ruler said. "They're highly skilled. If they don't want to be found, they won't be."

"I'm their commander," Gearwire said. "We *have* to find them."

"And I think we might understand the way they think better than your men, your Highness," Samuel added. "No offense, of course."

The giant grunted. "Very well. I'll have the guards show you where they picked up the trail. But you won't find anything."

"We'll see about that," Gearwire said, turning toward the door.

* * *

"You seem stressed," the Mysterious Man said as they hiked up the mountain pass.

Gearwire gave him a quizzical look. "The human race is facing imminent destruction, and half our team is MIA with the device we need to stop them. Of course I'm stressed."

"But that's not what's really bothering you, is it?"

Gearwire glanced over at him.

"That's not a worried-about-the-future look," the Mysterious Man explained. "Looks more like worrying about the past."

Gearwire sighed. "I'm the one responsible for this. I'm the one who set all this in motion. The blood of a whole world of innocents will be on my hands."

"This isn't on you, Gearwire," the Mysterious Man said. Gearwire started to protest, but the Mysterious Man cut him off. "No—listen to me." He drew one of his swords from the sheath on his back, its hilt slightly larger than the other.

"I killed my last team with the bomb in the hilt of this sword's twin," he said, his voice breaking a little at the end. "I drove my sword into the main generator and destroyed our base and everyone in it. When I came to my senses, I vowed I would never use explosives again."

He slid the weapon back into its sheath. "*That's* what having blood on your hands looks like."

Gearwire was silent for a long time. Then he said, "What makes you so sure our situations are that different?"

Before the Mysterious Man could answer, the giant who served as their guide came to a stop. "This is the place," he said, pointing to a dilapidated monastery just up ahead.

Gearwire nodded. "Thanks. We'll take it from here."

He walked up to the door and knocked. He waited a moment, but nothing happened. He raised his hand to knock again, but the door swung open. A giant stood in the doorway, dressed in the plain robes of a hermit.

The hermit looked puzzled, taking in the oddly dressed group standing in front of him. "Can I help you?" he asked.

"We're looking for some friends of ours," Gearwire said. "Three men and three women. They probably would have been dressed similarly to us."

The hermit shook his head, starting to close the door. "I already told you, I don't know where they are."

Gearwire stuck his foot in the door, forcing it open again. "It's important. Please. I need to know they're safe."

The hermit hesitated for a moment, glancing at the giants who were standing a respectful distance away. "Come in," he said at last. "I might be able to help you."

* * *

New Miami, South Floridian Republic
Forty-Three Hours Remaining

Timothy stood on the banks of the sea, staring into the black depths.

Somewhere down there is the next fail-safe device, he thought. *The Omnishield, I think?* He stifled a yawn, fighting off the wave of sleepiness that suddenly washed over him. He glanced up at the moon, which was just beginning to rise. He tried to remember the last time he had had more than an hour of sleep, then quickly dismissed the inquiry.

It would only make me more tired if I knew how long it's been. And we can't afford to stop and sleep now. We're running out of time. And there are still so many fail-safe devices left to collect.

"Timothy," Jewel called from behind him. "Are you ready?"

Timothy nodded, pulling on the helmet of his diving suit. Then, taking a deep breath, he marched into the sea.

The cold water woke him up at once, chasing any thought of sleep from his mind.

"Any idea how we're supposed to find the city from here?" Crystal asked over the radio built into their helmets.

"We just keep swimming," Timothy said. "We should be able to see signs of civilization."

"Like that?" Quill asked, pointing to the shell of an old building, mostly buried beneath the ocean plants.

Timothy paused, turning back to look. "No," he said after a while. "I think that's from the people who used to live here. Before this area flooded."

"Not to break up the history lesson, but we'd better keep moving," Crystal said. "We only have so much air in these tanks, and we can't afford to waste it sightseeing."

Timothy nodded and turned back away from the coast, swimming deeper into the sea. After a while, Jewel appeared beside him.

"You know, if not for the circumstances, this would almost be like a vacation," she said, watching a small school of glittering fish swim past.

A smile crept across Timothy's face. "Yeah," he said, nodding. "I wouldn't mind coming back here someday. Assuming we survive the week." He fell silent for a moment, then turned to look at Jewel. "Maybe we could both come back here together."

The silence that followed was agonizing. Finally, Jewel spoke.

"I'd like that."

* * *

They had been swimming through the depths of the sea for nearly half an hour when they first saw the city. It was composed of huge glass domes, anchored to the ocean floor by tarnished beams of some unidentifiable metal. Jutting out from the sides of the domes were large glass boxes, resting parallel to the ground.

Not a moment too soon, Timothy thought, glancing down at the dial that measured his remaining oxygen levels. *We would have had to turn back in just a couple minutes.*

"How do we get in?" Aksell asked, studying the outside of the domes.

"There's got to be an entrance somewhere," Quill said. "They helped fight in the Robot War, didn't they? They must've had a way to get in and out of the city."

"Let's try these," Madison said, treading water just underneath one of the boxes. "These things don't have floors. We could swim right up inside."

"Nice work," Timothy said, swimming up to join her. He pulled himself up out of the water into the city, quickly taking off his diving suit. A smile broke out across his face as he smelled the fresh air.

He knelt down beside the hole, helping the others up after him.

"Now what?" Quill said. "We don't know anything about this place. How are we supposed to find the fail-safe device here?"

"We're just going to have to ask," Jewel said, removing her helmet. She gestured towards the path in front of them, where rows of buildings stretched out before them. "Someone down there is bound to know."

After stowing their diving gear in the Infini-case in Timothy's chest plate, the travelers made their way to the buildings below. Few people were still out on the streets, and those that were seemed to be in a hurry to get home. The hustle and bustle seemed to be strangely stilled, however, when Timothy and the others walked past, the people eyeing them with suspicion.

We should have changed back into our street clothes, Timothy realized belatedly. *We stand out like a sore thumb dressed in our battle gear.*

Although, he added, noticing the unfamiliar style of the locals' clothing, *we probably would have stood out just as badly in our street clothes.*

As Timothy reflected on their poor choice of dress, Madison finally succeeded in flagging down a nearby pedestrian.

"Excuse me," she said. "Do you know where we might find the fail-safe device that's hidden here?"

The woman raised an eyebrow, staring at Madison as if she had grown a second head.

"I don't have the slightest idea," she said. "I don't think anyone does—unless maybe the military has it hidden away somewhere."

"Great!" Madison said. "Do you know where we might find them?"

"The military? Lady, how would I know that? I'm an accountant, not a politician."

With that, the woman turned and left, quickly disappearing into the crowd.

"That could have gone better," Crystal said.

"At least we learned something," Madison said. "If we want to know where the device is, we're going to have to find someone in the government who can help us."

"But in order to do that, we need to figure out where the government *is,*" Aksell said. "Assuming there even is a high enough official in this dome."

"We'll keep looking," Timothy said. "We're bound to find someone who's willing to help us, eventually."

For the next fifteen minutes, they did exactly that, but did not come much closer to finding an answer. They regrouped in a nearby alleyway, safe from the curious stares of onlookers.

Before they could figure out what to do, however, an armored vehicle pulled up in front of the alleyway, blocking the entrance. The door opened, and an athletic, brown-haired girl stepped out, seemingly no more than eighteen years old. She was dressed in all black and seemed to have some sort of weapon in her hand, although from this distance, Timothy couldn't quite make out what it was.

She walked into the middle of the alleyway, flanked by several others in similar apparel.

"We're with the CIA," she said, pulling out a metal badge and showing it to them. "We have a few questions for you."

"This is starting to get a little old," Crystal muttered. "Can't we go anywhere without being arrested?"

"I'm not sure they're arresting us," Quill said. "I don't know what the 'see-yi-yay' is, but I think if they were working for the government, they would have said so."

Timothy nodded. "You might be onto something there," he said quietly. He glanced around the alleyway, noting the several smaller paths that branched off from it. "Alright. When you hear me yell, scatter. We can meet back up at the same place we came in."

He looked back up at the agents, who had slowly been making their way closer.

"Go!" Timothy shouted. The Guardians of Kawts scattered, sprinting for the other roads as the agents opened fire.

Timothy could hear the bullets whizzing past him as he vaulted over an abandoned vehicle. He stopped on the other side, pausing to assess his route. As he prepared to make a mad dash for the exit, he saw Jewel go down out of the corner of his eye, lying motionless on the ground. Fear gripped his heart, and he ran back to help her, hoping with everything he had that she wasn't already dead. Something pinged off his armor, but he ignored it, his entire focus on getting to Jewel. He bent down beside her, dragging her to the relative safety of a nearby doorway. To his relief, she still seemed to be breathing, but for how long, he couldn't guess.

Something pinged off his armor again, narrowly avoiding hitting Jewel.

I've got to draw their fire away from her, Timothy thought, turning and running back into the center of the street. A shuriken was already in his hand, and he threw it at the nearest of the agents, dropping him to the ground. As he surveyed the battlefield in search of his next target, he had the chilling realization that he was the only member of his team still standing. The others lay where they had fallen, unmoving.

Timothy grabbed another throwing star, only to have it kicked out of his hand. He whirled around to see the girl who had led the agents standing behind him. Before Timothy could recover, she threw herself at him, tackling him to the ground. He reached for another shuriken, only for the girl to kick his hand away.

The girl tugged on Timothy's helmet, slowly beginning to remove it. Timothy realized what was happening and tried to stop her, but it was too late. She fired her weapon into the gap she had created, and everything went dark.

Chapter 12

"Sir! We're within slingshot range!"

High Command pulled up a hologram of Earth on the monitor in front of him. The map had been cobbled together from the recollections of several Earthen missionaries to the Orgwar hundreds of years prior. Of course, once the missionaries realized what the Orgwarian generals were doing, they had clammed up, and the Orgwar had quickly disposed of them.

Our picture is somewhat lacking, High Command thought, twirling the hologram aimlessly. *That must change if we're to obtain a swift victory.*

"Very good," he said, turning to face the Orgwarian technician for the first time. "Send out the scouts."

* * *

Timothy groaned and opened his eyes, blinking rapidly as he adjusted to the brightness of the room he found himself in.

What happened? he thought, his muddled brain struggling to remember.

There were a bunch of people in black suits. One of them shot me in the face. He shook his head. *It must have been a tranquilizer of some sort,* he realized, touching the spot where he had been shot. Aside from a small puncture mark on his chin, there was no sign of injury.

Either that, or I'm dead.

His mind went back to the memory of Jewel, lying prone in the street, and he had his answer.

There was no blood, he realized now. *She wasn't dying—she was just unconscious.*

I hope.

His mind set somewhat at ease, he examined the room he now found himself in. The room was only about six feet long in either direction and empty except for a cot bolted to the far wall. As expected, his captors had confiscated his armor, leaving Timothy with nothing beyond what he could manage to find inside the room itself. The door was solid wood, with no window, and Timothy knew without trying that it would be locked.

Defeated, he returned to the cot, thinking over the situation.

"Unless something changes, I'm stuck in here," he muttered. He sighed.

If there ever was a time when we needed God's help, this would be it, he thought, wondering how many hours had slipped away while he had been unconscious. He stared up at the ceiling and offered a half-hearted prayer, trying to ignore the part of him that insisted he was wasting his time.

Timothy had been awake for nearly fifteen minutes when he became aware of an irregular pounding sound coming from the other side of the wall. At first, he dismissed it as irrelevant noise, but after a while, he began to sense a pattern in it.

It's Morse code, he realized suddenly, the thought striking him like a bolt of lightning. He listened closely to the sound, straining his brain to remember enough of the letters to make sense of the message.

So-eone t-ere is so-eone t-ere is

Is someone there?

Growing excited now, Timothy whacked the wall twice to show he had received the message. After thinking for a moment, he gave his response.

Its T

There was silence for a moment, then the banging sound returned.

-uill -ere

Quill, Timothy thought. *Of course. He was the one who sent me that book of codes back in Kawts in the first place.*

Ere are us, Timothy pounded back, hoping the message was clear enough with the letters that he remembered. *Are all Oa?*

U need to practice ur code, Quill responded. He hesitated a moment, then sent, *Dont -no- —ere -e are. Cr-stal on m- le-t. No clue or A or - or -*

Timothy was silent for a moment, trying to decipher what Quill had said. The message repeated, and this time, he understood.

He doesn't know where we are. Or what happened to Aksell, or Madison, or Jewel.

-een -uestionin- e-er-one, Quill said through the wall. *A-out t-e -ission. I t-in- u r ne-t.*

Timothy frowned. He waited for Quill to repeat the message, but Quill had fallen silent. A few seconds later, the door swung open, revealing a fierce-looking young man who looked to be a few years older than Timothy. His uniform was a mottled blue color, though beyond that, there was no clue as to his identity. A gun of some sort hung at his belt, and for a moment, Timothy was tempted to make a grab for it.

"I wouldn't try that if I were you," the man said, resting his hand on the hilt of his weapon. "Not unless you'd like to spend a few hours unconscious. Which, from what your friends told us, would not be something you appreciate."

Timothy looked up at the man, Quill's last message finally clicking. *He was trying to tell me that they've all been questioned about the mission.*

"Let us go," Timothy said. "We're on a very important mission, and we don't have any time to waste."

"That may very well be true. But given that you broke into our city through a fishing portal in the middle of the night dressed for battle and asking about the location of one of the most powerful relics known to man, I think I'm justified in questioning your motives."

"He's got a point there," Timothy muttered to himself. Then, louder, he said, "What do you want?"

"Just the truth," the man said. "Nothing more, and nothing less."

Timothy nodded, taking a moment to collect his thoughts. Then he told the man the story of everything that had happened to them since they had left Kawts. The man listened carefully, occasionally making a note on the pad of paper he took from his pocket. When he had finished, the man put the paper back into his pocket and turned toward the door.

"Someone will be back to see you soon," he said. "Until then, just sit tight."

Then he was gone, leaving Timothy alone in the room again.

Only a few minutes later, the door opened again, and several soldiers marched into the room, dressed in a similar bluish uniform as the man who had questioned him.

"You're in luck," one of the soldiers said. "The Governor thinks your story is credible enough to give you a hearing."

The soldiers ushered Timothy into the hallway, where he was quickly reunited with the rest of his team. The soldiers shepherded them through the building, finally depositing them outside a nondescript door. A black-suited man stood guard outside, eyeing the newcomers with suspicion. One of the soldiers spoke to him, and the man nodded, opening the door.

"Right this way," the soldier said. Timothy started to step into the room, but the man stopped him. "Don't try anything foolish in there," he said, touching the hilt of his weapon. "Most of *us* don't use tranquilizers."

"Noted," Timothy said, eyeing the soldier warily. The soldier stepped aside, allowing him to enter.

The room he found himself in seemed to be a meeting room of some sort, a long oval table running down the middle of the room. Around the table sat various important-looking people, most of whom were wearing some sort of military insignia. At the far end of the table, flanking the man at the head, Timothy recognized the girl who had captured them and the man who had questioned him.

The soldiers filed into the room behind the Guardians of Kawts lining the back wall as the door slammed shut. The soldiers looked expectantly toward the man at the head of the table, whom Timothy took to be the Governor.

Durgan, he remembered, scrutinizing the man even as he did the same to them.

Durgan was an imposing figure, standing a bit taller than average and having the appearance of a battle-hardened warrior, despite his greying hair.

"General Staples says you've come here looking for the Omnishield," Durgan said. "Explain."

"There was a dictator in our hometown who made a deal with the Orgwar to invade Earth," Jewel said. "We were able to stop him, but he managed to send an S.O.S. to the Orgwar before he was defeated. They're on their way here as we speak."

"Who is 'we?'" the Governor asked. "There's no way the six of you defeated a dictator and his allies alone."

"There… there used to be more of us," Jewel said, her voice breaking. "We lost the rest of our team in Velikanov."

"I'm sorry to hear that," Durgan said. "But what makes you so sure that the Orgwar are really coming?"

"There was a scientist on our team—he was a close friend of Gearwire's," Timothy said, hoping to see some sort of recognition on the Governor's face. Durgan's face remained impassive, so he went on. "He examined the communication device after we defeated Ethos."

"And he also died in the explosion?" the man who had questioned Timothy interrupted. "That seems awfully convenient."

Durgan arched his eyebrows at this, but he said nothing.

"No," Timothy said. "During the battle, we also lost the Weather Belt. He's traveling back in time to meet with a group of scientists who he said might be able to rebuild the device."

"What was the name of this scientist?" a silver-haired general asked, his voice raspy.

"Dr. Maddium," Crystal said. "Thomas Maddium."

Durgan leaned back in his chair, rubbing his chin thoughtfully. "We are familiar with the name. He fought alongside Milkop Quawz in the Robot War."

Timothy exchanged a glance with Jewel.

I guess the Council wasn't completely wrong in thinking there was a connection between Milkop Quawz and Gearwire. I wonder what his real story is.

Was, he corrected himself, an image of the flaming ship plummeting to the ground flashing across his vision.

"So what?" another man asked. "You want the fail-safe devices to fight off the Orgwar?"

"Exactly," Jewel said. "It's the only way we have a chance at stopping them."

The man who had interrogated Timothy was on his feet in an instant.

"Maybe where you come from. But I'd like to see the Orgwar TRY to take South Florida!"

"Sit down, Devon!" Durgan snapped. "If the Orgwar invade, we don't stand any more of a chance than anywhere else! Our only hope of survival would be to pray they never learn we exist!"

"So you'll help us?" Madison said. "You'll let us have the Omnishield?"

"I didn't say that," Durgan said. "I only said that we'd have no choice but to help you if you were telling the truth."

"Wait," Quill said. "We have proof. We have a letter from the High Baron of Ellada verifying our mission."

Durgan looked intrigued. "And where is this letter?"

"It's in my chest plate," Timothy said. "There's a secret compartment."

"Very well," Durgan said. "We will look for it. In the meantime, you will be escorted back to your rooms. We will try to be brief," he said before any of them could object. "But you have to realize that we're going to need time to verify your story."

"That's very reasonable," Timothy said. "But remember, Dr. Maddium estimated that we only have about forty hours left before the Orgwar arrive. And most of the fail-safe devices are still unaccounted for."

Durgan nodded. "We will be as quick as we can. That much, I can assure you."

* * *

Nearly fifteen minutes passed before the Guardians of Kawts were summoned back to the meeting room. This time, the room was empty except for Durgan and two other people. Timothy recognized them as the man who had questioned him and the girl who had led the force that had captured them. For a long time, the Governor remained silent, staring off into space.

"After careful consideration, we believe we can trust you," he said. "We will allow you to borrow the Omnishield." Durgan studied the travelers for a moment before continuing. "On one condition."

"The Omnishield is a very powerful relic," he said. "And as much as we believe we can trust you, it's never wise to completely trust a band of dangerous strangers you don't know. Which is why we're sending two of our most trusted operatives with you."

Timothy frowned, glancing at the two others in the room. "I'm not sure that's the best idea," he said. "We all know each other very well, but we won't know what to expect from a pair of total strangers. It could jeopardize the mission."

"Plus, how can we be sure *we* can trust *them?*" Crystal said. "And for that matter, how do you know they won't stab us all in the back and take the fail-safe devices for themselves!"

"I appreciate your concerns," Durgan said. "But those are the only terms on which you're going to leave this city with the Omnishield. I can assure you, they are among our best agents, and they are completely trustworthy."

Timothy said nothing, sensing that it was a fight he wasn't going to win.

"These are the operatives who will be accompanying you," Durgan said, turning to the people on either side of him. "Agent Eva of the CIA, and Captain Devon of the South Floridian Army." He paused for a moment, then added, "My children."

"The operatives you're sending with us are your children?" Madison said.

"They're the only ones I trust completely on a mission like this," Durgan said. "But mark my words," he said, his expression hardening.

"If you harm them in any way, you will have all of South Florida after you."

Timothy swallowed hard, unable to stop himself from imagining the many ways this could go horribly wrong.

"You don't have anything to worry about," Quill said. "You can trust us."

"Yes. I believe I can," Durgan replied after a moment. Then he stood. "Devon and Eva will show you the way to the Omnishield."

"This way!" Eva said, slipping out the back door of the conference room with Devon right behind her. Timothy hesitated for a moment, then jogged after them.

He was surprised by how dark it was outside, the large overhead lamps dimmed to a fraction of their previous brightness. The streets were completely empty, giving Timothy the impression that much time had passed.

"How long were we out for?" he asked, eyeing the darkened city warily.

"Only an hour or two," Eva said, glancing over her shoulder at him. "The effects of our tranquilizers don't last very long. To be honest, I'm surprised it took you all as long as it did to recover."

"It's been a rough couple of days," Crystal said.

"So where is this device?" Aksell asked.

"I'm going to ask you not to mention that where people can hear you," Devon said through gritted teeth.

"You'll find out soon enough," Eva said with a smile. "And I promise you, you never would have found it otherwise."

Devon gave his sister a dirty look, and Timothy could hear him muttering something about giving out too much information. Eva, however, did not seem fazed.

"Relax, Dev. No one's going to figure out what we're talking about just based on that."

Devon frowned, but he said nothing.

"We sure meet some interesting people working for Gearwire, don't we?" Quill said quietly, coming up beside Timothy.

Timothy nodded, his attention still focused on their two newest teammates. *It's hard to believe they're siblings,* he thought, noticing the sharp contrasts in their personalities. His mind drifted to his own brother. *Then again, Maurice and I weren't exactly on the same wavelength most of the time either.*

"Tim…" Quill said hesitantly. "I've been thinking…" He hesitated, biting his lip. "I don't think God will let the Orgwar win."

Timothy looked over at him. "You know, you're the third person to say something like that to me since we left Alpen."

"Great minds think alike, I guess," Quill said with a smirk. Then his smile faded. "But seriously—think about everything that's happened to us in the last few months. I was dying, Tim. And then I wasn't."

"People recover from injuries all the time," Timothy said. "There's nothing miraculous about it."

Quill raised an eyebrow. "I know you don't believe *that*. And what about what happened in the Cold Room? You and I both know that the light we followed wasn't the door. It certainly seems like someone's looking out for us."

Timothy shook his head. "Even if there *were*, there's no guarantee they'd do it again," he said. "They didn't stop Henry from dying. Or Maurice. Or the rest of our team."

In spite of his protests, Quill's words stirred something in Timothy's memory, and he remembered the weeks after he had fled Kawts. He had completely run out of food and was on the verge of starving to death when he had stumbled across an apple tree.

Right after I prayed about it, he remembered now. *I mean, I had been praying about it before, too. But what if Quill's right? What if it was God intervening?*

"I don't know," Quill said with a helpless shrug. He sighed. "I'm pretty new to this whole God thing. I'm still trying to figure things out."

"That makes two of us," Timothy said with a wry smile.

"We're here," Jewel whispered, appearing beside the pair.

Timothy nodded. "Thanks for the heads-up."

He looked up to see an old, Victorian style building on the edge of town, the sign over the door marking it as a museum. By the time he reached the entrance, Devon's soldiers, whom he had sent on ahead, were already inside, clearing out any bystanders who happened to be in the way.

Devon and Eva came to a stop in the center of the museum, standing in front of a large display about the Robot War. Standing in one corner of the room was a replica of an old statue depicting several men standing guard over the planet. Most of them were people Timothy had never seen before, but standing near the middle were two that he recognized.

"That's them!" Madison said. "That's Gearwire and Dr. Maddium!"

Devon looked at her, his forehead furrowed. "That's... odd," he said, frowning. "This statue is a replica of one that was constructed after the Heroes War to commemorate the leaders of the different factions of heroes who fought in the conflict. That was the first time the Orgwar attacked. It was under that very statue that Dr. Thomas Maddium and Milkop Quawz found the relics those heroes left behind. If that truly is Gearwire and Dr. Maddium, more might ride on this fight than you think."

"What do you mean?" Jewel asked.

"If the man in that statue really is Dr. Maddium, it would seem that there's some time travel in play," he said. "And judging from what you've told us, it would seem rather unlikely that he's fought in the Heroes War recently."

Timothy nodded slowly, picking up on what Devon was saying. "Which would mean that his involvement hasn't happened yet. And if he gets killed by the Orgwar before that…"

"If that's the case, we're already in trouble," Crystal said. "Because Gearwire's dead. And I think I can pretty definitively say that he hasn't fought in any wars outside of Kawts in at least the last five years or so."

"We must be missing something," Quill said. "Some part of this we aren't aware of yet."

Devon nodded. "I hope you're right."

Eva turned away from the statue and walked over to the central display, a mural depicting a battle from the Robot War. Mounted in front of it were several relics from the battle, including a battered robot head and what seemed to be an early precursor to Gearwire's glue gun. In the very center, illuminated by a string of lights, were the fail-safe devices.

Devon removed a key from his pocket and handed it to Eva. She removed the ancient shield from the case and handed it to Timothy.

"You keep the Omnishield in a museum?" Aksell asked. "That's– that's– aren't you afraid someone will steal it?"

"Not at all," Eva said, a smile breaking out across her face. "After all, why would anyone steal a plastic replica of a national treasure? Especially when it would be much easier to rob the gift shop than the museum."

"You're hiding it in plain sight," Timothy said, reading the plaque mounted on the outside of the glass. "Everything else is a replica. No one would expect a museum to try to pass off a genuine artifact as a fake."

"That's genius," Jewel said.

Eva's smile widened. "I can't exactly claim the credit for the idea, but I can say that there are no recorded attempts to steal the device."

"Along those lines," Devon interrupted. "You aren't to breathe a word of this hiding place to anyone else. It's only safe so long as no one knows about it."

"We won't tell a soul," Crystal said.

"You'd better not."

"Enough of this chatter," Eva said. "We have a very important mission to get on with, do we not?"

Timothy nodded. "That we do."

Without saying another word, Devon led the group back to their entry point, nodding to the soldiers who were standing guard around it. The soldiers produced the gear they had confiscated, handing it back to the Guardians of Kawts. Timothy smiled as he felt the familiar weight of his armor once more.

"Just one more problem," Crystal said. "We don't have diving suits for you two. We weren't expecting company."

"Don't worry about that," Eva said with a smirk. She adjusted part of the gauntlet she wore, and her armor morphed into a diving suit of her own. Beside her, Devon did the same.

"All right," Timothy said. "Let's get going." Without waiting for a reply, he turned and dove into the water. The others followed suit, and after a short while, they had reached the coast once more.

* * *

Timothy watched out of the corner of his eye as the two Floridians removed their helmets, marveling at the sky above them.

They've probably never left their city before, he realized. *They've never seen grass or trees—or even the sun!*

"Enjoying the view?" Jewel asked.

Devon looked down at her, hastily trying to hide his amazement.

"It's different from what I'd imagined," he said.

"It's amazing," Eva said. "I've never seen anything quite like it."

"Just wait until we use St. Sandoval's medallion," Aksell said. "It'll get even weirder."

Eva smiled. "I can't wait."

Aksell suddenly became very intent on inspecting his weapons, his ears turning bright red.

"If you're going to be traveling with us, we might as well get to know each other," Madison said. "How long have you guys been 'trusted operatives?'"

Devon stared at her, his eyes narrowing. Eva, however, seemed to have no problem with the question.

"It's been about two years for me," she said. "I think Dev is up to year four at this point. All South Floridians are required to serve for at least two years after they turn sixteen. It's a holdover law from the Robot War, I think." She turned to look at the others. "How about you? You guys can't be much older than Devon and I."

"I've really only been doing this for a little over a year," Timothy said, realizing not for the first time how quickly his life had changed. "Since I was sixteen. And Quill and Aksell are about the same."

"I've only been officially training for about a year," Aksell said quickly. "But my dad's been teaching me stuff ever since I was a kid."

"Your father, the dictator?" Devon said, raising an eyebrow.

Aksell flinched, but said nothing.

"Jewel and I have been doing this since we were twelve," Crystal said. "It's a long story."

"I think we're going to have plenty of time on our hands," Devon said. "Assuming you don't have some sort of teleportation device."

"It's not quite a teleportation device," Quill said, pulling out the medallion. "But it'll get us where we need to go in record time." He glanced over at the newcomers. "You might want to hold on. Things are going to get a little weird-looking."

Chapter 13

Oria, Ellada

Gearwire made a slow circle around the city, searching for an open place to land the ship. He finally spotted a place just outside the capitol building and steered the ship toward it, barely avoiding crashing into two hovercars that were parked nearby. As the roar of the engines died away, Gearwire emerged from the cockpit, noting with satisfaction that the others were already gathering their gear.

Quickly, they filed out onto the launchpad, and Gearwire headed for the front door. The bored-looking sentry standing outside started violently when they approached, suddenly snapping to his feet.

"The High Baron is not accepting visitors today," he said. He adjusted his raygun so that it pointed toward the Guardians of Kawts. "You'd better get moving."

"It's important," Gearwire said. "The fate of the world may very well depend on it. Tell him Gearwire is here to see him."

The guards exchanged glances, but neither moved. "The High Baron is not accepting visitors today," he repeated.

"Let them in, Leander," a voice called from the other end of the corridor. Gearwire glanced behind him to see a man dressed in an ornate suit of armor and a long brown cape. The man looked vaguely familiar, although Gearwire wasn't quite able to place him.

"Let them in," the man repeated. "The High Baron is expecting them."

"But sir!" one of the guards protested, but the man silenced him with a wave of his hand.

"But nothing! Did you not hear them! This is an urgent matter! Open the door!"

"Yes, sir," the guard said. He slowly pushed open the door, and the man led the group into the throne room.

"Who are you?" Samuel asked as they walked past the guards. "And how could the High Baron possibly be expecting us?"

The man adjusted his plumed helmet. "I'm Alexander Drakos, the Baron of Information. And as for knowing you were coming-"

"Captain Gearwire! We heard you'd been killed in action!" the High Baron called out from the other side of the room.

"Then Timothy and the others actually made it over here," Gearwire said, relief flooding him. "Where are they?"

The Baron of Information grimaced. "I'm afraid you're too late. They left several hours ago. But between you, me, and the High Baron, I'm sure we can come up with something."

"How on earth did you manage to get here?" the High Baron asked. "Your young crewmembers told us you'd been shot down over Velikanov."

"We were," Gearwire said. "Fortunately for us, it'll take more than a couple of missiles to destroy my ship. But by the time we got everything sorted out, they'd already moved on. I was hoping we'd be able to meet up with them here. But from what the Baron of Information's been telling me, it sounds like we're too late."

The High Baron shook his head. "I'm afraid so. We gave them a copy of our map of the fail-safe devices. When they left, they were planning on heading to South Florida."

"They'll never get across the sea," the Mysterious Man said. "What are they thinking?"

"They have the Learner's medallion," the Baron of Information said. "They'll be fine."

Gearwire nodded absently, deep in thought. "Could you have some of your scientists build something for us? Some diving gear, or a one-man submarine, maybe?"

"The Baron of Technology perfected plans for such a device just last week," the High Baron said. "Baron Drakos? Can you send someone to fetch him?"

The Baron of Information nodded. "Right away. It's a good thing he's in town this week. Otherwise, you'd have to fly all the way over to his lab in Crete."

Baron Drakos left the room, and Gearwire asked the High Baron several questions about his missing crewmembers, most of which merely confirmed what he'd already suspected. After a few minutes, Baron Drakos returned, followed closely by the Baron of Technology, a dark-haired man named Exypnos.

The newly arrived Baron's eyes darted from Gearwire to the High Baron, then back to Gearwire.

"Baron Exypnos," the High Baron said. "Gearwire and his team need-"

Before the High Baron could finish his sentence, Baron Exypnos whipped out a gun from his armor and fired it at him. At the last moment, Gearwire tackled the High Baron to the ground, his military training taking over. The blast from Exypnos' gun hit the top of the throne, turning it into a melted heap of slag. But before he could take another shot, Gearwire had drawn his own weapon, firing it at the livid Baron.

As if sensing what was about to happen, the Baron dropped to the floor, causing Gearwire's shot to instead hit the throne room doors, sealing them shut. As the Baron readied his weapon for another shot, the Guardians of Kawts scattered throughout the room, spreading out to create less of a target.

The Baron took another shot at Gearwire, this time using the friction ray from the holster on his hip. The blast struck the ground at Gearwire's feet, and he went down, unable to get any traction on the frictionless floor.

The Baron whirled around and fired the ray at Idalbo as well, then fired his original weapon at Samuel. At the last second, the Golden Knight jumped in front of him, catching the blow on his chest plate. The force of the blast threw him against the wall, knocking the wind out of him. His armor smoked, but the invincium had held strong.

Whirling around, the Baron turned his attention to Adalbo and Penn, who were standing close together. He fired his blaster at them, missing Adalbo by inches but grazing Penn's arm. Penn's hooded cloak burst into flames, singeing his arm as he struggled to free himself from the burning garment. Howard and Idalbo ran over to help him. The Baron smirked as he watched them clump together, raising his weapon for a killing shot. As his finger tightened on the trigger, his weapon was suddenly knocked from his hand, and he crumpled to the floor.

Behind him stood the Mysterious Man, the pommel of his sword hovering in the air where the Baron's head had been seconds before.

"He'll have quite a headache when he wakes up," he said, slipping his sword back into its sheath. He kicked the Baron's weapons across the floor, making sure they were out of reach should the Baron regain consciousness once more.

"What just happened?" the High Baron demanded, looking around at his damaged throne room. "Why did Baron Exypnos try to kill me?"

"I think we might have found the Council's scientist," Gearwire said, pulling himself away from the frictionless patch of the floor. "I never would have guessed he was so high up. He must have thought we'd discovered him."

"I don't believe it," the High Baron said, looking at the prone figure of the baron on the floor. "And yet, he definitely tried to kill me." He paused for a moment, then looked over at Gearwire. "Are there any other traitors I should be worrying about before I call someone else in?"

"As far as I know, he's the Council's only supplier," Gearwire said.

The High Baron nodded. "Then send in the Baron of Security. And the High Doctor," he added, glancing at Penn's badly burnt arm.

As the Baron of Information slipped out the back door of the throne room, Gearwire frowned to himself.

With the Baron of Technology working for the Council, there's no way we'll be able to get the equipment we'll need to bring a large force down to South Florida, he realized. *Our only chance will be to catch up with the others in the Yellowstone Desert.*

* * *

Yellowstone Desert
Thirty-Eight Hours Remaining

"So you all really know Thomas Maddium?" Eva said. "One of the great heroes of the Robot War?"

"I think we might have known Milkop Quawz, too," Timothy said, remembering how Milkop's name continued to come up alongside Gearwire's. "Not that we'll ever know for sure now."

"You guys just don't see how cool that is," Devon said, his previous guardedness beginning to break down. "You were trained by some of the best warriors and military strategists of all time. Milkop and his crew are legendary!"

"Henry used to be part of our team, too," Jewel said, glancing over at Timothy. "I never really knew him well, but Timothy went on a few missions with him."

"What happened to him?" Eva asked.

"He died," Timothy said. A lump formed in his throat as the memories of Henry's death brought to mind the vision of Gearwire's ship exploding.

The group fell silent for a moment, and Timothy pulled out the map from Ellada. He glanced between the map and the towering shapes that stretched out in front of them on the horizon.

"I think we're here," he said after a moment. "Quill, take us back to reality."

Quill nodded, and a second later, the shapes lost their mirage-like quality, coalescing into a burnt-out husk of a city.

"Do you think anyone lives there?" Madison asked, staring into the ruins.

Timothy shook his head. "It looks abandoned."

"We just have to hope that whoever lived here didn't take the Laser Gauntlet with them when they left," Crystal said, shading her eyes against the sun.

"Assuming they *did* leave," Devon added. "As opposed to dying there."

Timothy shuddered, imagining a town full of corpses.

"We'd better get searching," Jewel said. "Split into pairs. We can cover more ground that way."

"Good thinking," Devon said. "Eva and I will take the north side."

"Quill and I can take the south," Madison said.

"Aksell? You and I are tackling the west," Crystal said.

"I guess that leaves you and me on the east," Timothy said, turning to look at Jewel.

Jewel nodded. "I guess so." They walked toward one of the ruined buildings in silence. Then Jewel said, "I'm sorry about putting you on the spot back there about Henry. I wasn't thinking."

"It's not really about Henry," Timothy said. "I've come to terms with the fact that he's gone. It's just… where does it stop? I thought it was bad when I lost Maurice. And Henry. But we just lost most of our team. Our friends. I can't lose anyone else."

I can't lose you, he added silently, unable to bring himself to say it out loud.

"I miss them, too," Jewel said. "Honestly, I think I'm still kind of in shock over the whole thing. All we can do is trust God."

Timothy shook his head. "I'd like to. I really would. But I'm not there yet."

Jewel nodded sympathetically. "I know what that's like. If you ever want to talk about it, you know I'm here."

"Thanks."

"Now let's find that fail-safe device."

* * *

For nearly half an hour, the Guardians of Kawts searched the abandoned city, searching for any signs of the Laser Gauntlet. The city was a good deal smaller than Kawts, or even Gearwire's Cave, but even so, they were unable to find the missing fail-safe device.

"I don't think it's here," Crystal said, meeting up with Timothy and Jewel in the town square. "Between the eight of us, we've looked everywhere."

"We'll have to keep looking," Timothy said, unwilling to accept defeat. "We don't have any other choice."

"Guys!" Eva shouted from somewhere above them. Timothy craned his neck to see her waving down at them from the top of a nearby clock tower, the massive clock mounted on the front having long ago stopped working. "You're going to want to see this!"

Timothy and Jewel exchanged glances.

"Do you think she found the Laser Gauntlet?" Timothy asked.

"I wouldn't be too sure about that," Crystal said.

"Only one way to find out," Jewel said.

"I'll race you to the top of the clock tower," Quill said, coming up behind the group.

Before anyone could respond, he took off toward the rickety old building, Timothy sprinting after him. Despite his best efforts, Quill quickly outpaced him, although Jewel easily beat him to the top with the help of Marathon's ring.

"Hey! No fair!" Quill was saying as Timothy reached the top of the tower. "You had help!"

Jewel smiled. "So did you, Quill," she said, pointing to the ring on his arm, which was glowing faintly.

"Come on, Tim," Quill said. "Back me up here. My ring doesn't give me any extra speed."

Timothy just shook his head, trying to hide a smile. "I didn't see anything, Quill," he said. "I just got here."

Quill rolled his eyes. "I see how it is," he said. "You'd rather-"

"As entertaining as this is, we did race up here for a reason," Crystal said, interrupting him. She turned to Eva. "Which would be…"

Eva nodded, pointing at something in the distance, beyond the outskirts of the abandoned town. "There's smoke. Someone else is here."

Chapter 14

Timothy retrieved Henry's old field binoculars from his chest plate, peering off in the direction Eva had indicated. His breath caught in his chest when he saw a lively campsite, only a short distance outside the town.

"What is it?" Quill asked, squinting. "What do you see?"

"People," Timothy said, lowering the binoculars once more. "There's an entire camp."

"Locals?" Devon asked.

"I don't have the slightest idea," Timothy said. "I've never been to this part of the world before."

"Maybe they'll be able to tell us what happened here," Aksell said, glancing over at Eva. "Maybe they know where the gauntlet is."

"It's worth a shot," Crystal said. "At the very least, they might have something to eat other than survival rations."

"I don't know about this," Devon said. "South Florida is pretty isolated from the rest of the world, but even there, we've heard stories about the nomads who roam these deserts. They're utterly heartless. They'd eat you as soon as look at you."

Eva shook her head. "Those stories are old, Dev. Even if they *were* true at one point, that was hundreds of years ago. And chances are, they've been heavily embellished."

"They didn't seem to be armed," Timothy said. "At least, they didn't have any weapons that I could see. Although it's hard to make out details from this distance."

"I say we give it a shot," Eva said. "We have Crystal and Jewel. And how many of the fail-safe devices? Even if they are hostile, we're more than capable of fighting our way out."

"I agree with Eva," Aksell said immediately. "We have nothing to lose."

Timothy turned to the others. "What do you think?"

Quill shrugged, and Madison said, "Do we have another option? We're kind of running out of leads."

"Let's do it," Jewel said. "But keep your weapons at the ready. Just in case."

"I still think this is a bad idea," Devon said, frowning.

Eva laughed and rolled her eyes. "Devon, you were the one who thought we should try to fight off the Orgwar. If we could do that, surely we could fight off a handful of nomads."

"That's different, and you know it," Devon said. "And besides, we're not supposed to be getting into battles. Dad told me to keep you safe."

"Really? Because that's exactly what he told me to do for you," Eva said, arching an eyebrow.

"Okay," Timothy said, cutting off Devon's retort. "We're going to check out the campsite." He looked up at Devon. "If you're concerned about it, you're welcome to stay behind and bail us out if we get captured."

"Fine," Devon said. "But don't say I didn't warn you."

With Devon's words still echoing in his mind, Timothy led the group out of the city and toward the campsite. Despite what he told the others, he had to admit that he was on edge, his hand hovering over one of his shurikens.

They were almost to the campsite when they heard a shout. Timothy whirled around to face the sound just in time to see a plainly dressed man sprinting toward the camp. He was shouting at the top of his lungs, but he was too panicked for Timothy to figure out what he was saying.

"Well, they know we're here," Crystal said. "Let's see what they do now."

They stayed where they were for a few minutes, watching the camp for any sign of what was coming. After what seemed like an eternity, a small group of men emerged from the camp and began walking toward them.

"Weapons down," Timothy muttered as the group drew closer. "Don't attack unless they make a move."

The men came to a stop in front of them, and Timothy now saw that they held a variety of battered weapons, ranging from an old musket to a very homemade-looking spear. For a moment, the men said nothing, but Timothy could tell from the way they held their weapons that they were unused to them.

"We don't want any trouble," one of them said at last, waving his gun at them in what Timothy suspected was intended to be a menacing fashion. In reality, however, the gun almost slipped from the man's hands, and he quickly shifted to a two-handed grip.

"Neither do we," Timothy said, raising his hands in the air. "We're just passing through. We were actually hoping you might be able to help us."

The man with the gun lowered his weapon, looking relieved. Beside him, an older man with a grey beard cuffed a younger man on the back of the head. "Those aren't Owenites, you dummy! Now get back to your post!" The older man shooed him off, muttering, "Kids. Afraid of their own shadows, I swear it." Then he turned to the third man. "Well? Are you going to ask them to join us by the fire? Or are you just going to stand there and let them freeze?"

"Of course," the man said, shifting awkwardly at the older man's rebuke. "I was just about to-"

"Then do it!" the old man said. "Don't just stand there jawin' about it!"

The man grimaced, then turned back to face the Guardians of Kawts. "We just put some coffee on the fire. We'd love for you to join us. You can ask us whatever you need to while we drink. Unless you had other plans..."

"That's fine," Timothy said, the tension draining out of his body. He nodded reassuringly to the others, then followed the two men into the camp.

As they walked closer to the cook fire, Timothy's suspicions were confirmed. Several wagons dotted the campsite, forming a rough defensive ring. Aside from the few battered weapons held by the sentries, there was no sign of anyone being armed. Their wagons were worn and dusty and looked like they had traveled quite a way.

Whoever else these people might be, they aren't warriors.

"I hope you'll forgive us for our... rough welcome," the man said. "But you can't be too careful. Not with the Owenites in the area. Blasted nomads. They got our guide a few days ago. We were hoping he'd be able to escape and catch up with us, but..." A troubled expression crossed his face, and Timothy knew what the man was thinking. If the guide hadn't come back by now, he probably wasn't going to.

After a few minutes of walking, they finally made it to the center of the camp, where a handful of others stood around the fire. Timothy quickly scanned their faces, searching for any signs of hostility. Though a few of them seemed to be suspicious of the newcomers, most just seemed curious.

While Timothy examined the crowd, the old man who had greeted them at the edge of the camp stood and began to pour out the coffee from a pot that hung over the fire. As he passed out mugs to the dozen or so people who had gathered around, the crowd began to quiet down.

By the time he got to the Guardians of Kawts, it was nearly silent.

"So," one of the sentries said as the old man sat down with his coffee. "What brings you out here? And what did you need our help for?"

Timothy glanced back at Jewel, who nodded slightly. He turned back toward the travelers and began to tell their story, though he was careful not to mention the exact reason for their quest, not wanting to make the people more on edge than they already were.

When he had finished, the man looked thoughtful. "I'm not sure how much we can help you with that," he said. "Unless you're just looking for more people to help you search. We're just passing through here ourselves. We're on our way to Cleanwater. Hoping to join the settlement there. Dawson might have known the answer to your question. But as I said earlier, he's… missing."

The man's words hit Timothy like a physical blow, though he hid his disappointment well.

It was a long shot, anyway, he thought. *Looks like there's nothing left to do but go back to the city for another look.*

"Well, thanks anyway," Madison said. "And thanks for the coffee. It feels like forever since we've had a warm drink."

The man smiled. "You're welcome. I assume this means you'll be leaving us?"

Timothy nodded. "I'm afraid it does. We still have to find the Laser Gauntlet. Before the—before it's too late," he finished, catching himself just in time.

"Well, you're always welcome at our fire," the man said. "For as long as we're both in the area."

Timothy gulped down the last of his coffee and stood up, the others following suit. "Thank you again for your hospitality," he said. Then he turned and headed back to the ruined city.

For nearly another hour, they scoured the city, looking through every room in every building. They had almost reached the center of the city when Devon ran up to them, a steely look in his eyes.

"There's a fire in the camp," he said, locking eyes with Timothy. "It's the nomads. I know it."

"It's probably just another campfire," Timothy said. "That's a pretty large group of people to cook for with only one fire."

"Normally, I'd be inclined to agree with you, Tim," Aksell said, jogging up alongside Eva. "But this is bigger than a campfire." He pointed behind him in the direction he had come, and Timothy's heart skipped a beat when he noticed the eerie glow on the horizon.

"That's not a campfire," he breathed, running up to the top of the clock tower. He skidded to a stop on the top platform, whipping out Henry's old binoculars. His heart sank when he saw the campsite.

Devon's right, he thought. *The settlers have been attacked.*

The others began to catch up with him, slowing to a stop as they saw the destruction in the distance.

"What do we do?" Madison asked, looking toward Timothy.

Timothy said nothing, running through the situation in his mind.

If we go down to help them, we're probably giving up all chance of completing our mission, he thought.

But the Laser Gauntlet doesn't even seem to be here anymore. We don't have a chance, regardless.

His mind drifted back to something Jewel had said the previous day.

'If we can't stop the Orgwar from invading, I'm going to do everything in my power to save as many people as I can before they kill me.'

"We help them," Timothy said, coming to a decision.

"What about the Laser Gauntlet?" Crystal asked. "I don't mean to seem callous, but if we don't find it soon, the entire planet is doomed. We're running out of time."

"We're not going to find it," Timothy said. "We've searched this entire town top to bottom and haven't found any trace of it. Whoever lived here must have taken it with them when they left. The least we can do is to help these people now, while we can."

"And when the Orgwar come?" Crystal asked. "What then?"

Timothy looked up at her, suddenly at peace with his decision. "Then we just have to keep saving as many people as we can before they kill us."

"Whatever we're doing, we'll have to act fast," Eva said. "It's only a matter of time before the nomads figure out we were at the camp earlier. If we don't hurry, they might be gone before we get there."

"If they are, we can track them down," Timothy said. But even as he said it, he couldn't help but think of another alternative to what Eva said—upon learning that they had visited the camp earlier in the day, the nomads might come looking for them. "But it will be best if we get there before they leave."

Scrambling down from the clock tower, they jogged back over to the camp, their weapons raised. The campsite was a mess, the trampled sand giving little indication of what had happened. Here and there small trinkets lay half-buried in the sand, but whether they were dropped by the nomads in their looting or the settlers in their flight was unclear. The camp seemed to be abandoned, and Timothy cursed himself for not leaving sooner.

We have to save them, he thought. *We can't be too late.*

They were almost to the center of the camp when they saw the first body. It was one of the nomads, a bloody ring on his shirt testifying to exactly how he had died. Up ahead, Timothy heard Quill give a shout. He abruptly stood up, running over to his friend. In the center of the camp, the old man who had greeted them earlier lay face down in the sand, an old pistol still clutched in his hand. Behind him, one of the wagons was on fire, its timber frame smashed to bits.

Timothy froze when he saw the body, images of Henry flashing across his mind.

"Is—is he dead?" Quill stammered.

Jewel knelt down beside the body, feeling for a pulse. The look on her face was enough to answer the question.

Timothy looked up sharply, alarm bells suddenly ringing in his head. He scanned the gaps between the wagons, popping a shuriken off into his hand. As he watched, he saw a flicker of movement behind the burning wagon. He opened his mouth to warn the others, but before he could finish, something heavy struck him in the back of the head, and everything went black.

Chapter 15

T.O.W.E.R. Headquarters
Twenty-First Century

D r. Maddium bolted awake. His eyes darted around the dark room, every inch of his body alert. From behind the half-closed door, he heard the murmur of voices. The tension drained out of him as he reassured himself that he was safe.

He climbed down from his cot and pushed the door closed. He was in a storage room in the center of the ancient superhero team's headquarters, which Dr. Grant had converted into a temporary bedroom. His usual quarters were currently occupied by another hero, one of the twins' ancestors.

Dr. Maddium glanced at his watch. There were still a few hours left before Dr. Grant estimated the device would be completed. Dr. Maddium had helped him and his companions for as long as he could, but eventually, he started nodding off and had withdrawn to the makeshift bedroom.

Now, sitting by himself in the darkened room, Dr. Maddium turned his thoughts toward what had awakened him.

It was a dream, he recalled. *About what will happen once the fail-safe devices are reassembled.*

"More of a nightmare, really," he muttered. "And yet-" He shook his head. "It seems too real to be a dream. It's too concrete. Almost like–like the other ones."

Almost unbidden, the other dreams came into his mind, the ones his old teacher had insisted were prophetic. Dr. Maddium remained still for a moment, replaying the new dream in his head. He found that he could still remember every minute detail, which only served to amplify his concerns.

"No," he said at last. "This is ridiculous. It's the stress, nothing more. I'm reading far too much into this." He lay back down and tried to go back to sleep, although he couldn't shake the small worm of doubt that his dream had been true.

No sooner had he drifted off than the dream began anew.

* * *

Yellowstone Desert
Thirty-Three Hours Remaining

Timothy groaned and opened his eyes, his head throbbing where he had been hit. He slowly sat up, taking a look around. They were in a camp of some kind, surrounded by clusters of tents. A fire burned a short distance away, and he could hear the distant murmur of voices beyond that. The others were lying nearby, their hands and feet chained together. Timothy's heart sank as he realized he was similarly bound.

It looks like they got everyone, he thought, doing a quick headcount. His eyes flickered back toward the still-unconscious members of their team, and his frown deepened.

I hope they're okay.

Timothy heard the clank of chains behind him and turned to see Jewel shuffling toward him, crouched low to avoid attracting the attention of the guards. A bruise was growing on the side of her face, and a trickle of dried blood ran down her forehead, but otherwise, she seemed to be fine.

"You're awake," she whispered. "We've been waiting for you."

"How are the others? Are they all still…"

Jewel nodded. "We're all fine. A little beat up, but we can handle it."

"So, what now? I assume we've been captured by the same people who attacked the settlers' campsite earlier."

"As far as we can tell. Although we haven't been able to confirm it for sure. They ambushed us and brought us back to their main camp. Aksell thinks we've been on the move for around three hours."

Timothy reached for a shuriken before remembering that their weapons had most likely been confiscated. "So, what's the plan? Or have we not figured that out yet?"

"They took all our weapons. And Marathon's rings," Jewel said. "Although as far as I can tell, they haven't realized what the rings are yet. The guards don't know about Crystal and my powers, but we're only going to get one shot at escaping."

Timothy nodded, taking in what Jewel was saying. "We need to fight off the guards and get our weapons back before they realize what's happening," he said. "It won't be easy. Especially not when some of us are still unconscious."

A smile flickered across Jewel's face. "Everyone else is already awake," she said. "We were just waiting for you."

Timothy felt a brief flash of embarrassment, but he recovered quickly.

"Do we know where they're keeping our gear?"

"There's a tent just outside this ring. We think that's where they're storing the things they stole from their prisoners."

Timothy nodded, examining the handful of guards that stood around the fire, glancing over from time to time at their captives.

They don't seem too vigilant, Timothy noted. *We can use that.*

Timothy thought for a moment, running through several possible strategies in his head.

"Alright," he said at last, keeping his voice low. "I think our best bet is if we pretend to get into a fight with each other. Like what happened with Aksell and Quill in Velikanov. When they come to investigate, we drop the act and attack them."

"Are you sure that will work?" Jewel said. "If we're already fighting, they'll probably be more wary than they might be otherwise."

"It's possible," Timothy said. "But I can't think of any other way to get them all over here at once. And if any get away, we might not be able to get to our weapons and rescue the settlers before they catch on."

Jewel nodded. "Fake fight it is, then," she said, then crept off to tell the others about their plan. When she was finished, she turned and gave Timothy a thumbs-up.

Timothy got to his feet and made his way over to Devon, the chains on his hands and feet clanking loudly.

"I told you we shouldn't have gone in to investigate!" he shouted. "This is all your fault!" He tried to throw a punch at Devon, but Devon sidestepped, grabbing Timothy's arm and throwing him at Aksell. Aksell, apparently just waking up, put Timothy in a headlock.

"Hey! Knock it off, you guys!" Quill said, stepping between Timothy and Devon. Devon shoved him aside, and was promptly tackled by Madison.

By now, the guards had noticed the commotion and had abandoned their meal, running over to their prisoners. Once they realized the cause of the fight, they began to laugh. Their smiles quickly turned to fear, however, as one of them suddenly froze, encased in a chunk of crystal.

Before the startled guards could figure out how to react, the remaining Guardians of Kawts were on them. Eva swept one guard's feet out from under him, taking his makeshift spear and impaling him with it in one fluid movement. She rifled through the man's pockets and pulled out a ring of keys, quickly unlocking her chains.

As the guards fell before the Guardians of Kawts, Timothy noticed one guard trying to escape. Before he could get too far, Timothy tackled him, using the chain around his wrists to choke the man out until he lost consciousness.

Timothy lowered the man's limp form to the ground, hoping he hadn't killed him. But even as he got to his feet once more, the others were already making their way toward the tent where the nomads were storing their gear.

Timothy ducked inside the tent, breathing a sigh of relief as he realized their suspicions had been correct. Their weapons were lying in a heap on the ground, mixed together with assorted weapons and bits of jewelry from the nomad's previous prisoners. Timothy quickly grabbed his armor, putting it on as best he could while Eva moved among the others, unlocking their chains.

"Alright. We need to find the settlers," Timothy said once the group was suited up once more. "Preferably before the rest of the camp realizes we've escaped. Any idea where they might be?"

Quill shook his head. "Most of us were unconscious when they brought us in. And they were here before we arrived."

"We'll have to split up," Eva said, inspecting the tip of a spear she found in the pile of weapons. "We can travel in pairs to cover more distance."

Timothy hesitated for a moment, then nodded. "We can each take one quadrant and meet up west of camp. If anyone doesn't show up, we'll know they ran into trouble."

"Sounds good to me," Quill said. "Madison and I will take the south side."

"I'll take north," Eva said.

"I'll come with you," Aksell said quickly.

Devon arched an eyebrow at him. "I'm not sure that's the best idea," he said. "You've gotten taken out pretty quickly in the only two fights I've seen you in."

"I know how to fight!" Aksell said, his face flushing. "And in both those cases, we were ambushed, remember?"

Eva smirked. "Give him a chance, Dev." She turned to Aksell. "Try to keep up," she said, then ducked out of the tent, heading north.

"I guess that just leaves the four of us," Jewel said. "Crystal? Do you and Devon want to take the west quadrant?"

"Sure thing," Crystal said. Then she and Devon charged out of the tent, leaving Timothy and Jewel alone inside.

"This day just keeps getting worse," Timothy sighed, shaking his head. "It's going to take a miracle for us all to survive through the week."

"If we're going to die, there's no one else I'd rather die with," Jewel said.

For a moment, neither of them spoke, Jewel's words hanging in the air over them.

Finally, Timothy coughed. "We'd better get going," he said. "Before the others think something happened to us." Jewel nodded, and the two of them slipped off toward the eastern side of the camp. In the distance, he could hear the cries of alarm as the nomads began to realize that something was not right.

I hope the others make it out all right, he thought, ducking behind a tent as a pair of heavily armed nomads ran past. He waited until they were out of sight before he relaxed, stepping out of the shadows.

"Timothy? I think we found them," Jewel whispered. "Look behind you."

Timothy turned to see the survivors of the attack on the settlers' camp, huddled together in a circle beneath the watchful eyes of about a dozen guards. A brief glance told him that the guards hadn't noticed his presence yet.

"Wait here," Timothy whispered back, sliding his staff into his hand and creeping up behind the nearest of the guards. After glancing around to make sure no one was watching, Timothy struck the man in the back of the head. The man dropped as if his legs had been cut out from under him, barely making a sound on the sandy ground. Before the other guards had a chance to react, Timothy threw several weighted shurikens toward them, dropping a few more before any of them were aware of what was happening.

A few of the guards tried to flee, but Jewel stepped in, quickly trapping them inside chunks of crystal. In spite of their efforts, however, one of the guards managed to escape in the confusion, narrowly dodging one of Timothy's shurikens.

We'll have to move fast, he thought, shaking his head in frustration. *They'll be back with reinforcements before long.*

Timothy recalled his weapons to his hand and approached the prisoners. They drew back in fear when they saw him, unnerved by the way he had seemingly materialized out of the darkness.

"It's okay," Timothy said, taking off his helmet. "It's me. I'm here to get you out of here."

"Are any of you wounded?" Jewel asked, stepping up beside Timothy.

The man who had first greeted them staggered to his feet. "The Owenites aren't too gentle with their prisoners," he said. "Most of us aren't injured too badly, but there are a few…" He trailed off, not daring to finish his sentence.

"So we'll need some way to transport them," Timothy said. "Any ideas?"

"We could use our wagons," the man said. "After they captured you, they brought most of our wagons along. I think they're storing them pretty close to here. If we're lucky, maybe the horses will still be harnessed up."

"Let's head for the wagons, then," Timothy said. "But we're only taking as many wagons as we need in order to carry everybody. We can't afford to try to bring all of them."

Slowly, the prisoners got to their feet, helping their wounded as best they could. Timothy stood back a few meters, scanning the area for any signs of the guards' return.

"We need to keep moving," he said. "It's only a matter of time before someone shows up to investigate."

"Someone already has," came a voice from behind Timothy. He spun around to see a tall man in a patchwork leather jacket standing over him. The man carried no weapon, which only made Timothy more wary.

"Dawson?" one of the prisoners said. "We thought you were dead! We thought the Owenites had killed you when you disappeared."

Dawson raised his eyebrow, a haughty smile spreading across his face. "Unfortunately for you, that's not the case. You'll find it's pretty near impossible to kill the chief of the Owenites!"

He led them into a trap. He was planning on kidnapping them all along.

Before the man finished gloating, Timothy swung his staff at him, hoping to catch him off guard. To his amazement, the staff swung right through the man's body.

"Nice try, little shadow," the chieftain said with a chuckle. "But you're going to have to do a little better than that." He swung a fist at Timothy, his skin turning into metal as he did. Timothy only half managed to duck out of the way, catching a glancing blow on the side of his head. Disoriented, Timothy barely managed to roll out of the way as the man slammed his fists into the ground where Timothy's head had been only moments before.

"Go!" Timothy shouted to the prisoners, who were frozen in terror. "Jewel! Make sure they get to the wagons! I'll meet you outside the camp!" For a moment, Jewel looked like she was going to protest, but then she changed her mind, doing her best to hurry the prisoners along.

Timothy sprang to his feet and jabbed his staff into the chieftain's stomach. Just before the staff reached him, the man turned into water, then quickly hardened into concrete as the staff entered his body. The sudden resistance almost yanked Timothy's arm out of its socket, forcing him to drop the staff. His opponent tapped the staff thoughtfully.

"Interesting..." he said, running his finger down the side. Immediately, the man's body began to transform into wood. Timothy's mind raced as he watched the transformation.

How do you fight a guy who can turn into anything he touches? he thought, glancing around the camp for anything he could use. His eyes landed on the campfire the guards had been warming themselves around, and suddenly, an idea struck him. He charged toward the man, yanking on the staff that was now sticking out of his body. The man staggered forwards, and before he could recover, Timothy shoved him straight into the blazing fire. The man screamed in agony, quickly transforming into water to avoid getting burned.

Timothy took advantage of the situation to snatch his staff out of what was left of the fire. Almost immediately, the chieftain began to change again, this time becoming pure fire. He swung a flaming hand at Timothy, who only barely managed to jump out of the way. Quickly, Timothy reached into his chest plate and pulled out one of his firefighting shurikens. When the man swung again, Timothy threw the shuriken through him. The weapon spewed water at the man, beginning to turn him into steam.

The man began to shift once more, but before he could fully get his bearings, Timothy yanked up the stakes of the nearest tent. He bundled the fabric up in his arms and charged at the chieftain, tackling him to the ground just as he changed into a solid once more. Before he could escape, Timothy drove the stakes into the ground beside him, pinning the man beneath the fabric. The man struggled underneath the canvas, and Timothy realized that it was only a matter of time before he freed himself.

He glanced back at the wagons and was relieved to see that they were already beginning to move. Timothy recalled his shuriken to his hand and ran off after them, making his way to the west side of the camp. The others were already waiting for them when they arrived.

"We need somewhere to lay low for a while," Eva said.

"Our best bet is to get back to that ghost town," Timothy said. "With luck, we might be able to mount a defense there."

Aksell glanced up at the sky, then out across the desert. "I think it would be back that way," he said, pointing off toward the west. Timothy raised an eyebrow, and Aksell said, "I might have been awake for most of our trip out here. When I saw you go down, I dropped too. In all the confusion, they never bothered to make sure I really was unconscious."

"We'd better make it quick," Jewel said, dropping down beside them. "The nomads are on their way here."

"We'll never be able to outrun them," one of the settlers said. "They'll be riding at top speed. We'll have to drag the wagons along with us."

"Everyone get in a circle," Timothy said, pulling the Learner's medallion from his chest plate. "Make sure everyone is connected to the rest of the group." Though confused, the settlers quickly did as Timothy instructed.

Here goes nothing.

He pulled the entire group into the in-between, hoping that the medallion would be powerful enough to transport so many people.

Immediately, the sounds of the chaos in the nomad camp vanished, replaced by an almost eerie calm.

Timothy almost laughed when he saw the bewilderment on the other's faces as they got their first look at the in-between. His mirth quickly faded, however, as the seriousness of their situation came back to him.

"Everybody, get aboard a wagon," he said. "We have a lot of distance to cover, and not much time to do it."

"Shouldn't we be treating the wounded?" one of the refugees asked.

"I'm afraid there's not much we can do," Timothy said. "None of us really have much medical knowledge. Unless a member of your party knows how to treat injuries."

"Only the old man and Dawson," the man replied. "And they're both…"

"Then we'll just have to focus on getting to the ruins," Timothy said. "We'll do what we can for them there."

Moving in the in-between, it only took them a short time to reach the ruins. Timothy jumped down from the wagon, jogging into the city to scout out the best place to stash what remained of the settlers' supplies. Once he had found a spot, he made his way back to the others and brought them back into reality. Behind him, he could hear several sighs of relief as the terrain resumed its natural form.

Timothy set Eva and Devon to work determining the extent of everyone's injuries, as the wagon drivers parked the wagons in the spot he had found. Satisfied that the others could handle things for now, Timothy walked over to Jewel.

"We need to come up with a plan," he said, keeping his voice low. "The nomads don't seem to be the type to just let us escape without a fight. They'll be here as soon as they can. And when they get here, we need to be ready for them."

Jewel looked around at the ruined town. "I'm not sure how we're going to do that. How can we make a ghost town into a stronghold in only three hours?"

"I know," Timothy said. "And that's not even considering trying to care for the wounded. The only medical supplies we have are a partially used first-aid kit."

"There's always this," Jewel said, allowing a bluish light to dance across her fingertips.

"That's what I'm afraid of," Timothy said. "But even that won't do any good unless we figure out where we can get supplies from later on."

"So, what do you want me to do?" Jewel asked.

"If any of them have life-threatening injuries, you and Crystal will have to freeze them," Timothy said with a sigh. "Just make sure you let their family members know about the side effects first. Less serious injuries, try to treat as best as you can. Like what you did with Draagetsew back in the ruins. Have everyone else comb this place for anything we can use to mount a defense. Or any supplies the people might have left behind."

Jewel nodded. "And what will you be doing?"

"I'm going to try to figure out how on earth we're going to defend this place."

Chapter 16

"I'm telling you, Tim—it'll work," Aksell said, shaking his head. "They won't know what hit them."

"It's not the effectiveness that I'm worried about," Timothy said. "If we do what you're suggesting, we'll be killing those nomads just as surely as if you pulled the trigger yourself."

"The guards back in Ellada were one thing, but these guys are literally trying to kill us. And if we hadn't shown up when we did, they would have enslaved all these people."

Timothy shook his head. "I'm not doing this. Gearwire would never approve of that."

"Tim… I don't know how many other ways I can say this. Gearwire is dead. It doesn't matter whether he would approve. And as much as you don't want to hear it, the fact that he was killed doesn't exactly say good things about the effectiveness of his methods."

Timothy sighed. "Have you ever seen a dead body, Aksell?"

Aksell gave him a funny look. "You know I have," he said, a warning note in his voice. "We both saw people die of that virus back in Kawts all those years ago. Including my mother."

"But you've never seen someone killed," Timothy said. "I've seen Blanks and attack drones and even your father kill more resistance members than I'd care to count. Most of them good people. And if fighting the Blanks has taught me anything, it's that not everyone who's trying to kill you is doing it by choice."

"That's different, and you know it," Aksell said. "Doing this is the only way we and these people are going to survive the week."

Timothy sighed. "Fine. We'll put it to a vote."

"That's all I ask," Aksell said.

The pair made their way over to where Crystal and Jewel were tending to the wounded, rounding up the remainder of the Guardians of Kawts as they went. When they had all gathered, Aksell proposed his plan. For a long moment, there was silence as they mulled over his words.

Then Eva said, "Sounds like a plan to me."

Devon nodded. "Quite a clever bit of strategy,"

Timothy glanced over at the others, trusting that they would back his objections. To his dismay, however, he found Crystal nodding in agreement.

"Desperate times call for desperate measures," she said, moving over to Aksell's side of the circle. "I'm not sure we really have another option here."

For a moment, nobody moved. Then, slowly, reluctantly, Quill separated himself from the line and moved toward Aksell. "Sorry, Tim," he said apologetically. "We have to do it."

Timothy waited for a moment longer, hoping that Crystal or Quill would change their minds. When they showed no signs of doing so, he sighed. "All right. Aksell, looks like you win. We'll do this your way."

"It'll work," Aksell said. "I promise."

* * *

Timothy looked out over the city from his perch at the top of the clock tower. He saw a faint cloud of dust appear on the horizon, and he brought Henry's old binoculars up to his eyes to examine it.

It's the nomads all right, he thought, recognizing Dawson at the front of the pack. Leaning over the edge of the railing, he shouted, "They're coming! Everyone! Into formation!"

The remaining Guardians of Kawts and the unwounded settlers quickly dispersed, making their way to their places atop the hastily constructed barricades. Timothy looked at the other man in the clock tower with him, a settler who had suffered a broken leg in the initial attack.

"Keep us posted on any major movements," Timothy said, starting to climb back down to the ground.

"I'll do my best, captain," the man replied, giving Timothy a little salute.

Timothy smiled sadly, the man's words reminding him of Gearwire's recent demise. He quickly shrugged the feeling aside, forcing himself to focus on surviving the impending attack.

He took his place on the wall, watching as the nomads drew nearer. The rest of the Guardians of Kawts were spaced out across the perimeter of the city, their weapons at the ready.

I feel so exposed up here, Timothy thought, fidgeting with one of his shurikens. He glanced over at Quill, standing halfway around the city. *I'm not used to fighting battles like this without a team behind me.*

But it's the only way we have a chance. We're the only ones here with any combat experience.

Timothy looked up at the approaching nomads once more, gauging the distance between them. He reached down and grabbed one of his shurikens, throwing it at the nearest of the nomads. The shuriken glanced off the man's arm with hardly enough force to scratch him, the distance being too great for the weapon to be effective. But Timothy's attack had been a signal as much as anything else, and Crystal opened fire, encasing the first few nomads in chunks of crystal.

Before the nomads could recover, Eva used the Gravity Ray on the sand between the two groups, causing it to float up into the air as a dusty curtain. As she moved on to the next part of the wall, Jewel used her powers on the levitating sand particles, fixing them in place to form a crystal wall.

Timothy could hear the nomads' shouts of confusion as they watched the wall rise up, seemingly from nowhere.

Give up, Timothy thought, praying that the nomads would somehow sense his thoughts. *Just give up and go home. This isn't worth your effort.*

For a moment, it seemed like Timothy's hopes might come true. The nomads were unnerved, some of them even shouting about some sort of curse. But then Dawson's voice rang out across the desert, ordering them to continue with the attack.

All we've done is buy time, Timothy realized, glancing around to see how far Eva had gotten. She was practically sprinting along the top of the makeshift wall, firing the Gravity Ray as she went. The yellow ring was on her arm, glinting in the early morning sunlight. She had gotten nearly halfway around the outside of the ghost town.

Let's just hope she gets back around before the nomads get over that wall, Timothy thought, listening intently as the nomads started trying to scale the walls. *They won't have much luck with that,* he thought, remembering how slippery the crystal could be. *But once they get some kind of ladder...*

Even as he had the thought, he heard the chieftain order his men to stop trying to climb the wall and find something to climb on to get over it. There was relative silence for a while as the nomads retreated, searching the area for anything they could use. A series of thumps against the wall confirmed that their search had been successful.

At that moment, Eva returned, out of breath from her sprint around the city.

"Get ready for round two," Timothy said, coming over to her. "It won't take them much longer to get over that wall."

Eva nodded, still trying to suck in as much air as she could. Then she straightened up again and repeated the process, this time firing at the sand between the two walls with the Anti-Friction Ray.

Hardly had she disappeared around the corner than the first of the nomads poked his head above the wall. Timothy threw a shuriken at it, and the man toppled to the ground, unconscious.

But now that the ladders had been constructed, the nomads began to pour over the wall, appearing faster than Timothy and Crystal could push them back. As far as he could tell, the nomads hadn't tried to attack from any other parts of the city, but it was only a matter of time before they did.

The first wave of nomads had reached the top of the wall now and jumped down to the ground below. The looks of terror on their faces were clear even from where Timothy stood as they plunged into the ground, sinking beneath the frictionless sand in a fraction of a second.

Timothy turned his focus back to the top of the wall, trying to ignore the unfortunate nomads' fates.

It was the only way, he told himself. *They'd have killed us all by now otherwise.*

The knowledge did little to reassure him.

By now, the nomads had caught on to their trap and were in retreat, scrambling back over the crystal wall as fast as they could.

Timothy heard a cheer go up from the settlers as they watched the nomads flee, but he knew that the battle was far from over. It would take the chieftain a little while to figure out how to counteract the frictionless sand, but once he did, the battle would begin again in earnest.

As he pondered what to do next, a low humming noise caught Timothy's attention, and he paused, trying to discern the source of the sound. For a moment, he worried that the chieftain had already figured out a way to circumvent their defenses. But as the sound grew louder, he realized that it was coming from overhead.

Leaving his post on the wall, Timothy ran back up to the top of the clock tower, scanning the skies for the source of the sound. His eyes finally came to rest on a distant speck on the horizon, which was rapidly growing closer.

As he peered through Henry's binoculars, he felt a chill run down his spine.

"What is it?" Jewel shouted up from the ground below him.

"It—it's Gearwire's ship."

"That's impossible!" Crystal said. "We watched the giants blow it up! How could they have survived that? And how did they find us?"

"Gearwire knew where the devices were hidden," Timothy said, allowing a flicker of hope to grow within him.

The ship grew closer, beginning its descent and kicking up gusts of sand. Now that the ship was so close, there was no doubt in anyone's mind that it was Gearwire's. The engines appeared to have had extensive repairs, but it was clearly still the same vehicle.

Timothy scrambled back down from the tower, just in time to hear Crystal say, "We don't know for sure who will get off that ship. It's possible that only a few of them survived. Or maybe someone else rebuilt the ship after it crashed."

Jewel shot a withering glance at her sister, but Crystal was unmoved. "I'm just saying that there are a lot of other explanations out there. Don't get your hopes up. Not yet."

The landing gear of the ship extended, and the ship settled on the ground, sinking ever so slightly into the sand. The cabin door slid open, and Timothy watched the opening, hardly daring to breathe.

Come on... Come on. Please be alive...

After what seemed like an eternity, Gearwire emerged from the ship, looking haggard but alive. One by one, the others filed out after him. Madison choked out a sob and ran toward Howard, hugging him fiercely.

"We thought you were all dead," she whispered.

"We almost were," Samuel said with a sympathetic smile. "It's a bit of a long story." He glanced at Gearwire, then quickly added, "I'll have to tell you later."

"Where's Penn?" Jewel asked. "Is he-"

"We got into a fight with the Baron of Technology back in Greece. Penn sustained some pretty serious burns. The High Doctor is looking after him," Gearwire said. "When we left, he was unconscious, but stable."

Timothy glanced at the Golden Knight, wondering how he was taking his former partner-in-crime's injury. The golden-clad warrior made no response to Gearwire's words, though Timothy thought he seemed a little more worried than usual.

Gearwire met Timothy's eyes. "Did you get the rest of the fail-safe devices?"

Timothy nodded, unable to keep the smile off his face, in spite of the circumstances. "We have the Gravity Ray, the Anti-Friction Ray and the Omnishield. But we couldn't find the Laser Gauntlet."

"Good," Gearwire said with a nod. "That means we still have a chance."

"We also have an army of vengeful nomads surrounding the city," Crystal said. "They want to kill us all."

"The sooner we find the Laser Gauntlet, the sooner we can get out of here," Gearwire said.

"It's not quite that simple," Timothy said. "We're not the only ones here." As quickly as he could, he explained to Gearwire the problem with the settlers and the nomad's chieftain. When he finished, Gearwire looked grave.

"That sounds serious. But now you have reinforcements." He turned around to face the others. "Mysterious Man! See if you can do anything for the wounded. There's a first-aid kit on the ship. See if you can get some of the other settlers to help you. The rest of you, take up positions around this town. Timothy? You and your team are going to help me get the Laser Gauntlet."

The Guardians of Kawts dispersed, and Timothy waved the others over.

"The gauntlet isn't here," Crystal said. "We searched everywhere."

"It's here," Gearwire said, crossing the main square. "Most of the scientists who worked on the Laser Gauntlet were from the country that used to sit here—America. The Robot War took a heavy toll on civilizations all around the world, but the damage here was especially bad. Especially after the robots triggered a volcanic eruption that wiped out most of the continent. After the fail-safe alliance broke apart, the scientists who built the Laser Gauntlet returned here to try to rebuild their civilization."

Gearwire fell silent for a moment, looking up at the skeletons of the buildings around him. "They built this town with a heavily armed facility in the center to house the Laser Gauntlet. But despite their best efforts, they found that the land could no longer support a stationary settlement. The towns were abandoned, and the people took up nomadic ways to survive."

"The same nomads as the ones who are trying to wipe us out?" Quill asked.

"Possibly," Gearwire said.

"Hold on," Devon said. "You guys told us it took you over a month to get to the Weather Belt. What makes you so sure you can get the Laser Gauntlet in time?"

"Allegedly, the Laser Gauntlet compound isn't as elaborate as the Weather Belt's," Gearwire said. "And unlike Alpen, they didn't have large quantities of invincium available to them. If we need to, we can blast our way through."

He came to a stop in the center of the town square, scanning the buildings. Finally, he marched over to what looked like the entrance to an abandoned mine, stomping his foot on one of the flagstones in front of it. An odd grinding sound echoed through the air, and Timothy's heart beat faster.

A secret passageway! He thought. *Of course! That's why we couldn't find it!*

Gearwire stared at the yawning hole, his hand coming to rest on the hilt of his sword. He said something under his breath that none of them could quite make out, then stepped forward into the ruin. One by one, Timothy and the others after him. No sooner had the last of them entered than the door slid shut, plunging them into darkness. A few seconds later, the lights flickered on, revealing a long hallway, an intricate mural running all the way down on both sides.

In spite of himself, Timothy examined the mural with interest, brushing his fingers over a tiny painted Martian. A little ways further down, several strangely dressed people stood facing off against each other. One of them appeared to be a green alien of the same type as the first one, and close beside him stood a man who seemed to be little more than a stick figure with a doorknob for a head. A chill ran down Timothy's spine when he noticed the five rings that adorned the arms of one of their opponents.

It's Marathon, he realized, recognizing the legendary first wielder of the rings which he and his friends now wore. *This must be a history of some kind.*

"There's no door," Crystal said, snapping Timothy back to the present.

"That's impossible," Aksell said. "Why would they make this hallway without a door?"

He turned a shade paler when he saw the looks on the others' faces.

"It's a trap," Gearwire said. "The question is, what kind?"

As if in answer to his question, the walls began to move, sliding slowly toward each other. Eva was the first to react, jamming the spear she had taken from the nomad's camp between the walls. The spear began to bend slightly, and Crystal quickly encased it in crystal.

"We have to find a way out of here!" Gearwire barked, his glue gun in his hand as he glanced around in search of the exit. "Try the walls—if we can find a hollow spot, we can blast our way out!"

Timothy looked back toward the mural, hardly noticing anymore the painstaking detail that had been added to the painting. His heart sank as he glanced down the length of the hallway.

Even with all of us looking, we're going to have to be really lucky if we're going to find the door in time.

His eyes came to rest on a portion of the mural depicting the forging of the fail-safe devices. A glimmer of an idea began to form in his mind as he scanned further ahead on the mural. A few feet further down, there was a large portion of the mural dedicated to the fail-safe devices, surrounding them in a glowing starburst.

"What better place to put an emergency exit than behind the fail-safe devices?" he muttered. He reached out and knocked on the wall. It was hollow.

The spear groaned ominously, and Timothy realized they had only a few seconds before it shattered. "I think I found something!" he shouted. "There's a hollow spot over here!"

Jewel was by his side in an instant. "The fail-safe devices," she said. "Of course."

"I think it's the exit," Timothy said. "It would make sense, symbolically. The fail-safe devices will save you from the trap."

"It's worth a shot," Gearwire said. "Everyone in front of the fail-safe devices!"

The sound of the spear snapping echoed through the corridor, and the walls lurched forwards before resuming their previous pace. The walls continued to move closer, the trap showing no signs of changing.

Out of the corner of his eye, Timothy saw Gearwire raise his glue gun, ready to fire it in a last-ditch effort to save them. The wall was only inches away from the group, and Gearwire's finger tightened on the trigger. Timothy tensed, waiting for the inevitable pressure of the walls crushing the air from his lungs.

He felt something give in the wall behind him, and he staggered backwards into the opening that had suddenly appeared. The wall swept them through the opening, stopping when it hit the opposite wall. The group was once again plunged into darkness for a moment before the lights flickered on once more.

Timothy spun in a quick circle, scanning the room for new dangers. A low grinding noise emanated from the ceiling, and he looked up to see a wall of spikes descending toward them.

Great. Just what we needed.

Timothy glanced around the room to find that, as expected, there was no visible exit.

"Fan out!" Gearwire shouted. "We need to find a way out of here!"

The Guardians of Kawts scattered, inspecting the walls and the floors for any sign of an escape route.

The spikes were only inches above their heads when Devon shouted, "I found a hollow spot!"

Gearwire wasted no time waiting to see what the trap would do next, whipping out his glue gun and blasting a hole in the floor. The glue was still sizzling on the edges of the hole when Eva jumped down it, throwing herself into the unknown without any hesitation.

One by one, the others followed suit, only barely making it before the spikes reached the floor. Like the previous trap, it did not reset once they left, sealing them deeper inside.

"I really hope there's a back exit somewhere," Quill's voice said from the darkness.

"There has to be," Madison said. "If they didn't want *anyone* to ever get the device, they would have just destroyed it."

"The next question is, where's the next trap?" Crystal asked. "Gearwire?"

"Stay here," Gearwire's voice called out. "I'm going to check it out."

Timothy heard the clang of his metal feet on the ground, walking deeper into the room. Suddenly, a web of blue lasers sprang out of the darkness, illuminating Gearwire's silhouette a few feet in front of them.

"Great," Crystal said. "Just what we needed."

"We'll never get through in time if we have to work our way through them one by one," Jewel said.

"What if we use the rings?" Quill said.

Gearwire shook his head. "Too risky. Besides, we can't all use the rings at the same time."

"Why don't we just block the source of the lasers?" Aksell said.

"My thoughts exactly," Gearwire said, reloading his glue gun. He fired his weapon, taking out several laser generators, as well as a good portion of the wall.

Crystal and Jewel joined him, impaling the generators with little shards of crystal. Madison sent one of her grenades skittering across the floor, taking out a few clusters of the lasers. Quill and Timothy took out their fair share as well with their stun rifle and shurikens. After a few minutes, only a few lasers were still functioning, and those were easily avoided as they crossed the room toward the exit.

The building above them creaked ominously, and Timothy realized with a shudder that their solution had taken its toll on the building's structural integrity.

If we don't find the Laser Gauntlet soon, we might be buried alive.

Gearwire came to a stop in front of the exit door, frowning thoughtfully. "Timothy. Hand me your staff," he said at last. After a moment of hesitation, Timothy complied. Staff in hand, Gearwire slowly turned the handle of the door, pushing it open with the tip of the staff.

As the door opened, something flew out of the darkness toward them. Timothy jumped backwards, a shuriken ready in his hand. But no enemy materialized, and after a moment, he let down his guard.

"Just what I thought," Gearwire said, inspecting the end of Timothy's staff. A small dart was embedded in the end of the staff, and he pulled it out of the wood. "Poisoned," he said, holding the dart up to the light. He thrust the door open and fired his glue gun in the direction the dart had come from, turning the launcher into a heap of molten slag. Then he led the way into the next room, tossing the staff back to Timothy.

The lights came on as they entered, revealing a wall full of heat-seeking missiles aimed right at them.

"Gearwire? What-" Quill began, but before he could finish, the missiles launched, barreling toward them. The Guardians of Kawts scattered, only barely evading the first attack. The missiles exploded against the wall, unable to change direction quickly enough. The building shuddered, and a piece of plaster fell from the ceiling.

As soon as the missiles exploded, another set launched, streaming toward them. Gearwire blasted the nearest two out of the sky with his glue gun, moving with almost superhuman speed. Another missile flew toward him, and he rolled out of the way, knocking it off-course with a blow from his sword.

Jewel sprinted around the room, the yellow ring glowing brightly as she encased several of the missiles in chunks of crystal. The crystalized missiles fell to the floor, exploding on contact. Quill managed to take down a few of the missiles with his stun rifle before being forced to drop to the ground, narrowly avoiding being blown up himself.

"We aren't going to make it out of here like this!" Timothy shouted, ducking under a missile in the nick of time. The missile exploded against the wall behind him, shaking more chunks of plaster loose from the ceiling. The blast of the explosion threw him off his feet, sending him sliding across the floor.

Timothy's vision swam as he looked around the battlefield. Gearwire alone seemed fully capable of standing his ground against the missiles, but even he seemed to be tiring, his movements increasingly desperate.

I have to figure out how to stop this, Timothy thought, realizing that the brunt of the missiles were currently focused elsewhere. He struggled to his feet, his eyes catching on a thick steel door halfway across the room.

The control room, he thought. *It's got to be.* He sprinted toward the door, readying one of his shurikens as he did. He had almost reached the door when he heard the sound of a missile screaming toward him. He dropped to the ground, and the missile crashed into the door, blowing it to pieces. Shrapnel ricocheted off Timothy's armor, but none of it penetrated deeper.

Timothy scrambled to his feet and ducked inside. The room was empty except for two things. The first was the Laser Gauntlet, lying on an adobe pedestal in the center of the room. The other was a massive switch mounted on the wall. Timothy ran over to it and yanked it down, hoping that it was, in fact, what he thought it was.

For several tense seconds, nothing changed. Then, slowly, the sounds of the explosions died away, finally coming to a stop altogether. Timothy stepped outside to see the others slowly getting back to their feet. They were singed and bleeding, but they were all alive.

The Guardians of Kawts began to take inventory, checking themselves for injuries and making sure everyone was accounted for.

"I found the gauntlet," Timothy said, jogging over to the rest of the group. "It's in the control room over there."

Gearwire nodded wearily and marched toward the gauntlet. Slowly, the group crowded into the control room, which was only barely big enough to fit everyone at once. Timothy removed the gauntlet from the pedestal and handed it to Gearwire. A grinding noise echoed through the room, and a thick metal door slid down from the ceiling, locking them inside. Timothy tensed, prepared for whatever the ruins would throw at them next. The room began to move, sliding upwards through the complex. After a few moments, they came to a stop, and a soft ding echoed through the room. The door slid open again, revealing the same hallway they had started in, the bright morning sunlight shining through the open doorway.

Chapter 17

"How are our defenses holding up?" Gearwire asked, marching up to the Mysterious Man.

"It's been quiet since we arrived. But Adalbo's scouting out the area as we speak. We'll have more information once he gets back."

As if summoned by his words, Adalbo appeared on the horizon, frantically flying toward them. He landed on the ground, his beetle-like wings folding back into his shell. "They're coming," he said. "They've built a bunch of bridges that are long enough to connect the two walls without touching the sand."

Gearwire nodded, deep in thought. "We'll have to break the attack now. If we can do that, we have a chance. If we can't deal them a decisive defeat, they'll just keep coming."

"What do you want us to do?" Eva asked.

"We fight," Gearwire said, his face settling into a familiar frown. "The same way we always have. If we're lucky, the nomads won't have realized that you've gotten reinforcements." He paused for a moment, scanning the group in front of him. "Eva, you seem to be competent with the fail-safe devices. Once their bridges appear, I need you to blast as many of them as you can with the ray guns. Doesn't matter which one."

Eva nodded. "Whatever you say, captain."

"They're coming!" Idalbo shouted from the makeshift wall, notching one of his quills into his bow.

Gearwire nodded and ran off to the wall, not wasting any time on additional instructions.

The battle that followed was heated, the hordes of nomads pouring over the wall only barely kept at bay by the Guardians' skillful defense. Each of them knew well that if any of the nomads got through their lines, the battle was over.

The battle had been raging for some time when Timothy saw a familiar face appear at the top of the wall. Dawson. Quickly, he whipped one of his shurikens at the enemy chieftain, but the weapon simply whizzed through his body, the man having once again turned himself into air. He grinned wickedly and continued to cross the bridge.

Eva blasted the bridge he was on with the Gravity Ray, and it began to float up into the sky. Dawson broke into a run, jumping down from the bridge and landing on the ground. The impact was enough to have severely injured anyone else, but in his present form, the chieftain didn't even seem to notice.

Dawson turned his skin into a shiny metal that Timothy strongly suspected was invincium. Then he charged toward the nearest of the defenders, pulling his fist back to attack.

The Golden Knight stepped forward to meet the charge, but Timothy shouted, "Stop! He can turn into any substance he touches! You'll never beat him!"

His warning came too late, and the chieftain collided with the Golden Knight. The resulting shockwave threw the Golden Knight backward, slamming him against the ground. Dawson staggered to his feet, slightly dazed by the unexpected strength of the impact. Before he could turn and charge them again, Jewel encased him in a chunk of crystal, immobilizing him.

A hush fell upon the battlefield, everyone's eyes on the frozen chieftain. While everyone watched, Madison picked up the chunk of crystal the man was trapped inside, the red ring on her arm glowing. Then she threw it as far as she could, sending it sailing back over the wall. Before it could hit the ground, Eva zapped it with the Gravity Ray, and it began to float upwards, narrowly avoiding shattering open on impact.

Then, as if a spell had been lifted, the nomads turned and fled, scrambling back over the wall as fast as they could. When they reached the other side, they didn't stop, abandoning their siegeworks and mounting their horses. Mere minutes later, they were gone, a cloud of dust the only evidence left of their presence.

"Well, that's one way to handle that," Timothy said as he watched the nomads disappear. He smiled at Jewel. "Nice work."

"That's our cue to leave, I think," the Mysterious Man said, helping the Golden Knight to his feet. "I don't want to be around when that gravity ray wears off."

The Golden Knight shook his head. "They'll be back sooner or later. Men like that chieftain don't surrender easily."

"I'm afraid you might be right," Gearwire said. "Until we can get the settlers to Cleanwater, they'll still be in danger."

"We can fly them there, can't we?" Quill said.

"The ship isn't big enough to take them all at once," Gearwire said. "And we don't even have the time for one trip, let alone multiple."

"We can't just leave them to fend for themselves," Madison said.

"I wasn't suggesting we do that. Even if we didn't have the settlers to worry about, I would be wary about leaving someone with that kind of power unmonitored. You said that he called himself an Owenite?"

Timothy nodded. "Why? Does that mean something?"

"Stella Owens was the name of an ancient hero from before the Robot War. Called herself the Alchemist."

"Which means… what for us, exactly?" Crystal asked.

"Hopefully nothing," Gearwire said. "But if he's got the same powers as the Alchemist, he might be even more formidable a foe than we know."

Idalbo and Adalbo exchanged glances. Then Idalbo said, "Captain? Adalbo and I will stay back with the settlers. We'll keep them safe until you come back after dealing with the Orgwar."

"You won't stand much of a chance against the chieftain," Gearwire said. "And if the nomads come back, you won't be able to hold the entire settlement by yourself."

"With all due respect, none of us really have much of a chance against the chieftain," Adalbo said. "But I can fly over the wall and start dismantling their siegeworks. When they return, they'll have to start from scratch. It might be enough to delay them until you get back."

"And I can keep them at bay for a while with my quills," Idalbo said. "Like it or not, unless you're willing to leave more than two people behind, Adalbo and I are your best option."

Gearwire sighed. "You're right. But that doesn't mean I'm happy about it." He was silent for a while, then said, "Very well. As soon as the Orgwar have been defeated, we'll come back and finish the job." He glanced up at the sun, gauging how much time they had left.

"Everyone else, back to the ship," he said. "We have a lot of ground to make up."

"What's going on?" one of the settlers asked, running up to them. "You can't just leave us here! Dawson will be back!"

"We have to finish our mission," Gearwire said gently. "But I'm leaving two of my best men behind. They'll hold the nomads off until we return." The man started to protest, but Gearwire cut him off. "It's the best we can do. If we don't complete our mission in time, we're going to be facing much worse than those nomads."

The man nodded, reluctantly acknowledging Gearwire's words.

Satisfied, Gearwire turned back toward the rest of the Guardians of Kawts.

"All aboard!" He shouted. He turned to Timothy, and in a quieter tone, he added, "Timothy—meet me in the cockpit. We need to debrief."

Timothy nodded. "I think Jewel should be there too," he said. "She was leading this just as much as I was."

"Very well," Gearwire said, nodding. "I'll meet you *both* in the cockpit."

With that, he disappeared into the ship. The rest of the Guardians of Kawts filed in after him, battered, exhausted, and covered in sand. A few short minutes later, they were airborne once more, heading off to the location of the next fail-safe device.

After checking to make sure there were no unexpected obstacles, Gearwire set the ship to autopilot, pivoting in his chair to face Timothy and Jewel.

"It seems we've missed quite a lot," he said. "You seem to have collected two new crewmembers, for one," he added, one eyebrow raised. "And I would very much like to know how you six managed to collect three fail-safe devices before we could catch up with you."

Timothy and Jewel exchanged glances. Then they told the story of everything that had happened since the ship had been shot down. Gearwire listened intently, only interrupting occasionally with a clarifying question. When they finished, there was silence in the cockpit for a while.

"You two never cease to impress me," Gearwire said at last. "You're a formidable team."

Timothy nodded absently. "Now that you're back, there is something you should know," he said. He hesitated a moment, then continued, "Before you showed up to break us out, back in Velikanov, Quill and Aksell got into a fistfight. They seem to have worked it out, but Aksell's still kind of butting heads with almost everybody."

Gearwire nodded. "Ah. I suspected something of that sort might happen. Of course, I also intended to be here to mediate." He shook his head. "I wouldn't be too concerned about it. You and Aksell have been on opposite sides of a war that's had a formative influence on who you are today. Some conflict was inevitable."

"If you knew there were going to be problems, why did you let Aksell come with us?" Jewel asked.

"He needed it," Gearwire said after a long silence. "I could see it in his eyes. He had realized the full weight of what it meant for him to have been helping the Council, and now he needed to make up for the wrongs he'd helped the Council commit. He needed to prove himself to me. And, I suspect, to the five of you as well."

Timothy nodded slowly, the explanation for many of Aksell's words and actions over the last day and a half suddenly becoming clear. Yet something in Gearwire's tone made him pause. He looked up at his leader's face, suddenly realizing the truth.

Aksell reminded Gearwire of himself. Everything he just said about Aksell—it's true for him too. That's why he let Aksell come with us.

He glanced over at Jewel, and he could tell that she had realized the same thing.

Should we say something? he wondered, locking eyes with Jewel. Jewel gave an almost imperceptible shake of her head, and Timothy let the matter drop.

"If that's everything you have to report, you should go back to the cabin and get some rest," Gearwire said. "You've more than earned it."

Timothy nodded, the chaos of the last few days finally catching up to him.

Unless you count being tranquilized or knocked out, I think it's been more than a day since I last slept, he realized.

He left the cockpit, settling into one of the long benches that lined the outer walls of the cabin. Despite his exhaustion, it took him some time to fall asleep, his mind worrying over the Orgwar's impending arrival. As he began to drift off, he became aware of someone talking. Sighing, he opened his eyes, hoping that the person was talking to someone else.

He groaned when he realized who was speaking. It was the Golden Knight, talking in his sleep again.

He's getting more coherent, he thought as he lay there, trying to fall asleep again. *Back in the Weather Belt complex, I could only understand a word or two.*

"You can count on me, sir," the Golden Knight muttered. "Ayrton won't let you down." He said something almost inaudible, then garbled something that was either Quawz or Kawts.

Timothy frowned, something about what the Golden Knight had said tugging at his memory. In his sleep-deprived state, it took him a few minutes to figure out what. Then it hit him.

Ayrton! That's the name of the guy that Dr. Maddium said was killed during Milkop Quawz' rebellion. The one he said Gearwire believed was his fault. I wonder how the Golden Knight heard about him?

He puzzled over this new question for a few minutes before finally giving up, realizing it wasn't important. He closed his eyes once more, and this time, faded off to sleep.

Chapter 18

Xiangcun, Zhongguo
Twenty-Four Hours Remaining

Timothy yawned and opened his eyes, feeling the gentle humming of the engines dying away. Though he was still a little tired, he felt refreshed, and hopeful that they had a chance.

As the others began to wake up, Gearwire emerged from the cockpit, dark circles under his eyes.

Gearwire hasn't slept a wink since we left Alpen, Timothy realized, suddenly feeling guilty for sleeping. *He's the only one who knows how to fly the ship.*

Timothy stood and made his way over to Gearwire's side. For the first time, he realized how ragged a band they seemed—hardly anyone was without minor cuts and bruises, and their clothes and uniforms were torn and covered with sand. The Golden Knight still had one arm in a sling from where he had been injured fighting the robotic guardians of the Weather Belt.

If the Orgwar don't kill us, this mission might, he thought, a wry smile crossing his face at the bedraggled state of their team. *When this is all over, I'm taking a long vacation.* His mind flitted to Jewel, and he added, *Maybe Jewel and I can both take a vacation. We have a lot of things to sort through.*

By now, the rest of the Guardians of Kawts were fully awake, and Gearwire led them outside into the night.

By the light of the moon, Timothy could make out the capital city of Zhongguo, nestled inside a shallow valley between a ring of hills. Clusters of boulders dotted the ridge surrounding it, standing like resolute sentries in the darkness. With Gearwire in the lead, they began their trek down to the city, hoping that, for once, they could get one of the fail-safe devices without any trouble.

There's only a few more fail-safe devices left, Timothy thought, trying to remember the exact number. He glanced down at his watch, and his relief quickly turned to fear.

We have less than twenty-four hours to find the last four.

Absorbed in his thoughts, Timothy almost didn't register the sudden flash of movement behind one of the boulders. His forehead furrowed as he squinted into the darkness, readying a shuriken as he did so. He was about to dismiss it as a false alarm when a man suddenly jumped out from behind a boulder beside the path in front of them, waving a gun in their direction.

Timothy froze, his mind struggling to explain how a Blank had just appeared in front of them. As he looked up at the man's face, his question was answered.

That's not a Blank, he realized. *That's Taranis in a Blank suit. But what's the old track manager doing way out here? I thought we captured him when the Council fled Kawts.*

"Stay back," Taranis said, his alarmingly large mustache wriggling with glee. He chuckled, mistaking Timothy's surprise for fear. "That's right. Stay back, and no one gets hurt," he said. With his other hand, he pulled a sack from his belt. "Hand over all your valuables," he said. "I'm sure a group as well-dressed as you fine people can spare a little something for an old wanderer?"

Gearwire reached for his glue gun, and Taranis immediately pointed his weapon at him. "Now, now. There's no need for that," he said. "We wouldn't want to hurt ourselves, would we?"

He's gone completely insane, Timothy thought. *Why would he try to take on a heavily armed group by himself? Unless...*

Timothy glanced upward, his eyes narrowing. A chill ran down his spine as he realized that a small army of men were crouched on top of the boulders, their guns drawn.

"Gearwire...?"

"I see them," Gearwire muttered, his eyes fixed on the bandit and his compatriots. He scanned the ridge with the practiced eye of an experienced general. "On my signal," he said, staring down Taranis.

With almost unnatural speed, Gearwire unholstered his glue guns, gluing two boulders' worth of bandits to the rocks before anyone had fully realized what was happening. Timothy followed Gearwire's attack up with a few well-placed shurikens, sending several of the sternest-looking bandits tumbling to the ground. Quill managed to get a shot off with his stun rifle, dropping the bandits' leader before he could determine the source of the attack.

"Fall back!" Gearwire shouted. As if warned by some sixth sense, he dove behind a low boulder just as the remaining bandits opened fire. The Guardians of Kawts scrambled for cover, most of them ending up behind a large cluster of rocks.

"What now?" Timothy shouted, flinching as a bullet ricocheted off a rock near his head.

"I don't know!" Gearwire shouted back, loading a new cartridge into his glue gun. He rolled out from behind the relative safety of the boulder to fire at the bandits. As the bandits returned fire, he ducked back behind the rocks.

We won't be able to stay here long, Timothy realized as the bullets pinged off the rocks around them. *It's only a matter of time before someone gets hit.*

Ignoring the bandits for a moment, Timothy glanced around the area. The Mysterious Man and Howard were nowhere to be seen, and Timothy hoped that they had found cover somewhere else. Aksell crouched a few feet away, holding a pistol he had taken from one of the first bandits to fall. Weapon in hand, he seemed like a completely different person, coolly popping up from the rocks to take a few shots at the bandits before crouching down once more.

"I don't think we've been pinned down this badly since the last stand at the watchtower," the Golden Knight said, ducking back behind the rocks.

Timothy gave him a funny look. He opened his mouth to ask the Golden Knight what he meant, but Crystal beat him to it.

"What do you mean, 'the last stand at the watchtower?' There hasn't been a battle there since Milkop Quawz' rebellion."

The Golden Knight blinked, his forehead furrowing in confusion. "I… I'm not sure," he said. "It just… seemed fitting somehow."

Timothy frowned.

Something's definitely going on with him, he thought. *I hope whatever it is, it isn't serious. We need every man we've got right now.*

Another volley of bullets zinged off the rocks, and Timothy let the matter drop, directing all of his focus toward preventing the bullets from finding his unarmored friends. There was a brief lull in the firing, and Gearwire crawled over to where Timothy was.

"Can you make it to the ship without being seen?" he asked in a low tone.

Timothy surveyed the coverless terrain. "I think so. It might take me a while, though."

"Retrieve the fail-safe devices. They're our best shot at turning the tables on these thieves."

Timothy nodded, then slunk off towards the ship, staying low to the ground to avoid detection by the sharpshooting bandits in the rocks above. Even in the darkness, it took him the better part of an hour to get back to the boulders with the fail-safe devices.

The battlefield was almost the same as when he had left it. The Mysterious Man and Howard were still missing, and the bandits were still perched atop the rocks. Devon had caught a bullet in the leg, but thanks to Jeff's medical database and Gearwire's first-aid experience, it appeared that he would live.

Timothy handed the fail-safe devices to Gearwire, who waved everyone over. As bullets whizzed overhead, he looked out at the faces of his crewmembers.

"We need someone to man the fail-safe devices," he said. "One of us needs to go in there and destabilize the bandits' position to give us the opening to strike."

"I'll do it," Eva said. "I've used the devices before."

"Eva, come on," Devon said. "It's too dangerous."

Eva arched an eyebrow at him. "You're one to talk. This is no more dangerous than that time back in Key Reef."

"That was different!" Devon shot back.

"Maybe I should do it," Aksell said. "Just in case."

Eva glanced over at Gearwire, who remained silent. "I could beat either of you in a duel, and you know it," she said. She looked at Gearwire. "I'm the one who's going to use the fail-safe devices."

Gearwire nodded slowly. "Very well." He handed her the devices, ignoring the anxious looks on Devon's and Aksell's faces. Eva buckled the Omnishield onto her arm and slipped the Laser Gauntlet onto her opposite hand. Then she picked up the two rayguns, clenching and unclenching her fingers as she tested the grip.

As Timothy watched, Eva rose out of the cluster of rocks, the invincium Omnishield protecting her from the bandits' bullets. Before the bandits could come up with a counter, she fired the Anti-Friction

Ray at the rocks, causing them to slide to the ground. She followed this up with a blast from the Gravity Ray, and the rocks floated up out of the way. As the bandits scrambled for cover, a cloud of leaves swirled among them, obscuring their vision.

It looks like Howard's alive, at least, Timothy thought, recognizing the effects of Howard's telekinetic mask. He glanced over at Madison as Gearwire gave the order to attack, hoping that she too had seen what he'd seen. Then he vaulted over the rocks, smashing into the scattered bandits before they could recover.

With Eva wielding the fail-safe devices, the bandits quickly fell before the Guardians of Kawts' counterattack. A few short minutes later, the remaining bandits broke and fled, disappearing into the darkness. Over a dozen bandits lay sprawled on the ground, unconscious or wounded. Five others were dead, killed at some point during the fighting.

Timothy looked at the bodies of the dead bandits, his stomach churning. He closed his eyes and took a deep breath. Visions of the dead resistance soldiers flashed across his mind, and for a moment, he saw Henry lying dead among the bandits. He shook his head to clear it of the image.

No. Henry's not here. He's in a better place. He felt a slight twinge of regret. *But are they?*

"We sure showed them, huh?" Aksell said. "That's one bunch of bandits that isn't going to be robbing anyone again!"

Timothy grimaced, Aksell's words making him feel nauseous.

It's like he hasn't registered that the bandits were real people, he thought. *That they had their own friends and families and hopes for the future.*

As if knowing his thoughts, Gearwire appeared beside him, his lips pressed into a tight frown. "The death of any man is always a tragedy, regardless of their character," he said, reaching out and closing the eyes of one of the dead bandits. "Even our victory celebrations ought to be like funerals in that way."

"Very well said," a new voice said. Timothy turned to see a small group of men on horseback waiting on the edges of the battlefield. "One of our great sages once said something very similar." As Timothy watched, the man in front dismounted from his horse, taking a step toward the group.

Gearwire looked up at the newcomers, letting his hand casually come to rest on the handle of his glue gun. "That's far enough," he said, nodding toward them. "Who are you?"

The man at the front of the group raised his hands in surrender. Now that he was closer, Timothy could see that he was young, no more than twenty-five or thirty. "We don't mean any harm to you," he said. "You've done us a great service in breaking up those bandits. They've been plaguing this area for weeks."

"If these bandits have been such a big problem, why didn't you stop them?" Quill asked.

The man gave a sad smile. "It's a bit more complicated than that. My confederates and I are no longer permitted to enter the city, under pain of death. But if you'll consent to come with us back to our camp, we can tell you the whole story."

"We're in a bit of a hurry," Aksell said. "We're on a very important mission."

"I wish you well," the man said. "Although I'm not sure you'll have much success going through official channels."

Timothy raised an eyebrow. "What do you mean?"

"Come with us to the camp. I promise you it will be worth your while."

Timothy turned toward Gearwire, watching to see how he would respond. Gearwire studied the horsemen for a second, his eyes narrowed. "You don't even know what our mission is about."

"I know you're armed, and you're foreigners. Around here, that alone is enough to get you arrested. Trust me on this one. They weren't too pleased when I first came here either."

Gearwire studied him for a moment longer before responding. "You've made your point. We'll come with you. But if you can't give us the information we need in a few minutes, we're going to have to take our chances by ourselves. Too much is at stake to wait."

The man nodded. "I won't waste your time. I'm Mikio," he added, bowing.

"You can call me Gearwire," Gearwire said. "Now, let's get to your camp. We don't have much time."

* * *

"So, what brings you and your men to be fighting bandits all the way out here?" Mikio asked Gearwire as the Guardians of Kawts crowded into a large tent in the center of the encampment. Only Devon and Eva were not present, Eva helping the camp medic tend to the bullet wound in Devon's leg.

"We're here for the fail-safe device." Gearwire said. "There's an alien invasion force on its way to Earth as we speak."

Mikio looked startled at Gearwire's announcement. "The day has finally come," he said, talking more to himself than to anyone else. Then he looked up sharply. "I'm afraid you're just a few months too late."

"What do you mean?" the Mysterious Man asked. "What happened?"

"I suppose I should start at the beginning," Mikio said. "I grew up on an island off the eastern coast of the empire. I wasn't much older than some of your companions when I came here to join the Dun Pai."

"And who are the Dun Pai, if you don't mind my asking?" Crystal interjected.

Mikio frowned, giving her a disapproving look. But he answered anyway. "We're an order of Junzi Ru—I believe your word for it would be Confucians. Our order has been responsible for protecting and keeping the device you seek for centuries, trained and at the ready to use it when the time arose."

"That's great!" Quill said. "So, what's the problem?"

"Our order has never been particularly popular with the emperor," Mikio said. "We were always there to remind him of his responsibilities to his people. A few months ago, he decided he'd had enough of us and seized our facility and our assets—including the fail-safe device."

"Do you know where it is now?" Gearwire asked.

"If it still exists at all, only the emperor would know its location," Mikio said. "But he'd never agree to meet with you."

"We've gotten a lot of experience with breaking and entering in the last few days," Timothy said. "We'll get in to meet with him whether he wants us to or not."

Gearwire nodded. "Timothy, you and the Mysterious Man and I will go pay the emperor a visit. The rest of you, stay here until we get back."

"You'll need someone who knows the city," Mikio said. "I'll come with you."

"Me too," Quill said.

Gearwire shook his head. "I appreciate the offer, but this is a stealth mission. We need to get in and out as quietly as possible." He glanced toward the east, where the sun was just beginning to peek out over the horizon. "Preferably before the city wakes up."

"If we're wanting to get this done before sunrise, we'd best get moving," the Mysterious Man said. "Lead the way, Mikio."

* * *

The city was eerily quiet this early in the morning, the occasional light in the windows the only sign of life. As they hurried through the empty streets, Gearwire activated the device built into his robotic legs, taking on the appearance of the first pedestrian they encountered.

Timothy saw Mikio start violently as he watched the transformation. Timothy couldn't help but smile as he remembered the first time he had seen Gearwire use the device.

"If you think that's unsettling, imagine seeing yourself run past," he muttered to Mikio.

Mikio gave him a strange look. "You all are a very eccentric bunch."

As day broke over the city, the small team arrived at the palace, a sprawling complex topped with golden, trapezoidal roofs.

"This is the place," Mikio said. He glanced back at Gearwire. "How are you planning to get in?"

Gearwire looked at Timothy and nodded. Timothy removed a grappling hook from his chest plate, flinging it over the wall.

The hook clattered to the ground, catching on part of the gold-plated gate. Timothy gave the rope a tug to make sure it was solid, then scrambled up the wall, followed closely by the Mysterious Man. Only a few minutes later, all four of them had reached the inside of the palace, Gearwire changing shape once more to resemble a passing guard.

Under Mikio's skillful guidance, the team slowly made their way toward the emperor's quarters. The floors creaked loudly beneath their feet, making Timothy wince. Mikio looked apologetic, but he said nothing.

When I first opened Quill's box, I never expected I would wind up breaking into a palace halfway across the world trying to find a superweapon to stop an alien invasion, he thought, scanning the ornately decorated hallway in front of him. *It's hard to believe so much has changed in such a short time.* Quill's words to him in South Florida floated to the surface of his mind, mingling with the words of Samuel and the monk from Velikanov.

Maybe they're right. Maybe everything that's happened has been part of some divine plan. I mean... what would have happened if I hadn't been chased out of Kawts last year? If I hadn't thought the Council killed Samuel?

Henry's death flashed before his eyes. *If I hadn't been there, would Ethos have discovered our base? Or what about the Council's raid on the church in Kawts? Half the team would have died if I hadn't shown up when I did. Is it possible that-*

"The emperor's rooms are just around the corner," Mikio whispered, snapping Timothy out of his reflections.

"How many guards?" the Mysterious Man asked.

"Just one," Mikio said. "People don't usually get this far."

"I've got this one," Gearwire said, unholstering his glue gun. He loaded a capsule into the chamber and stepped around the corner, gluing the startled guard to the wall before he even realized there was a threat.

Mikio surveyed the immobilized guard with professional interest. "Impressive," he said. "You're a good shot."

"I've had a lot of practice," Gearwire said, slipping his weapon back into its holster.

Mikio said nothing, marching up to the door of the emperor's quarters and giving three quick knocks. For a moment, nothing happened. Then, as the echoes died away, a rather sleepy voice came through the door.

"Yes?" it snapped irritably. "What is it?"

Mikio glanced back at the others before responding. "It's Mikio, Your Majesty. I need to speak to you on an urgent matter."

"Mikio? You're not welcome here. Get out of here before I have you removed permanently."

"It's urgent, Your Majesty. You know I wouldn't be here if it weren't."

There was silence for a long moment, then the sound of a deadbolt sliding open. There was a long pause, then a voice from the other side of the door called, "Come in."

Mikio pushed open the door, and the little band followed him inside. They were in what was evidently the emperor's bedchamber, a lavishly decorated room lined with paintings and tapestries from several different eras. In the middle of it all stood the emperor himself, staring crossly back at them.

"Speak," he commanded.

"The Orgwar are coming," Gearwire said. "We have less than a day until they arrive."

"Why precisely is this my problem?" the emperor asked.

In an instant, Gearwire had crossed the distance between him and the emperor, heaving him off the ground by his collar. Timothy could hear the barely contained rage in his voice as he spoke. "Because, you fool! The Orgwar aren't coming here for vacation. It's an invasion party! And what do you think they'll target first?"

"Rulers and leaders?" the emperor stammered, turning several shades paler.

Gearwire nearly threw the man back to the ground. The emperor staggered, barely avoiding falling to the floor. "Important cities! And how do you expect your people to defend themselves against the Orgwar when they couldn't even stop a band of robbers!"

"So, you've had a run-in with the bandits, I take it?" the emperor said, massaging his throat. "If you're still alive, I take it they are not. We are deeply indebted to you for your help. For that, and for your timely warning, I will overlook your crimes against me as long as you leave town before sunrise."

"We have no interest in staying," the Mysterious Man said. "We're only here for the Telekinesis Gauntlet. We need it to stop the Orgwar. Once we have that, we'll be on our way."

The emperor began to play with his fingers, swallowing hard. "Ah… I'm afraid I cannot do that," he said at length, eyeing Gearwire warily.

"Why not?" Gearwire asked, his eyes narrowing.

"We… ah… destroyed it," the emperor said.

Silence hung over the group for a moment. Then the Mysterious Man said, "It's definitely a setback, but it's not an insurmountable one. Just give us the blueprints."

"Ah… we destroyed those too."

Chapter 19

Blancstadt, Alpen

Draagetsew was helping a contingent of builders reinforce the castle walls when a messenger ran up to him.

"President Draagetsew! There's something you need to see!"

The four-armed mutant straightened up, placing the large stone he had been carrying onto the ground. "What is it?" he asked.

"You'll have to come and see, sir," the messenger replied. "Tapfer is waiting for you at Elgae's Spire."

Draagetsew nodded and jogged off toward the castle keep, making his way to the tallest tower. Tapfer didn't seem to hear him when he entered, his gaze fixed on the sky through a pair of binoculars.

"Tapfer? What's happening?" Draagetsew asked, somewhat unnerved by the guard's preoccupation.

"Do you see that speck on the horizon?" Tapfer asked, pointing.

Draagetsew followed his finger, squinting to make out what he was referring to. "I think so," he said. "Why?"

"It's a ship."

"Gearwire's?"

Tapfer shook his head. "I've never seen anything like it before. It's like someone took a bunch of metal bubbles and compacted them as tightly together as they could without popping them."

Draagetsew took the binoculars from Tapfer's hands and peered through them, examining the strange ship in greater detail. The ship was wide and flat, yet strangely lumpy-looking. It seemed quite compact, and its hull had a strange sheen to it that Draagetsew had never seen before.

"The Orgwar," he said, dropping the binoculars once more. "They're early."

"I think this may just be an advance party," Tapfer said. "It seems to be all by itself, and it doesn't seem nearly big enough to be the Orgwarian flagship."

"A scout," Draagetsew said. "Come to scope out our weaknesses before the mothership arrives." He remained silent for a moment, glaring at the ship. Then he straightened up. "Have the rest of the Kriegerhelden meet me up here as soon as possible. We've got an alien to harass."

* * *

The king's words hit Timothy like a sledgehammer.

"You did what?" the Mysterious Man shouted. Beside him, Gearwire's face was completely devoid of emotion. He sat down on the floor, all the fight draining out of him.

The king shifted, eyeing Gearwire warily. "We destroyed it." He swallowed hard. "You must understand, it was much too dangerous to-"

"That was our only chance at defeating the Orgwar," the Mysterious Man said, shaking his head. "The blood of the world is on your hands." Gearwire stood in silence, staring blankly at the wall.

"So that's it?" Mikio asked. "After everything you all have done, you're just giving up?"

"The Orgwar aren't here yet," Timothy said. "If we hurry back to Kawts, we might still be able to prepare a defense. We do have half of the fail-safe devices..."

"And leave our allies to die?" the Mysterious Man said, shaking his head. "I can't do that again."

"There is one more thing we could try," Mikio said. "It's a long shot, but if there's a chance it can save the world..."

"What is it?" Timothy asked, feeling a glimmer of hope returning.

"Shortly after I joined the Dun Pai, one of our members was expelled. Seems he was a bit of a kleptomaniac. But once upon a time, he was the keeper of the plans for the Telekinesis Gauntlet."

"You think he might have something?" the Mysterious Man asked.

"I don't know," Mikio said. "As I said, it's unlikely, but stranger things have happened."

Timothy looked over at Gearwire, awaiting his response. For a long time, Gearwire said nothing, seeming to hardly have heard Mikio's words. Finally, he returned to the present, a dogged determination appearing in his eyes.

"Take us to him."

Mikio nodded. "Follow me."

Timothy followed Mikio out of the throne room, keeping a close eye on Gearwire and the Mysterious Man.

I'm not sure how much more of this Gearwire can handle, Timothy realized, noticing for the first time that their leader seemed to be running on tenacity alone. *He's been... off ever since we started this mission. Something is weighing on his mind—other than the Orgwar,* he added.

As Timothy pondered what to do, the little band slowly made their way to the edge of town, arriving after several minutes at an old house just outside the town boundaries. The building had clearly seen better days, the paint peeling away in places and the front porch sagging alarmingly.

"Are you *sure* this is the right place?" the Mysterious Man asked, eyeing the building skeptically. "If I didn't know any better, I'd think this building has been abandoned for a while."

Mikio nodded his head towards the building, and Gearwire stepped forward. He had only gone a few steps before a voice rang out from inside the house.

"Not a step further!"

Timothy looked up towards the source of the sound and noticed a telling glint from one of the house's upper windows.

The barrel of a rifle.

Gearwire stopped walking, but he seemed otherwise unfazed by the man's challenge. "We don't mean any harm," he said. "We're looking for something very important, and we were told you might be able to help us."

The voice laughed. "I'm sure you are," the man said. "And then that twitchy monarch of ours will promptly confiscate it from me."

"It's a matter of life and death."

"Look, mister, I don't know what you're trying to pull, but if you so much as *lean* closer to my house, I will shoot you."

"Xu! It's me, Mikio," Mikio said, stepping forward to join Gearwire. "This is Dun Pai business."

The gun disappeared from the window, and for a long, agonizing moment, there was silence from the house. Then the front door swung open, revealing a grizzled old man with a scar on his cheek. His right hand still held the rifle, but it was no longer aimed at them.

"You must really be desperate if you're coming to me," he said. He set the gun down on a table just inside the door. "Come on in," he said, stepping aside.

Slowly, everyone filed into the house, crowding into the man's cluttered living room. Looking around, Timothy quickly realized that the man was more than just a kleptomaniac—he was a complete pack rat, with random objects stuffed into nearly every crevice of the room.

How does he find anything in this mess? he wondered, glancing with growing dread at the maze of stuff. *This is even worse than the Council's Records Room!*

The man made his way around the group, taking a seat on a barely-visible couch. He leaned back, inspecting his visitors carefully. "How can I help you today?" he asked.

Timothy glanced back at Gearwire, waiting for him to answer. When he said nothing, Timothy turned back toward the man. He began to explain the situation, trimming out all but the necessary details.

"Interesting," the man said, rubbing his stubbly chin. "I've got good news and bad news," he said at last. "The bad news is, I don't have the Telekinesis Gauntlet. Wish I did. Would have been a nice addition to my collection."

Timothy deflated, but the man lifted a finger. "However," he said. "I think I might have a bootlegged copy of the blueprints around here somewhere."

He looked around the room for a moment, a look of deep concentration on his grizzled features. Then he leapt into action, rifling through a nearby pile of junk.

"No, not that," Timothy heard him mutter. "Not that either." He was silent for a while, then he chuckled. "So that's where that went! I was wondering what happened to you!"

Mikio cleared his throat. "If you could go a little faster, that would be great," he said. "They are in a bit of a time crunch."

"Right. Right," the man said. He sat up and looked around the room again. He made a clucking noise with his tongue, then began digging through a different pile a few feet away.

He's never going to find it at this rate, Timothy thought, frowning. Turning to the nearest stack, he began to rummage through it, scanning the contents of the boxes for anything that resembled blueprints.

"Hey!" the man shouted. "Hands off!"

"Look," Timothy said, turning to face him. "You clearly don't know where the plans are. If we wait for you to find them by yourself, the Orgwar might be here before we even find them. If it's that important to you, you can rearrange your stuff after we leave."

"Fine," the man muttered. "Just don't break anything."

Timothy nodded and returned to his search, this time joined by the others. In the end, it was the man himself who found the papers, well over an hour after they started looking.

He stood up suddenly, triumphantly holding a roll of papers over his head. With a flourish, he slapped them down on the table, shoving a pile of mechanical bits out of the way. "Here they are," he said with a grin. He rubbed his hands together in anticipation as Gearwire picked up the papers.

The room fell silent as Gearwire carefully unrolled the crumpled documents. He brought them close to his face, inspecting them carefully.

"There's some information missing," he said at last, lowering the papers. He sighed, a glimmer of hope returning to his eyes. "But I think there might be enough here to allow us to recreate the device."

"I never thought I'd be thanking you for stealing from us," Mikio said, looking over at the man.

"Don't mention it," the man said. "You're preventing a hostile alien force from enslaving all of humanity. The way I see it, we're even."

Gearwire nodded and handed the papers to Timothy, who slipped them into his chest plate. Without saying another word, he turned and led the way out of the house. Once everyone had gathered on the lawn, he looked at Mikio. "Can you take us to the infirmary back at your camp? We need to check on Devon. See if he'll be able to make the trip."

Mikio nodded. "Of course." Retrieving his horse, he led the Guardians of Kawts back to the exiles' camp. As they approached the medical tent, a man ran outside to meet them, the front of his shirt stained with blood.

"How's the patient?" Mikio asked.

"He's sleeping now," the other man said. "I had to sedate him for the operation."

"Is he going to be okay?" Gearwire asked.

The doctor nodded quickly. "He's lost a fair bit of blood, but he should be fine. He won't be able to travel for a few weeks, though."

Gearwire exhaled heavily, running his hand through his hair. He looked older somehow, as if the last few days had literally drained him of life. For a long time, he said nothing, his tired brain struggling to come up with a solution.

"We'll have to come back for him later," Eva said. Timothy looked up at her, surprised by her words. "We're running out of time," she said. "Dev and I knew the risk we were running when we joined you. If he were awake right now, he'd be saying the same thing."

"Eva..." Aksell started. "Don't you think maybe you should..."

"Stay here with him?" Eva finished. Her voice caught. "Of course I do. More than anything, I want to be here in case anything happens. But if things go well, we'll only be gone for a couple hours. And if they don't..." She broke off, unable to finish her sentence.

Gearwire stared at Eva for a moment. For a second, it looked like he was about to reject her suggestion altogether. But then he nodded.

"You're right. We have to keep moving," he said.

Timothy frowned, watching Gearwire from the corner of his eye.

Sooner or later, he's going to break. I just hope it's not before we complete our mission.

Chapter 20

Timothy stared out the window at the sea below, finally giving up on sleep for the time being. A dark shape on the water caught his attention, and he turned to look at it. Tired as he was, it took him a few moments to register that he was seeing a reflection. Craning his neck to get a better look, he glanced upward. A strange-looking ship was flying just above theirs, scanning them with some sort of energy beam.

Timothy stood up abruptly, leaving his book on his seat as he quickly ducked into the cockpit. "Gearwire?" he said, glancing behind him to make sure the door was shut. "I think we're being followed."

Gearwire turned to look at him. "What do you mean?"

"There's another ship flying over us," Timothy said. "It looks like it's examining us."

Gearwire frowned. He pressed a button on his console and spoke into the ship's intercom. "Everybody hold on. We're going to take evasive measures." He took his finger off the button and returned it to the controls. As Timothy quickly sat down in the copilot's seat, Gearwire suddenly threw the ship in reverse, nearly throwing him to the floor.

Unprepared for the move, the other ship shot past them, becoming visible from the cockpit for the first time.

"The Orgwar," Gearwire said, the color draining from his face.

"They're already starting to arrive." Then his fear hardened into determination. "Timothy. I'll need you to man the guns. On the panel beside you should be a large grey button. That'll activate the defense system."

Timothy quickly did as Gearwire directed, practically punching the button. A dull clang reverberated through the ship, and Gearwire muttered something to himself under his breath.

"The guns are down," he said, flipping a switch on the control panel. "The access hatch must have been damaged in the crash. We're going to have to do this the hard way. Hold on."

He jerked the wheel to one side, causing the ship to swerve away from the Orgwarian ship at a forty-five-degree angle. The Orgwarian ship gave chase, firing at them with a laser gun mounted just underneath the cockpit. Gearwire angled the ship into a downward spiral, somehow managing to avoid the deadly energy bolts that rained down around them.

Timothy's ears began to ache with their sudden descent, and his heart leapt up into his throat. He glanced over at Gearwire, but he looked completely calm and in control, piloting the ship with ease.

If I didn't know better, I'd say he's enjoying this, Timothy realized as he watched the former rebel general work. His reflections were cut short, however, when Gearwire thrust something into his hand. Timothy glanced down at the object. It was one of Gearwire's glue guns.

"Take this and open up the cabin door," Gearwire said, swerving out of the way of another barrage of energy blasts. "When I give the word, fire this at the cockpit. You'll have to hold down the button on the side."

Timothy nodded and staggered toward the cockpit door, struggling to maintain his footing as Gearwire continued dodging the Orgwarian ship's attacks. Finally, he managed to reach the exterior door of the cabin and swung it open. The ship suddenly swerved, and Timothy almost fell out into the water, stopped at the last moment by the Mysterious Man's arm around his waist. As the adrenaline began to fade, Timothy steadied himself and lined up Gearwire's weapon with the enemy ship. The ship swerved one final time, then Gearwire shouted over the intercom.

"Now!"

Timothy pulled the trigger on the gun, making sure to press the button on the side like Gearwire had directed. Superheated glue spewed out of the weapon, splattering all over the Orgwarian ship's cockpit. The glue began to eat through the outer hull. Nausea threatened to overwhelm him as he heard the pilot scream. Then the ship spiraled into the ocean, quickly disappearing beneath the waves.

Timothy stared at the spot where the ship had gone down, breathing heavily.

What did I just do? he wondered, the Orgwarian pilot's screams echoing in his head.

We didn't have any other choice. We had to do it.

He forced himself to put those thoughts aside, desperately trying to ignore the small voice in the back of his head that told him he was wrong.

✳ ✳ ✳

Onslow, Australia
Eighteen Hours Remaining

The ship touched down in Australia a few hours later. Timothy's eyes widened as he took in the full size of the city, noticing the towering skyscrapers and the seething mass of people that filled the streets.

Yet even the sight of the sprawling city wasn't enough to completely take his mind off what had happened on the flight over. No matter how hard he tried, his mind kept coming back to the death of the Orgwarian pilot, his ship plunging into the sea.

Did he have a family? Timothy wondered. *Do the Orgwar even have families? I don't even know if he was attacking us willingly. Maybe some Orgwarian equivalent of the Council brainwashed him. Or blackmailed him.*

Gearwire emerged from the cockpit, his face drawn and haggard. "We need to find the capitol building," he said, interrupting Timothy's reflections. "According to the map, the fail-safe device should be there."

"In that case, we'd better get a move on," Eva said. "That's a big area to navigate in such a short amount of time."

Gearwire nodded mutely, sliding open the door. Eva climbed out of the ship, followed by the rest of the Guardians of Kawts.

Timothy craned his neck back in an attempt to take in the full size of the buildings as they entered the city.

"Wow," Quill breathed, his mouth hanging open in astonishment. "I don't think I've ever seen so many people in one place before."

Timothy heard Gearwire's sharp intake of breath at Quill's comment and turned to look at him. The former rebel leader had stopped moving, staring helplessly at the crowded streets ahead of them.

"So many people," he choked out, his hands beginning to shake. His breathing grew quicker. "They're all going to die. The Orgwar are going to kill them. We don't have enough time to– to–"

"Gearwire?" Timothy said, jogging over to him. "Are you okay?"

Gearwire seemed to take no notice of Timothy's presence. By now, the others had also noticed something was wrong, and had turned to see what was the matter.

"Gearwire!" Timothy repeated, and this time Gearwire looked up at him.

"We… have to stop them," Gearwire panted. "We need… to find the… the boots."

Timothy exchanged glances with Jewel, who had come over to help.

"You take the others and find the fail-safe device," Timothy said, coming to a decision. "I'll take Gearwire back to the ship."

Jewel nodded, turning back to face the others. As they disappeared deeper into the city, Timothy focused his attention on Gearwire.

"Gearwire? Can you hear me?"

"Ye… yes."

"I'm going to get you back to the ship."

"I'll be… fine. We need… to complete the… mission," Gearwire managed.

Timothy shook his head. "Jewel and the others can handle it."

Gearwire still made no attempt to move, and Timothy reached out and took his hand. Gearwire recoiled, but then slowly gave in.

Is this what Dr. Maddium was warning me about? Timothy wondered as he led Gearwire back to where they had left the ship. He glanced over at Gearwire, who hardly seemed aware that he was moving. When they arrived, he brought Gearwire to one of the chairs in the cabin, ducking into the cockpit for the first aid kit.

By the time he returned, Gearwire seemed to be in a slightly better state of mind, though he now clutched the hilt of his sword.

Timothy tried to remove the weapon from his hands, but Gearwire shied away.

"Don't…," he gasped, with surprising vehemence. "I… I *need* it."

Timothy backed away, studying his commander with a mixture of worry and awkwardness.

What am I supposed to do in this situation? he thought as he watched Gearwire's breathing slowly return to normal.

"Is… is there anything I can do to help?" Timothy asked tentatively.

"No!" Gearwire snapped. "Just… I'll be fine."

Timothy fell silent once more, having nothing left to do but watch.

They had been staring silently at each other across the cabin for nearly thirty minutes when Jewel appeared in the doorway.

Timothy leapt to his feet, immediately fearing the worst.

"What happened? Is everyone okay?"

"We're fine," Jewel said. "Samuel sent me to come get you. We have a lot of old ledgers to skim through, and he wanted your help."

Timothy glanced back at Gearwire, who smiled at him weakly.

"I'll be fine here by myself," he said with a shuddering sigh. "Go."

"Alright," Timothy said, unconvinced. "But I'm taking a radio beacon with me. If you need anything, just contact us."

"I'll be fine," Gearwire repeated through gritted teeth.

With one last glance back at Gearwire, Timothy followed Jewel back out of the ship.

As they neared the city once more, Jewel stopped and turned to look at Timothy.

"Take my hand."

"What?" Timothy said, caught by surprise.

"If we're physically linked, the ring's power should apply to you, too," Jewel said quickly. "That's Crystal's theory, anyway."

Timothy nodded, hoping that Jewel couldn't see his face flush. "Right. Of course." He took Jewel's outstretched hand, and they took off at a run, their speed boosted by the yellow ring on Jewel's arm.

Timothy couldn't help but smile at the puzzled stares of the people they passed on the street as they raced toward the rest of the team.

We must be quite a sight, he realized. *It's not every day you see two unusually dressed teenagers sprint down the street at superhuman speeds.*

He turned toward Jewel to say something about it, but the look of intense concentration on her face stopped him.

Moving as fast as they were, it only took them a few minutes to reach their destination, an impressive window-filled building in the heart of the city.

"Is the fail-safe device hidden in the library?" Timothy asked, noticing the sign in front of the building.

"It's complicated," Jewel said. "Apparently, the government sold the fail-safe device to pay off its debts a few decades ago. So now we're here, sifting through years' worth of old government documents in the library archives."

In spite of the situation, Timothy couldn't help but smile. "I never would have guessed that this would all come back to a library," he said, remembering how influential the secrets of Kawts' library had been in setting him on his path to join the Guardians of Kawts.

Jewel smiled back. "That's why Samuel wanted you. You're one of the fastest readers we've got."

"Then we'd better get moving," Timothy said, pushing open the doors and entering the library.

It didn't take him long to locate the others, their now-tattered battle gear making them stand out from the other library patrons. Timothy and Jewel made their way over to them, joining them at the table they had commandeered.

"Find anything yet?" Timothy asked.

Samuel started violently, noticing his presence for the first time. "Not yet," he said as the tension drained out of him. "It's a bit like looking for a needle in a haystack. But it'll go faster now that you two are back." He pulled a reddish tome from the stack on the table beside him and handed it to Timothy. "Get reading. We're looking for anything relating to the Hover Boots. That's the fail-safe device of this region."

Timothy sat down beside Jewel, skimming the pages of the ledger for anything that seemed relevant. He stifled a yawn as he turned the page, the sleep deficit of the last few days beginning to take its toll on him. He shook his head and resumed his task.

Several minutes passed, and Timothy suddenly started awake. He glanced around, making sure no one had noticed that he'd nodded off. He tried to find his place again, but the text swam on the page. Beside him, Jeff was speeding through his second ledger, spending hardly more than a second on each page.

Some help I am, he thought, rubbing his eyes. *I'm barely staying awake right now.* He squeezed his eyelids shut for a moment, then turned his attention back to the ledger, struggling through a dozen more pages before starting to nod off again. He stood up and walked among the shelves. Then the process repeated itself.

"I think I found something," Quill said. It had been almost an hour since they had started searching, and Timothy was no longer the only one who was starting to nod off. "It looks like the Hover Boots were sold to Onslow Modern History Museum—should be somewhere in town, right?"

"Good work," Samuel said. "Eva?"

Eva removed a map of the city from her back pocket and unfolded it on the table. As she examined it, her expression grew more somber.

"I... don't see anything," she said. "There doesn't seem to be a museum here with that name."

"Maybe the name of the museum changed," Timothy suggested.

"Or maybe the museum doesn't exist anymore," Crystal said. "If the boots have been sent to another town, we might never find them."

"Only one way to find out," Samuel said. "Time to consult the index."

Chapter 21

Orgwarian Flagship
Twenty Hours From Earth

"We've lost contact with scouts two, five, and six," the Orgwarian technician reported, turning to face the High Command.

"Locations?" High Command asked, staring once more at the hologram of Earth.

"Number two went down over a mountain range known as the Alps. Number six went down in Southeast Asia. And number five was over the ocean when we lost contact."

"Why was number five over the ocean?"

"He was following an airship, sir. It's the only sighting of a flying vehicle the scouts have reported so far."

High Command said nothing, mulling over this new information. After a moment's hesitation, the technician added, "Sir? There's one other thing. Before he went down, the pilot of ship number five reported picking up signs of Orgwarian tech on board. It was a very distinctive energy signature…"

"The rings," High Command said. "He thinks he found the lost rings of Admiral Groor."

The technician nodded. "Yes sir. That's it exactly."

"Send out the Inspector. If those rings are still on Earth, I want them recovered. In the right hands, they could severely hinder our plans."

The technician nodded, trying not to think about the dark, grim-faced Inspector. "Right away, sir," he said, returning to his seat.

What have we done? he asked himself as he sent the coordinates on their way.

* * *

"Just like old times, eh?" Samuel asked as he and Timothy pored over the drawers of cards that made up the library's index.

Timothy smiled, remembering all the time he had spent indexing newspapers as Samuel's apprentice. "It's hard to believe that the fate of the world is coming down to this."

Samuel chuckled. "You all have come a long way since then," he said, his face growing more somber. "I remember a time when you steadfastly refused to believe anything bad about the Council. And here you are now—helping to end their threats for good."

"And Aksell, too," Timothy said, glancing back at the table where the others were busy sifting through the articles they had already found. "I don't think we would have beaten the Council without you," he realized aloud.

Samuel waved a hand dismissively. "I was a Blank when you defeated them the first time," he said. "And I wasn't exactly much help back in Alpen, either."

"No…" Timothy agreed. "But you helped Madison with her quest for answers about her father's fate. And then Quill. And then me. If not for you, Gearwire may very well have never discovered the truth about the Blanks. And I wouldn't be part of this team right now. I wouldn't be the person I am now."

"I have no doubt that if I'd stayed silent, the twins or your brother Maurice would have convinced you sooner or later," Samuel said. He glanced back at the others. "Speaking of the twins, how long are you two planning to keep up this charade?" he asked, a wry smile on his face.

Timothy stared at him, not sure what he was referring to.

"You and Jewel," Samuel said. He glanced over his shoulder to where Jeff was standing, flipping through the cards at an alarming rate. "Jeff, if you wouldn't mind turning your audio sensors off for a moment, I'd like to have a word with Timothy."

"Affirmative," Jeff said, his characteristic whirring sound growing slightly quieter.

"What about me and Jewel?" Timothy asked, hoping that Samuel's words wouldn't carry over to the others.

Samuel gave him a look. "Don't try to pull that one on me. You know exactly what I'm talking about."

Timothy sighed. "Is it really that obvious?"

"Maybe not to some people. But you forget that I've known both of you for years. Frankly, I'm surprised you didn't get together back in Kawts."

"It's complicated," Timothy said.

"Is it really?" Samuel asked.

"We agreed not to discuss it until after this mission is over," Timothy said. "There's too much at stake. I don't want to be worrying about Jewel when things get dangerous."

"You're worrying anyway," Samuel said with a small smile. He was silent for a moment, then said, "I've told you the story of what happened with Jane and The Race. What I didn't tell you was that we were really close—perhaps something more than friends. But I never actually told her how I felt before she disappeared." He shook his head. "That, more than anything else, was what I've regretted these last forty years."

He smiled. "This is probably one of the most dangerous and desperate missions you have ever gone on. But that's all the more reason you two should talk about how you feel. Before you no longer have that option."

Timothy sighed, Samuel's words reminding him of something Quill had said to him a couple days prior.

"I suppose you're right," he said. "I really should-"

"My apologies for interrupting," Jeff said, beginning to whir loudly. "But I think I may have found something." He tugged a card free of the drawer and handed it to Samuel.

Samuel took it, quickly scanning the contents.

"What is it?" Timothy asked.

"News article," Samuel said. "'Onslow Modern History Museum Closes.' Looks like it happened quite a few years back."

"So we've reached a dead end."

"Not yet, we haven't," Samuel said. "Jeff? If you could track down this article for us, that would be great."

Jeff nodded stiffly. "Affirmative."

As Jeff wandered off into the stacks in search of the article, Timothy turned to Samuel. "Where do you want me?"

"Why don't you go let the others know? I'm going to go consult my professional colleagues."

Timothy nodded, making his way back to the table where the others waited.

He hadn't been there long before Samuel and Jeff returned, bearing a battered box and a bound volume of newspapers, respectively.

Samuel dropped the box onto the table, removing the lid. "Looks like a lot of the museum's papers ended up here when they went bankrupt," he said. "With any luck, between this and the article, we'll be able to find the current whereabouts of the device."

Quill pulled a stack of papers from the box. "We'd better get looking, then. We're running out of time."

* * *

"I've got it!" Madison called, waving the page in question overhead. "The Hover Boots were auctioned off to a Mr.... Ethan Brewer. Address: 45 Aria Road."

"Perfect," Samuel said. "You guys go over there and see what you can find. I'll stay here for a bit. I'm going to see if I can find out anything about Mr. Brewer. Just in case."

"Just make sure you get back to the ship before we leave," Timothy said. "Once we get the Hover Boots, we're going to have to move on right away. If you're not there, we might not have time to go looking for you."

"Don't worry about me," Samuel said. "I wouldn't miss the ending of this story for anything."

"Alright," Eva said. "Let's move."

She pulled out the map of the city they had acquired, and soon, the Guardians of Kawts were gone, hurrying off to what they hoped was the location of the Hover Boots.

As they made their way toward the address they had found, Timothy glanced over at Jewel, who was near the back of the pack. His conversation with Samuel floated to the surface of his mind. He hesitated a moment, then took a deep breath and made his way over to her.

"Jewel?" he asked, his heart beginning to beat faster. "Could I talk to you for a minute?"

Jewel nodded. "What is it?"

It's too late to back out now, Timothy thought, trying to ignore his stomach flip-flopping. He took a deep breath, then he spoke.

"I know we agreed not to talk about this until the mission was over," he said, his words spilling out almost faster than he could think them. "But even if we beat the Orgwar, we might not both live to see it. And I don't want something like that to happen-" He shook his head. "What I'm trying to say is that Crystal was right. I really do like you." He hesitated for a moment, then added, "As more than a friend."

The silence that followed was unbearable. Then Jewel smiled.

"That's exactly what I tried to tell you back in Alpen."

Timothy exhaled heavily, realizing for the first time that he had been holding his breath.

"Whatever I do once we get back to Kawts, I want to do it with you," Jewel said. "We've been dancing around this for far too long. It's time we stopped pretending to ignore it."

Timothy smiled. "I'd like that."

* * *

"This is the place," Eva said, coming to a stop in front of a moderately sized house surrounded by an iron gate. She glanced back at the others, her gaze lingering on Aksell for a moment longer. "If it's all right with all of you, I'll take the lead on this one."

Timothy felt the others' eyes on him as he considered Eva's request. Slowly, he nodded.

"Great," Eva said. "First order of business: getting this gate open."

Withdrawing a small pouch from her pack, she set to work on the lock of the gate, coaxing the tumblers into position. After a few seconds, the lock clicked, and the gate swung open.

Eva made her way to the front door of the house, the others close behind her. She pounded on the door, taking one last look behind her, as if verifying that the others were still following her lead. There was a short pause, then the door was opened by a young man in his late twenties. He froze when he saw the Guardians of Kawts standing on his doorstep, his mouth hanging open slightly.

"We've come for the Hover Boots," Eva said. "The fate of the world depends on it."

The man stared at her, glancing between Eva and the rest of the Guardians of Kawts. For a moment, it looked like he was going to slam the door shut in their faces. Then he stepped to the side, pulling the door open.

"Come in," he said, though Timothy noticed he kept fiddling with his fingers. As the Guardians of Kawts filed into his living room, he walked along the edge of the room, keeping as far away from them as possible.

"The Hover Boots are a family heirloom," he said, turning to face them at last. "I'm not just going to hand them over to you. At least, not without some sort of incentive..."

"How does avoiding being killed by an alien invasion force sound for an incentive?" Crystal asked, quirking her eyebrow.

"Oh, so there's aliens involved," the man said, rolling his eyes. "Of course! Why wouldn't there be!"

"You don't understand," Quill said. "There's a ship of Orgwarian soldiers on their way here as we speak."

"Which I only have your word for," the man said. "I think I'll take my chances."

"I don't think you fully comprehend your position here," the Mysterious Man said, straightening up to his full height. The darkness of his tone gave him an aura of menace, and Timothy was glad that they were on the same side.

The man looked up at him. "How so?"

"There's a dozen of us, all heavily armed. There's only one of you."

"So this is a robbery, then," the man said, examining something on his sleeve. "So be it. You'll never find what you're looking for without my help."

"We have all the time in the world," the Mysterious Man said. "We'll tear this place to pieces if need be."

"I beg to differ," the man said. "Considering the number of rare artifacts I collect, I don't take security lightly. I triggered the silent alarm as soon as you came in here." He glanced out the window. "I'd say you have… five minutes until the police arrive."

Timothy glanced over at Eva, a weighted shuriken already ready in his hand. Eva subtly shook her head, and Timothy put the weapon away.

"What's your price?" Eva said.

"Five million," the man replied, turning away from the window.

Eva shook her head. "That's far too much. Five hundred thousand."

"Five hundred thousand?" The man laughed. "You must be joking. It's worth far more than that. Besides, it's a family heirloom."

"We both know that isn't true," Eva said. "You only purchased them a few years ago."

"Fine. Four million."

"This is a vitally important mission for the survival of humanity as we know it," Eva said. "Surely one million would be more than fair."

"Again, I only have your word on that," the man said. "And since you want it so badly, that seems like more of a point in my favor, wouldn't you say?" He glanced out the window again. "Three minutes."

"We'll go two and a half million," Eva said. "Final offer." She looked pointedly at the rest of the Guardians of Kawts standing beside her. "How confident are you in your hiding place?"

The man hesitated. "Fine. Two and a half million. Up front."

"We can't do that," Eva said. "We'll get you the money by the end of the week."

The man's expression soured. "No money, no deal."

"You think I just carry around a few million dollars in cash in my pockets? We'd have to retrieve the money from South Florida first."

"Then go back there and get it," the man said. "I'll wait."

"We can't," Eva said. "Immanent alien invasion, remember?"

"I'm just supposed to trust that you'll honor a two and a half million dollar debt? What do you think I am, stupid?"

"As a matter of fact, I do," Eva said, her tone shifting abruptly. She crossed to the mantelpiece and pried loose a false panel. She reached into the cavity behind it and pulled out a pair of boots. "If you wanted to keep these hidden, you shouldn't have kept glancing over here after I asked you about your hiding spot."

The man opened his mouth to protest, but Eva cut him off. "You'll get your money. Don't worry. Now, if you'll excuse us, we have places to be." She turned toward the door, and everyone hurried to get out before the police arrived. Only once they were safely out of earshot of the house did they slow to a stop.

"That was amazing!" Aksell said. "You tricked him into giving us the boots for nothing!"

"We are going to actually pay him eventually," Eva said, handing the boots to Timothy, who slipped them into his chest plate.

"How?" Quill asked. "We don't *have* that kind of money."

"South Florida can afford it," Eva said. "And besides, I bet a few other countries might be willing to chip in," she added, looking over at the Mysterious Man and the Golden Knight.

"I'll see what we can do," the Mysterious Man said. "Kawts is in a bit of a precarious place itself at the moment. But Samuel's the one you'd need to talk to about that."

"We'll figure something out," the Golden Knight agreed. "I could probably pull a few strings with the Merchants' Guild."

Timothy glanced at him out of the corner of his eye.

What strings does he think he's going to pull? he wondered. *I don't think he's ever even visited any of the shops in Kawts—certainly not enough of them to have any connections like that.*

His mind drifted to the Golden Knight's other strange comments over the last few days. Suddenly, a thought struck him.

The Golden Knight once told me he had no memories of his life before working with Penn. What if his memories are coming back?

* * *

As Timothy boarded the ship once more, Gearwire pulled him aside. He looked better now, though the drawn, haggard look on his face had only deepened since he had left.

"Is everything okay?" Timothy asked. "Are you okay?"

"I am now," Gearwire said. He hesitated for a moment, then added, "I think I owe you an explanation about what happened earlier."

Timothy shook his head. "As long as you're okay-"

"I need someone on this ship to know. If we manage to stop the Orgwar, I want there to be someone who can give an accurate account of my final hours."

Timothy suppressed a frown. *There he goes again,* he thought. *Why is he so convinced that he's not going to survive this mission?* For a brief moment, he considered asking Gearwire about it, but then he changed his mind. *Gearwire seems to be in a precarious enough place right now without me adding to it. We'll find out soon enough.*

Gearwire was silent for a long moment, trying to decide where to begin.

"I wasn't expecting there to be so many people," he said at last. "I haven't seen a city that populous since before the Robot War. When Quill pointed it out, everything came crashing down at once. I—I thought of the ruins of cities just like these that my original crew and I arrived too late to save. And I thought of what will happen to this city even now if we can't stop the Orgwar. This will be one of their first targets. If they don't just blast it into oblivion, they'll send raiding parties to gather slaves until the entire city becomes a ghost town."

Gearwire's voice became more choked up, but he kept talking. "All those hundreds of thousands of people—each priceless in the eyes of God… the thought of them being slaughtered or reduced to objects by the Orgwar…"

He fell silent, and for a moment, Timothy feared he would suffer a relapse of what had happened a couple hours earlier.

"It overwhelmed me," Gearwire said at last. "I'm sorry—I haven't had an episode like this in almost a decade."

"There's nothing to apologize for," Timothy said, breaking the silence that followed. "And we're going to stop the Orgwar."

Gearwire smiled weakly. "We have to," he said. "I don't think I can stand any more blood on my hands."

"This isn't your fault," Timothy started to say, but before he could finish, Gearwire turned away, vanishing back into the cockpit.

Chapter 22

The Defender's Starship
Twenty Hours From Earth

"**M**aurice! We're picking up a transmission!" Ally said, pulling off one of her headphones.

The Defender turned to look at her. "From Earth?" he asked, his heart beginning to beat faster as hope returned.

Maybe they can still be warned. Maybe they'll be ready to fight off the invasion!

Ally nodded. "It is coming from Earth," she confirmed. She hesitated, then added, "But the message is in Orgwarian."

The Defender's face fell. "We're too late."

"Actually, I'm not so sure we are," Maverick said, his eyes glued to one of the display screens. "The message looks like it's coming from an Orgwarian scout ship. The flagship still hasn't reached Earth."

"What's the message?" the Defender asked.

"It's a mission report," Ally said, still listening to the message with one ear. "The pilot found a ship flying over the ocean. He found some energy signals that seem to match some old Orgwarian technology." She looked up at him. "Does 'the energy signatures match exactly with the rings' mean anything to you?"

"The Orgwarian rings," Maurice said, a chill running down his spine.

"If the Orgwar get their hands on those, they'll be even more powerful. Was the scout able to take them?"

Ally shook her head. "Not yet. But the ship realized they were being followed. They're taking evasive action."

A tense silence grew on the bridge as the trio waited to hear the outcome of the fight. "The signal went dead," Ally said at last. "I think the scout lost."

"I'm not sure how," Maverick said. "The other ship was unarmed."

"Either way, the damage will already have been done," the Defender said. "High Command knows that someone on Earth has the Rings. He won't stop until he gets his hands on them."

"Let's just hope that whoever was on that ship can keep ahead of the Orgwar until we arrive," Maverick said.

The Defender said nothing, instead sending up a silent prayer.

* * *

Aurora Research Base, Antarctica
Eleven Hours Remaining

"Are you sure we're in the right place?" Quill asked, staring out of the window as the ship settled onto the ground. "I don't see anything but snow."

Timothy followed his gaze, taking in the wide expanse of snow for himself.

"My internal GPS confirms that we are within half a mile of the city," Jeff said. "Any feeling that we are lost is illusory."

"The city's underground," Gearwire said, emerging from the cockpit. His eyes were bloodshot, and he looked like he was about to collapse.

"Only the entrance was visible from the surface, but even that will have been buried by the snow after all these years."

His eyes landed on Timothy, and he said, "Timothy, if you could get out the coats Draagetsew put in the cargo hold, that would be great."

Timothy nodded and ducked into the back of the ship, rummaging around for a few minutes before finding what he was looking for.

Hopefully, this goes better than the last time we were in a place like this, he thought, shivering as he remembered how he and Quill had nearly frozen to death inside the ruins. He returned to the cabin and began to distribute the coats.

"I think we're a few short," Crystal said, doing a quick count of the remaining coats.

"That's all I could find," Timothy said. "I could take another look…"

"We lost a lot of our supplies in the crash," Gearwire said. "That's probably all we have left."

"If that's the case, maybe you should sit this one out," Jewel said, looking up at Gearwire.

Gearwire shook his head. "I'm coming with you."

"You should stay with the ship. Get some rest," Jewel said.

Especially after what happened in Australia, Timothy added silently.

"I can't. I need to see this through to the end."

"With all due respect, captain, you've been going for almost two days straight," the Mysterious Man said. "You need to get some sleep so you don't crash the ship into the ocean."

"We've got this one," Timothy said gently. "We need you to be ready to handle whatever comes next. Regardless of whether we succeed."

"If we need help, we can always call you with the radio beacon," Madison said.

There was a long pause, then Gearwire nodded. "Fine. But take Jeff with you. And this," he said, handing Quill one of his glue guns. "You should be able to use it to quickly melt through the snow once you find the entrance."

Timothy nodded and passed out the coats. Samuel led the group out of the ship onto the snowy plain beyond. The air was bitingly cold, and little clouds of steam rose up when they breathed.

"Where do we even start?" Quill asked, squinting to see through the swirling snow. "It could be anywhere."

"We can have Jeff scan the area," Samuel said. "If he can diagnose broken bones, he should have some way to see through the snow."

"Affirmative," Jeff said, moving even more stiffly than normal because of the cold. "Activating x-ray vision."

A strange whirring sound began to emanate from his head, and he stared at the snow beneath their feet, his robotic eyes seeming to bulge out.

A sudden roaring sound filled the air, and Timothy turned to see another Orgwarian ship rapidly approaching. It seemed a little larger than the first one, and it seemed much more compact. Instead of the strange silvery metal of the first ship, this one was dark, almost black, with a strange greenish sheen.

Timothy reached for a shuriken, his eyes never leaving the approaching ship. "Stay down," he whispered to the others. "Maybe it won't see us."

"It's going to see us, Timothy," Crystal said. "We're wearing all sorts of bright colors in the middle of a snowy tundra. He'd have to be blind *not* to see us."

"Jeff? Any luck finding that city?"

"Negative. No traces of human inhabitation have been located."

"Well, keep looking. It looks like we might have our hands full pretty soon."

The ship had stopped moving now, hovering in the air as it scanned the area with a greenish light similar to the one on the other ship. When the light passed over Timothy and the others, it flashed red.

"That doesn't look good," Aksell said. "What do you think they're-"

Before he could finish speaking, a barrage of lasers shot out from the underbelly of the ship, streaming toward them. The Guardians of Kawts scattered, narrowly avoiding the lasers as they vaporized the snow beneath their feet. As the ship readied for another shot, Gearwire charged outside, firing his glue gun like a madman. Several of his shots hit the ship's hull, but the thick armor plating prevented the shots from melting all the way through.

The Orgwarian ship ignored his attacks, continuing to fire on Timothy and the others. Crystal and the Mysterious Man broke away from the group, adding their strength to Gearwire's. After a moment's hesitation, Aksell and Eva joined them.

The Orgwarian turned to face the new threat, but before he could get a grip on the situation, snow flew up from the ground, swirling around the ship. Timothy caught a glimpse of Howard through the blizzard, a look of intense concentration on his face.

"Go!" Gearwire shouted, waving them away. "You have to find the city! We'll hold him off!"

Timothy fought back the urge to reply and forced himself to his feet. Despite his concerns, he knew Gearwire was right.

He's after us anyway, he thought. *The sooner we can get away, the better.*

"You heard Gearwire," Timothy said as the others stood up around him. "We've got to find that city. Jeff?"

"Continuing scanning procedure," Jeff said, slowly examining the snow beneath them.

"We don't have time for this," Madison said. "You'll have to scan as we go!" she shouted, heaving Jeff up off the ground and taking off at a run away from the battle behind them, the red ring glowing on her arm.

The others hurried after her, eager to put some distance between them and the Orgwarian ship. For the next quarter of an hour, they ran through the snowdrifts, searching for the entrance to the hidden city.

We can't keep this up for too much longer, Timothy thought, glancing up at the sky. The sun was almost directly overhead. *We only have about twelve hours left. What do we do if Jeff can't find the city?*

Before he could worry about it further, an alarm chimed, and Jeff looked back up at them. "I have located a potential entry point," he said. He took a few steps away from the group. "Directly beneath my feet is a metal structure."

Timothy nodded to Quill, who moved over to where Jeff was standing. He gently pushed the robot to the side, then fired Gearwire's glue gun at the spot he had indicated. A dense cloud of steam rose up as the superheated glue ate through the snow, creating a narrow shaft down to the thick metal door below.

Jewel jumped down into the hole and tugged on the door. It didn't budge, and for the first time, Timothy noticed the keypad mounted on the outside.

"Let me try," he said, sliding down into the hole. He pulled a shuriken from his chest plate and placed it onto the lock. The specially designed weapon went to work, ferreting out the proper combination.

It seems to be taking longer than usual, he thought, frowning. *I hope the mechanism still works. What if the snow seeped into the system—there might not be anything for the shuriken to work with.*

After several minutes of tense waiting, the shuriken clicked and fell silent. Timothy pulled it off the keypad and pulled on the door handle. It turned, but the door remained firmly shut.

"Well, it's unlocked now, anyway," he said, looking up toward the top of the hole, where the others waited. "But the door's still not opening. I think it might be frozen shut."

"If it really is unlocked, I might be able to get it open," Madison said. "Hold on." She hopped down into the hole beside Timothy and Jewel, grabbing onto the handle. Timothy shimmied to the other side, trying to stay out of Madison's way in the crowded space. Madison pulled on the door, the red ring on her arm beginning to glow. For a moment, the door remained frozen in place. Then, slowly, it began to creak open.

"What do you see?" Howard called down.

"Nothing," Timothy said, shaking his head. "Just a pitch-black tunnel. Hopefully, this is it."

He glanced around the bottom of the hole, then stepped into the inky blackness. As the others climbed down after him, he inspected the walls and floor of the corridor, checking them for any signs of traps. He found nothing, but his experiences in the Weather Belt complex had made him wary.

"Find anything?" Jewel asked, coming up beside him.

"It should be safe," Timothy said, looking over to her. "But I'd still be careful."

Jewel nodded. "Lead the way."

As the others filed into the tunnel behind them, Timothy and Jewel began their march into the bowels of the structure. After several minutes, they noticed a glimmer of light in the distance and made their way toward it.

As the light grew closer, Timothy realized he could no longer feel the biting cold from outside.

It's getting warmer, he thought, unzipping his coat. *There must be some kind of heating system.*

"Fascinating," Howard murmured beside him, staring up at the ceiling of the tunnel. "Just think of all the systems they'd have to design to survive down here. Ventilation, lighting, a monster of a heating system... and that's not even mentioning food and water! Are you seeing this, Jeff?" he asked, turning to the robot. "That must be an electrical line. Which means we must be close to-"

Before Howard could finish his sentence, the hallway opened suddenly into a large, brightly lit room. It was mostly empty, the only feature of interest being an abandoned guard tower up against the opposite wall, positioned in front of a massive metal gate which Timothy assumed led deeper into the city.

They approached the tower slowly, not entirely sure what to expect. Nothing moved inside the structure, and Timothy realized that it no longer posed any threat. He removed the lock-picking shuriken from his chest plate and set it against the gate. After a few moments, the gate unlocked, and Timothy pushed it open. It slid open without a sound, the relative cold having kept it perfectly preserved for centuries.

Timothy and Jewel led the way down the new tunnel, which grew warmer and warmer the further down it they went. By the time they emerged into the next room, they had abandoned their coats altogether, packing them into Timothy's chest plate.

Timothy scanned the new room carefully, wary for any signs of danger. He relaxed a little when he realized that the room was filled with houses, people milling around on the streets.

"I can't believe we're underground right now," Quill said, coming up beside him. "This looks just like Kawts. They even have trees!"

"Fascinating," Howard repeated. "There must be some sort of hydroponics system below the streets. And the light! You can hardly tell it's artificial!"

"We're going to stick out like a sore thumb dressed like this," the Golden Knight said, pointing to the nondescript grey of the citizens' clothing. "It won't take them too long before they call in someone to investigate. Especially since this place seems to have been pretty isolated from the outside world."

Just like what happened back in South Florida, Timothy thought, nodding.

"We'd better keep moving, then," he said. "The deeper we can get before they come looking for us, the better."

"It's a shame we're in such a hurry," Howard said as they rushed through the city. He looked around at the buildings and people that they passed. "If I could only spend a few hours in their research archives…"

"We might be here a little longer than expected," the Golden Knight said. "Armed guards incoming at twelve o'clock."

Timothy's heart sank as he looked toward where the Golden Knight had indicated.

"Here we go again," Quill muttered.

"We don't have time to go through all this again," Madison said. "We still have one more device to find before we fly back to Kawts."

"If it comes down to it, we can fight them off, right?" Quill said.

"Negative," Jeff said. "Reinforcements are en route."

"So what do you suggest we do?" Quill shot back. But before Jeff could answer, the Antarcticans spoke.

"That's far enough," one of the soldiers said. She took a long look at the ragged band, suspicion written across her face. "It has been over a hundred years since we've last had visitors from the outside world. Why are you here?"

"We wouldn't have come if it wasn't important," Jewel said. "The fate of the world depends on it."

The soldier's eyes narrowed. "And what do events on the surface have to do with us?"

Timothy glanced at the curious civilians who lingered nearby. "If you don't want to cause a panic, I suggest we discuss this somewhere a little less… public," he said.

The woman considered this for a moment, then nodded. "Very well. There's a police station a few blocks from here. Will that do?"

Timothy nodded. "That will be fine," he said. "Thank you."

Without saying a word, the soldier turned and led the group to the station.

She's let us keep our weapons so far, Timothy thought. *That's a promising sign.* He frowned as a new thought occurred to him. *Or it means she's confident enough in her troops' ability to take us out if we try to use them.*

As the group filed into the back room of the police station, the woman turned to Howard. "Now, what is this great danger you all were talking about?"

"The Orgwar are coming," Howard said. "Their invasion force will be here in only a few hours. We've spent the last two days gathering the fail-safe devices in order to defeat them."

"You're here for the Amplifier," the woman said, narrowing her eyes. The seconds ticked by slowly as she considered Howard's words. "This is too big a decision for me to make on my own," she said at last. "I must deliberate with the rest of the Board. Wait here."

Without saying another word, she left, leaving the Guardians of Kawts alone in the room.

The minutes dragged by, a tense silence having settled over the group.

"What do you think the Council is going to do with us?" the Golden Knight asked at last.

Timothy looked at him, his heart sinking. *Not the Golden Knight, too! It's bad enough worrying about whether Gearwire's losing his mind!*

"The Council isn't going to do anything to us," Howard said gently. "We arrested them a few days ago, remember?"

The Golden Knight shook his head, as if puzzled. "Sorry. I don't know what came over me."

"That's the third time this has happened since we left Alpen," Howard said. "Are you sure you're okay?"

The Golden Knight said nothing for a long time, then he sighed. "I've been having these dreams lately," he said. "They started a few months ago, but they've been more frequent since I broke my arm in the Weather Belt complex. I think they're memories. I think I'm starting to remember who I was before my time fighting alongside Penn."

"And what do you remember?" Timothy asked, his curiosity overwhelming him before he could think the better of it.

"I lived in Kawts," the Golden Knight said. "I think I was involved in Milkop's rebellion." He shook his head. "I wish I could remember more. It's all so hazy."

* * *

Gearwire's Ship

"Why is it so hazy all of a sudden?" Aksell shouted, shielding his eyes against the blinding snow.

"It's Howard's mask!" Crystal shot back. "He's covering their escape!"

"Well, I wish he wasn't covering the Orgwar's movements, too!"

"Aksell!" Eva's voice called from the blinding snow. "Catch!"

An oblong object sailed through the air, and Aksell only barely managed to catch it before it hit the ground. He looked down at the object in his hands. It was the Friction Ray.

Aksell nodded approvingly, holstering the pistol he had been using before.

All at once, the snow fell to the ground again, and the remaining Guardians of Kawts stood face-to-face once more with the Orgwarian ship.

With visibility restored, the ship opened fire, forcing Aksell to dive to the ground to avoid getting incinerated.

As he rolled back to his feet, he managed to get off a few shots with the Friction Ray, but the blasts simply glanced off the alien metal of the Orgwarian vessel.

"This isn't working!" Aksell shouted as the Orgwarian opened fire once more. "We need to try something else!"

Out of the corner of his eye, he saw the Mysterious Man approaching the ship. For a long moment, he did nothing. Then he reached his hand back and drew one of his twin swords from its scabbard, his eyes vacant. His hand trembled as he stared at the weapon in his hand. Then his expression hardened, and he charged at the ship, plunging his blade into a chink in its armor. For a moment, he hung there, dangling by his sword. Then he let go and dropped to the ground. Above him, the sword suddenly exploded, blowing a hole in the side of the ship.

"Woo!" Aksell shouted. "That's what I'm talking about! That'll show those aliens whose planet this is!"

As the smoke cleared, however, Aksell's heart sank. The pilot of the ship had emerged from his damaged vessel, seemingly unscathed. In his hands was a large blaster.

Aksell gulped. *Timothy had better hurry back with the Amplifier.*

* * *

Aurora Research Base, Antarctica
Ten Hours Remaining

"I'm afraid we can't give you the Amplifier."

"I'm not sure you're understanding the situation here," Howard said tentatively. "The fate of the entire world is at stake. If you don't give us the device, humanity is doomed."

The woman frowned. "No, we understand you. I really am sorry.

To tell the truth, we mostly do believe you. But I'm sworn to act in the best interest of my nation. As a hidden city, we may survive an alien invasion. But if we give you the Amplifier, we'll all be dead in hours."

"What do you mean?" Madison asked, a note of fear creeping into her voice.

"The Amplifier is the only thing keeping our city alive." She eyed the group carefully, weighing her next words. "If you leave your weapons here, I can show you what I mean."

Howard glanced at Timothy and raised an eyebrow. Timothy's eyes narrowed, examining the woman's face for any sign of malice. Finally, he gave a slight nod.

"We accept your terms," Howard said. One by one, the Guardians of Kawts placed their weapons down on the table. "You will be returning these to us once we are done?"

"They will be returned to you when you leave the city."

After making sure none of them were carrying any hidden weapons, the woman led them out of the building and down a series of winding back streets. Despite the gravity of their situation, Timothy could tell that Howard's scientific curiosity was only growing stronger as they began to walk up a steep hill in the center of the hidden city. They finally came to a stop in front of a thick steel wall, seemingly the only thing that connected the city below to the artificial sky above.

"Take a look in there," the woman said, pointing to a window embedded in the wall. Timothy peered through the window, which was near the top of a massive cavern. Filling the bottom of the cavern was a massive furnace with a strangely shaped device mounted on the front. He put his hand on the door and was shocked by how warm it was.

"The Amplifier is the thing that makes this heater strong enough to warm our entire city," the woman said as Timothy stepped back from the wall. "Without it, the city would completely freeze over in a matter of hours."

"Can't you invent something to replace the Amplifier?" Quill said. "I mean, look at this place! If you can build all this, surely you could work around not having the Amplifier!"

The woman nodded. "We certainly could," she said. "But by then, it would be too late. You only have a few hours, and it could take weeks to figure out an adequate workaround. And then we'd have to come up with a way to get the Amplifier out. It's too hot inside that room to enter without protection."

"She's right," Howard said. "Even with the best minds working on it, coming up with a solution for a problem that big isn't feasible in such a short window. Even if you could solve the problem in time, there's not likely to be time left to implement it."

The woman nodded appreciatively. "We would help you if we could. But our hands are tied."

"That is not strictly true," Jeff said, his characteristic whirring growing louder as his processors heated up. "Based on the current state of our quest, we will already have to stop somewhere to rebuild one device. The plans for the Amplifier are not needed to keep the furnace at full strength, and should be sufficient for our purposes."

The woman stared at the robot for a long moment. Then she nodded. "That we can do." She bent down and pressed on one of the rivets that made up the wall. It disappeared into the wall, and a small drawer slid out a few feet away. She removed an ancient roll of papers from the drawer and handed them to Howard.

"Go," she said. "Save the world. I'll have a few officers meet you at the entrance with your gear."

"Thank you," Howard said, bowing deeply. Then they took off, running back through the town and out to the ship. They scrambled out of the tunnel, taking a moment to collapse their entry shaft behind them. The snow settled back into place, the only sign of the city's presence a slight indentation in the snow.

The battle between Gearwire's crew and the Orgwarian ship was still raging by the time they reached their companions. The Orgwarian had abandoned his ship, the smoking crater caused by the Mysterious Man's sword still plainly visible. The Guardians of Kawts seemed to be holding the alien at bay for the moment, but Timothy could tell that they were tiring.

"Get onto the ship," Timothy said to the others, dropping his voice to just above a whisper. "I'll hold him off until then."

"Not by yourself, you won't," Jewel said. "We'll do it together."

Timothy nodded. "Let's go."

The little band ran toward the ship as fast as their legs could carry them, Timothy and Jewel taking their place beside Gearwire on the front lines.

"We've got the plans for the Amplifier," Timothy said, throwing one of his shurikens at the approaching alien. His shot went wide, as if repelled by a magnet. "It's all they were willing to give us."

Gearwire grunted in acknowledgement, his focus remaining on the battle in front of him.

"Everybody to the ship!" he shouted, throwing himself to the ground as the Orgwarian fired a high-powered laser just over his head. The laser struck Gearwire's ship instead, leaving a scorch mark behind.

The Guardians of Kawts did as Gearwire had ordered, and before long, only Timothy, Jewel, and Gearwire remained.

"On my signal, we break and sprint for the ship," Gearwire said, his face grim. He fired one last shot at the approaching Orgwar, then jumped to his feet.

"NOW!"

Timothy ran toward the ship, zigzagging slightly to make it harder for the Orgwarian to aim at him. Gearwire reached the ship, disappearing into the cockpit by the time Timothy arrived. Timothy scrambled up after him, then turned back to see what had happened to Jewel.

Jewel was right behind him, the yellow ring on her arm glowing as she sped toward the ship. As she began to climb up to the cabin, the Orgwarian pursuing her came to a stop, taking aim with his weapon.

"Jewel! Give me your hand!" Timothy said, realizing that she would never make it to the top before the alien fired.

Jewel threw up her hand, and Timothy grabbed it, pulling her inside moments before the blast from the Orgwarian's weapon reached the ship. Before he could take another shot, Timothy slammed the door shut, and they slowly lifted up into the air.

His heart pounding in his chest, Timothy reached down to help Jewel to her feet.

"Are you okay?"

Jewel nodded. "I'm fine. Thanks to you."

For a moment, neither of them moved, still holding onto each other's hands. Suddenly, the ship lurched beneath their feet, causing them to stumble apart.

"Just a little bit of turbulence," Gearwire said over the ship's intercom. "I'd recommend you stay in your seats for a bit."

Jewel and Timothy quickly found their seats, and Timothy's thoughts turned back toward their mission.

Only nine hours to go, and we still have to collect one more device, rebuild two of them, and make it back to Kawts to meet Dr. Maddium. We can do it.

We have to.

Even so, he couldn't quite dispel his uneasiness. They were running out of time.

Chapter 23

Ankoay Ruins, Madagascar
Seven Hours Remaining

As the ship touched down outside an ancient stone ruin, Gearwire staggered out of the cockpit. He seemed like he was about to pass out, and the light had gone out of his eyes. It was clear to Timothy that sheer willpower alone was keeping him going.

For a long moment, he simply stood there, blocking the exit. Finally, he said, "I don't expect to make it out of here alive."

This must be what he was trying to warn me about back in Alpen, Timothy realized. *He was thinking about one stop in particular. That's why he saved this one for last.*

But what does he think is going to happen?

"Samuel, you'll need to fly the ship back to Ellada so you can rebuild the Amplifier and the Telekinesis Gauntlet," Gearwire said. "Jeff can tell you how to pilot the ship."

"What are we up against here?" Quill asked.

Gearwire ignored the question. "After that, you need to go back to Kawts to meet Dr. Maddium. He can help you get the devices connected together." His eyes met Timothy's, and he said, "Promise me you'll do this. Whatever happens."

"I promise," Timothy said. "We won't let you down."

Gearwire nodded, his face flooding with relief. "Don't let the Orgwar win," he said. "No matter what it costs." Then he opened the cabin door and ran out into the ruins.

Timothy and a few others ran after him, catching up to him just as he entered the central compound. As soon as they stepped inside, the door slid shut behind them, the vine-covered facade concealing a strangely high-tech interior.

The inside of the building was nothing more than a single large room, well-lit, but otherwise empty.

"You weren't supposed to follow me," Gearwire said, staring vacantly at the wall.

"Where's the device?" Timothy whispered.

"I don't know."

"Spread out!" Timothy said. "Look for anything that might hide the fail-safe device!"

"You won't find it," Gearwire said, shaking his head.

"We will," Timothy assured him. "We have to."

For nearly half an hour, the Guardians of Kawts scoured every inch of the room, searching for any hint to the device's location. All the while, Gearwire stood resolutely in the center of the room, staring up at the ceiling.

Timothy stepped back from the wall, frowning.

"What do we do now?" Madison asked. "There's nothing here."

"Maybe we're just looking in the wrong place," Quill suggested. "Maybe we were supposed to come in through a different entrance." He jogged over to the door and tried to pull it open, but to no avail. Madison came over and joined him, pulling on the door with all her might. The ring on her arm glowed like a star, but the door didn't budge.

"You won't be able to open it," Gearwire said, still in the same spot he'd been in since they'd entered the ruins. "Not unless they let you." He turned his face back toward the ceiling. "You've had your fun!" he shouted. "You've watched my team search this entire room! Now answer me! Or will you leave us in silence forever?"

He's gone insane, Timothy thought. *He's completely lost it!*

"That was our plan, yes," a voice came from the ceiling. Timothy jumped, his heart pounding.

No, he's not crazy, he thought, looking around for the source of the sound. *Something else is in here with us.*

"But since you insist, we'll indulge you. It'll be nice to have some new conversation partners for a change. At least until you all starve to death."

"Who are you?" Crystal stammered, staring up at the ceiling.

The voice chuckled disdainfully. "We're dangerous abominations, not to be trusted," it said. "Or didn't they tell you?"

"They're robots," Gearwire said softly. "Seven robots of uncommon intelligence who joined the side of humanity in the Robot War. They fought against their own kind simply because it was the right thing to do. Their captain gave his life in the final battle."

"You're very well-versed in our history," the voice in the ceiling said. "Unfortunately for us, our captain was the only one of the seven the humans ever really trusted. With him gone, it was only a matter of time before people grew suspicious of those of us who remained. To protect humanity, the remaining world leaders came up with a plot to take care of the threat. They imprisoned us here, trapping our minds on the mainframe of this ruin and destroying our bodies."

"And in so doing, they made a grave mistake," a new voice chimed in. "They condemned us to be the protectors of the only thing that could protect them from us."

"That's why we're here," Gearwire said. "We need your part of the fail-safe device."

The voice laughed. "What part of this did you not understand? We've been trapped here for hundreds of years because of mankind's treachery. We owe you nothing."

"You don't understand," Eva said. "The Orgwar are coming! They're going to take over the world! It's only a matter of time before they find you too."

"So be it," the voice replied. "At least we will take the human race with us to our graves."

"The ones who did this to you have been dead for centuries," Gearwire said. "Your quarrel is not with those who are alive today. Don't take your wrath out on them. Give my team the device. I will stay here and pay the price."

"Why should we be content with you when we have all of humanity in our power?"

"Because I was one of those who did this to you. I was on the council that condemned you. I helped design the programs which were later used to imprison you. And when they made the details of their plan known to me, I did nothing to stop them."

"Who are you?" the voice asked in a softer tone, and Timothy suspected that it was a different robot now speaking.

"The man who was once your friend," Gearwire said, staring into one of the cameras mounted on the walls.

"Milkop?" the second voice asked.

Gearwire nodded.

"It doesn't matter," the first voice said. "He betrayed us too, just like the others. He admitted it himself."

"I voted against this," Gearwire objected. "As did Thomas. Our biggest sin was not doing more to prevent it. If you want to take your frustration out on me, go ahead. But let the others leave with the device. There's no reason that everyone should perish because of the mistakes of a few, long dead."

A sudden cacophony arose as the six robots argued amongst themselves, creating a nearly deafening sound. After a lengthy deliberation, they one by one fell silent.

"We have nothing against this generation," a voice said, and Timothy noted with interest that it was the second voice speaking. "We shall allow you to have the device. We ask but one thing in return—that you set us free."

"You have my word," Gearwire said. "As soon as the Orgwar are defeated, we will return to get you out of here."

"How do we know you'll actually come back?" the first voice demanded.

"I will remain behind as collateral," Gearwire said, staring defiantly at the ceiling.

"Your word is sufficient," the second robot said. "You always were a friend to us, regardless of what you may have done to assist our captors." A panel in the wall slid open, revealing a sleek metal mask. Gearwire took the device and handed it to Timothy.

"I will come back," he promised as the Guardians of Kawts filed out of the room.

"We know," the voices replied as the door slid shut once more.

* * *

Timothy sat near the door of the cargo hold, staring vacantly across the cabin. After a while, Quill came and sat down next to him.

"That was crazy, wasn't it?" he said. "I mean, I wondered what Ethos meant when he called Gearwire 'Milkop' back in Blancstadt, but I never guessed it involved angry robots from the distant past."

Timothy smiled halfheartedly. "He fought in the Robot War," he said absently. "I think Dr. Maddium might have mentioned those guys to me before." He sighed heavily. "Honestly, worrying about who Gearwire used to be is pretty low on the list of things I'm concerned about right now."

"What's at the top?"

Timothy hesitated a moment, reluctant to put his thoughts into words. Finally, he said, "Are we doing the right thing here?"

Quill gave him a funny look. "What do you mean?"

Timothy sighed. "Using the fail-safe devices to destroy the Orgwar's invasion."

"You're joking, right? You remember the part where if we don't stop them, they're going to kill everyone."

"I'm not saying we shouldn't stop them," Timothy said. "I'm just… wondering if we have to blow them all up in order to do that."

Quill was silent for a moment. Then he said, "Is this about what I said earlier about forgiving the Council for turning me into a Blank? Because I don't think that really applies to the Orgwar…"

"And what makes you so sure of that?" Timothy said. "I killed one of them earlier, Quill. And… he screamed."

"That doesn't make him human," Quill said.

"What does?" Timothy asked. "I mean, what about Jeff? Or those other robots back in the ruins. They were in pain. They were angry. They'd been wronged." He turned to look at Quill. "This whole time, we've been trying to follow Gearwire's no-killing rule. And I still believe it was the right thing to do. But where do we draw the line?"

"We can't give the Orgwar the chance to attack us," Quill said after a long pause. "Killing them might be wrong, but it's the only option we have. I think they're past the point of negotiating."

"Yeah. I suppose you're right," Timothy said. "What other choice do we have?"

* * *

Baron of Technology's Laboratory
Four Hours Remaining

With Aksell acting as their guide, the Guardians of Kawts flew toward the former Elladan Baron of Technology's laboratory, touching down near the coast of Crete just a few hours later.

Gearwire burned a hole through the front door with his glue gun, and Aksell led them to the Baron's primary workshop. Howard immediately got to work, unrolling the plans for the Telekinesis Gauntlet. Gearwire and the twins hovered nearby, lending a hand wherever they could. The others stood around and watched, waiting anxiously as the minutes ticked by.

Finally, Howard seemed to have had enough, and he turned to face them. "Why don't you all go fetch the supplies we're going to need?" he said with a strained smile. "It's a little difficult to focus with you all staring over my shoulder."

Chastened, the remaining Guardians of Kawts left the lab and spread throughout the compound, searching for the parts Howard had requested.

Timothy, Aksell, and Quill wandered through the building, trying to find where the Baron had stored his supply of scrap metal. Instead, they stumbled upon a room full of filing cabinets. Overcome with curiosity, Timothy opened one of the drawers, leafing through the papers inside.

These are the Baron's research notes, Timothy realized, spotting a file marked 'Ethos' among them. He pulled the file out and began to page through it.

"What've you got there, Tim?" Aksell asked, coming over to stand beside him. He looked over Timothy's shoulder as he flipped through the notes.

Timothy heard his friend's breath hitch as he turned the page. He looked over at Aksell, a questioning look on his face. Aksell had gone as white as a sheet, eyes glued to the page. Timothy looked down at the paper in his hand, and suddenly, everything made sense.

'Development of GL-47 Virus: Experiment 32a'

Of course! The Baron would have been the person that Ethos hired to create the virus he used in Kawts, Timothy realized. He glanced at Aksell again, and everything clicked into place. *The same virus that killed Aksell's mother.*

"What's going on?" Quill asked, coming up to the two of them. Timothy handed him the file, and he fell silent.

"What—what does that mean? Why does the Baron have notes on the virus?" Aksell stammered.

Timothy exchanged glances with Quill, both of them thinking the same thing.

"That's one of the things that led us to join Gearwire's crew in the first place," Quill said. "The virus that came through Kawts all those years ago—the Council commissioned someone to design it. Evidently, that person was the Baron."

"But Ethos—my mother… Why? How-"

Timothy shifted uncomfortably.

I can't believe I didn't put it together sooner! If the Council designed the virus and had access to the cure the entire time–

Then Edeline dying of the virus was intentional.

"Any luck finding those parts?" Samuel asked, poking his head into the room. A shadow crossed his face as he saw Aksell. Frowning, he stepped closer.

"Is everything all right?"

"We found the Baron's research notes on the virus," Timothy said.

"Ah. That," Samuel said, a sympathetic smile on his face. He turned to look at Aksell. "I think you deserve an explanation."

Aksell looked up at him, tears streaking down his face. "You all knew about this?" he asked. "Why didn't you tell me?"

"I didn't know most of the story myself until after the Battle of Kawts," Samuel said. "And since then, we've had more... pressing matters to attend to." He paused, unsure of how to continue.

"Your grandfather," he said at last, licking his lips. "Ethos the Eighth. He was a cruel, brutal man. Several people in Kawts, including your mother and my predecessor at the library, decided that he had to be stopped. They orchestrated an assassination, which resulted in your father coming to power. At the time, they believed that he would bring freedom to Kawts and undo the wrongs of his father."

Samuel paused, his mind going back to the early days of Ethos' reign. "And publicly, at least, that's exactly what he did. He renounced his father's policies and revoked the worst of them. But that's where he stopped. And worse still, many were secretly reimplemented 'for the good of Kawts' after he declared the nomads to be dangerous enemies. Edeline and the rest of the rebels were dismayed to discover that Ethos the Ninth was actually worse than his father—every bit as evil, but considerably better at hiding it."

He shook his head. "Most of Kawts' citizens welcomed his reforms gladly, not realizing that they weren't any better off than before. That's when Gearwire arrived. He set up camp on Mount Elbrus and made contact with the already existing rebel forces in Kawts, working in tandem with them as partners. Gearwire led one faction, and your mother led the other. Somehow, Ethos learned the identities of several of the rebellion's leaders in Kawts. He needed to get rid of the organization before it could take root. So he arranged for the production of this virus and secretly infected those he knew were working for us. You and the other Council members were all inoculated before the virus was ever released. Once his targets were dead, Ethos pretended to have discovered the cure and distributed it among the people, maintaining his image as a benevolent ruler."

"Why?" Aksell said at last. "Why not just turn them into Blanks like everyone else? Why did he have to kill her?"

Samuel bit his lip. "I don't know for certain. But if I had to guess, I would say that it was a misguided sense of love."

"No. Ethos is a monster."

"As I said, I don't know for sure," Samuel said. "But I believe that Ethos saw it as an act of mercy—he believed that being turned into a Blank was a fate worse than death—and he loved your mother too much to condemn her to life as a brainwashed puppet."

Samuel fell silent, his words hanging in the air. Finally, Aksell spoke.

"I—I think I'll wait on the ship," he said, his voice shaky.

Before anyone could object, he left the room and made his way outside. Timothy slowly followed him, making his way as far as the main laboratory.

"What's wrong with Aksell?" Eva asked as he disappeared into the ship. To Timothy's surprise, she seemed genuinely worried.

"He's just gotten some hard news," Timothy said. "He'll need some time to process it."

Eva nodded, then, after a moment, she started off after Aksell, vanishing into the ship as well. A few minutes later, she returned, alone.

"You're the only person he wants to talk to right now," she said to Timothy. "He asked me to come get you."

Timothy nodded, leaving the laboratory and boarding Gearwire's ship. Aksell was sitting on one of the benches, tears running down his cheeks. Timothy sat down beside him, and for a long moment, neither of them spoke.

"No wonder you all thought the Council was evil," Aksell said after a while. He fell silent again, struggling to speak.

"You know, it's not even the fact that Ethos killed my mom," he said at last. "I mean, that's terrible too, but I'm used to her being gone. The worst part is that I understand why he did it." He looked up at Timothy. "There's too much of him in me."

"Aksell-"

"No. Let me finish. I have helped him do terrible things. I've killed people because he told me they were enemies. If not for Quill and Samuel, I probably would have killed you all back in Alpen. When we get into trouble, my first thought is almost always one of Ethos' methods. If you guys hadn't been there to rein me in, who knows where we'd be right now."

"You're not Ethos," Timothy said. "You helped us stop him. You saved all of us."

"That doesn't count," Aksell said. "Not after what I helped him do. You would all be better off without me. Safer, too."

There was silence for a moment. Finally, Timothy said, "Aksell? Do you remember a couple days ago, when you asked me about that funeral service?"

Aksell nodded. "You said something about some guy coming back to life, right? I have to admit, after everything we've been through, that wouldn't be terribly surprising to me right now."

"I wasn't very specific when I was explaining it. The truth is, there's more to it than that. I didn't want to say anything because I was still trying to figure out what I thought about it myself." He hesitated a moment, then said, "But I think it might help you."

Aksell looked up at him, waiting.

"Like I said, the coming-back-to-life thing is only part of it," Timothy said. "The main part of the story is about how God came down to Earth to pay the price for everything we've ever done wrong." He trailed off, remembering all the friends who had died in the fight against the

Council. "He gave his life for us."

"I don't deserve that," Aksell said, shaking his head.

"Neither does anyone else," Timothy said. "That's the point."

Aksell looked up at him. "You sound like you really believe that."

Timothy paused, then, to his surprise, found himself nodding. "I do," he said at last, realizing for the first time that it was true. "I have to."

"It seems too good to be true," Aksell said with a wry laugh. "It's too easy—a clean slate, just like that? Just because some guy died a few thousand years ago?"

"In a way, I guess it is," Timothy said slowly, more to himself than to Aksell. "But that doesn't mean it isn't true."

A metallic clanging drew their attention, and Timothy turned to see Jewel standing in the doorway of the ship. "Howard's almost done with the rebuilding," she said. "Everyone's on their way over here."

Timothy nodded. "Thanks for letting us know."

Jewel smiled and ducked back out of the ship once more. After a few minutes, the others began to file into the ship, taking their seats along the wall as Gearwire turned the ship toward Kawts once more—and the final fail-safe device.

* * *

As the ship levelled out, Timothy made his way back to the cargo hold. For a long time, he stood in silence, mulling over everything that had happened since he had joined Gearwire's crew. Now that he was looking for them, he realized he could see several places where God had intervened in his story.

Like that time Quill was healed in Alpen. Or that light that guided Quill and I out of the cold trap. Or even what happened in Velikanov, he realized.

If we hadn't met that hermit, we never would have been able to get this far. We never would have met Eva and Devon. Or been able to rescue those settlers in the Yellowstone Desert.

As he thought back to what he had said to Aksell, he knelt down on the floor of the cargo hold and began to pray.

God, I know I've done a lot of things I shouldn't have. I've sinned against you and against my friends. And yet, you've still been guiding me every step of the way. And you let yourself be executed to save me. I don't know how much longer any of us have. Maybe we'll all be dead by the end of the night. But I want to follow you with whatever time I have left.

As Timothy opened his eyes, he knew, for the first time since they had left Alpen, that everything would be alright.

Chapter 24

City of Kawts
Less Than One Hour Remaining

When Gearwire landed the ship just outside the old rebel base, there were only minutes until the arrival of the Orgwar. They found Dr. Maddium in his lab, rewiring the Council's mind control helmet to restore it to its original purpose. He showed no signs of noticing the others as they entered, his attention focused on what he was doing.

"Were you able to rebuild the Weather Belt?" Gearwire asked.

"Yes," Dr. Maddium replied, still not looking away from the device in front of him. "I got back about an hour ago. Do you have the rest of the fail-safe devices?"

"We do," Gearwire said. "Every last one." He frowned. "Thomas, is something wrong?"

"No, not at all," Dr. Maddium replied, shaking his head. "I'm almost done here. Bring the devices to that hill outside of Kawts. I'll meet you all there in a few minutes."

Gearwire nodded and left the room, although Timothy noticed that he didn't seem satisfied with Dr. Maddium's answer.

He's probably just worried, Timothy thought. *We're all a little strained. It's been a long week.*

It only took them a few minutes to reach the location Dr. Maddium had mentioned, and Timothy removed the fail-safe devices from his chest plate one by one, placing them together on the grass. Dr. Maddium arrived several minutes later, carrying the Weather Belt and the Control Helmet. Then, moving with practiced familiarity, he began to put the devices together, locking them into place to form what looked like a suit of armor.

As the last piece clicked into place, he stepped back, tears in his eyes. "There it is," he said, his voice catching. "The device that will save the planet. Wearing this, an individual should be able to go up and destroy the Orgwarian flagship before it reaches our atmosphere." He glanced up toward the sky, searching for any sign of the invasion force. "They'll be here any minute. We should get suited up."

"Which one of us is going to actually man that thing?" Quill asked.

"It'll have to be someone who's immune to the Council's Blanking device," Gearwire said. "The same gene that makes a person susceptible to Blanking will also make it nearly impossible to interface with the Control Helmet."

"And there's one other problem," Dr. Maddium said. "Whoever goes up to destroy the ship won't make it back. The suit wasn't designed to go into outer space. The pilot will have only just enough time to take out the ship before they run out of oxygen."

Dr. Maddium's words hung in the air as the Guardians of Kawts looked at each other, wondering which of them would have to die in order to save the planet.

It has to be me, Timothy realized with startling clarity. He didn't know how or why he knew, but the conviction was overwhelming. Along with the certainty came a strange sense of peace, despite the immensity of what he was about to do.

"I'll do it," he said, stepping forward.

"No," Gearwire said, stepping between him and the suit. "I will."

Timothy shook his head. "It has to be me, Gearwire. I can feel it."

"He's right," Dr. Maddium said with a sigh. "It has to be Timothy."

Gearwire stared at him, bewildered.

"I had a dream, Gearwire," Dr. Maddium said, looking his friend in the eye. "All night long, the same dream playing over and over. I tried to convince myself it was nothing. But so far, everything has played out exactly as it did in the dream. I don't know why, but it's essential that Timothy be the one to use the devices.

Timothy nodded at Dr. Maddium, giving him a weak smile. Dr. Maddium nodded back, the reason for his sorrow now becoming clear. Timothy took a step closer to the armor, glancing up at the sky.

"I won't let anyone else die for my mistakes!" Gearwire shouted, tears pooling in his eyes. As he looked around at the other Guardians of Kawts, his composure began to crumble. "I won't have your blood on my head too!"

Gearwire's words struck home, but Timothy forced himself to ignore them, beginning to put on the armor. Gearwire started to walk toward him, intent on stopping him.

Dr. Maddium tried to hold him back, but Gearwire shoved him aside. The Golden Knight was the first to react, grabbing Gearwire from behind and pinning him down as Timothy donned the armor.

"Sorry, old friend," he said. "Doctor's orders."

Gearwire seemed to have lost it completely, tears streaming down his face.

"I've already caused the deaths of too many people!" he shouted. "MacGregor! Henry! Edeline! Elijah! Ayrton! Dolan!"

As Gearwire continued to list off names, a strange change came over the Golden Knight. He blinked and looked around, looking like a man newly awakened from a dream.

"Milkop Quawz," he said quietly. Gearwire froze, momentarily pausing in his struggle against the Golden Knight's grip.

"You didn't kill Ayrton," the Golden Knight said. "He was turned into a Blank by the Council after they squashed the rebellion. But somehow, he—I, escaped." He looked at Gearwire with wonder. "It's all there. Everything that happened before I became the Golden Knight. You didn't kill me, Gearwire."

Gearwire stared up at him, examining the Golden Knight's face. "How? But you're… You look nothing like-"

"It's me," the Golden Knight said with renewed conviction. Gearwire stopped struggling and fell to the ground, covering his face with his hands.

Timothy turned his attention to the helmet of the fail-safe devices in his hands, the only piece of the armor he had yet to put on.

"Well, I guess this is it, Tim," Quill said, trying to hold back his tears. He swallowed hard, then choked out, "Thank you. For everything."

"It's been an honor to serve alongside you," the Mysterious Man said, his eyes moist.

"Everyone in Kawts will know what you did for them," Samuel said, tears streaming down his face. "I'll make sure of it."

"You don't have to do this, Tim," Aksell said suddenly. "We can find another way. I-" His voice broke. "I just got you back. And we still have so much to talk about."

"I need to do this," Timothy said. He gestured to the rest of the Guardians of Kawts. "They'll all be here for you."

"They don't know me like you do," Aksell said. "They wouldn't understand."

"I think you'd be surprised," Timothy said, forcing a smile. "They have some experience with this sort of thing."

Aksell fell silent, at a loss for words.

Jewel pushed through the crowd toward Timothy, her eyes red. They looked at each other for a moment, and Jewel gave him a sad smile. Then, to Timothy's surprise, she reached over and kissed him.

How long it lasted, Timothy wasn't sure. But all too soon, Dr. Maddium pulled him away. "It's time," he said, looking up at the large grey shape which had just appeared in the outer atmosphere. He shook Timothy's hand. "I'll see you later," he said, glancing skyward. For a moment, Timothy was confused, but then he realized the scientist's meaning.

He's talking about Heaven, he realized. *Somehow, he knows.*

Dr. Maddium released his hand and stepped back. "The armor is controlled by your thoughts," he said. "Just put on the helmet and tell it to activate. The suit's AI will tell you anything else you need to know."

Timothy nodded and slid the helmet onto his head. An energy field spread out from the armor, covering his entire body with a yellowish sheen. The shield began to shift, morphing into an invincium coating that covered the entire suit. Timothy looked up at the Orgwarian ship, which was rapidly getting closer. He took one last glance back at Jewel, noticing the tears that stained her cheeks. Then he tore himself away, forcing himself to focus on what he had to do next.

Take me up there, he thought, and the armor shot into the air, rocketing upwards at a fearsome pace.

By the time he reached the upper atmosphere, Timothy's breath was becoming labored.

I'm only going to have one shot at this, he realized. He flew up level with the ship, ignoring the suit's warning about the low oxygen levels. The ship slowed down, settling into position for an attack.

Yet, despite the urgency of the situation, Timothy hesitated.

How many of the aliens on that ship are just following orders? he wondered. *How many don't want to be there at all?*

As he wavered, he remembered what the monk had told them about St. Sandoval back in Velikanov.

He died trying to convince them of the same thing that Quill and Samuel and Jewel have been trying to convince me. What's the difference between us? *If I can't kill another human, can I really destroy the Orgwar?*

But what other choice is there?

Awaiting instructions, the computer said.

All at once, Timothy had his answer.

Can you hack into the ship's computer system? Timothy asked, trying to keep his breathing level as the amount of air left in the suit grew lower and lower.

Affirmative, the computer replied. *Establishing connection now.*

A few seconds went by, and Timothy felt like his throat was closing up.

Come on, work faster!

Connection established, the computer said.

Good. Erase any mention of Earth from their databanks. Disable their weapons. And send them somewhere far away from here!

Affirmative, the computer replied. After a couple of seconds, the Orgwarian ship suddenly changed direction, then vanished from sight as it sped away through space.

Awaiting further instructions, the computer said.

There was no reply.

Epilogue

The sound of laughter greeted Jewel as she stood outside the house that had once belonged to Councilman Ethos. She hesitated in the doorway, half tempted to turn around and go home.

"Are you coming or not?" Crystal asked, standing just inside the hallway.

Jewel sighed. "Yeah. Just give me a minute."

It had been nearly a month since the Orgwar's attempted invasion, and things were finally starting to return to normal. The Council had been transferred to Kawts, their trials scheduled to begin in the next few days. Idalbo and Adalbo had returned to Alpen a week prior, vowing to come to Kawts' aid should they be needed. And still, no sign of Timothy had been found, despite Howard and Dr. Maddium's best efforts.

Jewel made her way into the building, joining what remained of the Guardians of Kawts in the cozy living room. She sat down beside Madison on a couch near the door.

"I'm glad you could make it," Madison whispered.

Jewel smiled weakly. "I had to be here to see Penn and the Golden Knight off."

Aksell and Eva emerged from the kitchen, carrying a tray of cookies between them. Devon had returned to South Florida as soon as he was well enough to travel, but with Idalbo and Adalbo's return to Alpen, the two Floridians had been offered places as members of the Guardians of Kawts, though they had yet to accept.

Aksell set the tray down on the table in the middle of the room. "This baking stuff is harder than it looks," he said. "Hopefully these are better than the last batch," he added, grinning at Eva.

Eva grinned back, and Jewel turned away, trying to quash the bitterness that threatened to rise within her.

"I believe it is customary to give a toast upon such occasions," Jeff said, in a voice rather unlike his own.

Because it probably isn't, Jewel realized, remembering what Crystal had told her about the robot. Until Gearwire and Dr. Maddium could get around to building individual bodies for each of them, the minds of the robots from the ruins were all sharing a body with Jeff—at his own suggestion, of course.

"Who's going to give that toast?" another voice snapped from within Jeff. "You?"

"I'll do it," Gearwire said, getting to his feet. For a long moment, he was silent, looking out at the faces of his crewmembers. For the first time in a long time, he seemed at peace.

"This team has been through a lot," he began. "We've fought by each other's sides against some of the greatest evils of our time. We've eaten, trained, and laughed together." A cloud crossed his face. "And we've grieved together. We've lost good friends, good people." He trailed off, his voice catching.

"Today we celebrate a different kind of ending," he continued once he found his voice again. "Ayrton—the Golden Knight—has been a part of this team almost since the beginning. And he's fought beside me even before that. Now he and Penn are leaving us to become the guardians of the people of the Yellowstone Desert." He lifted his glass, looking around once more at his team. "To new stories."

"To new stories."

As everyone lowered their glasses once more, a hush fell over the group. The silence was suddenly broken, however, by a messenger bursting into the room. Jewel recognized him at once as one of Gearwire's former agents in Kawts.

"Gearwire! There's something you should see—outside the northern wall!" He glanced at the others, then added, "You all might want to see this too."

Jewel leapt to her feet, rushing after the messenger.

Did they find Timothy? Could he somehow have survived?

By the time they reached the northern wall, a small crowd had already begun to appear, gathered around a strange ship that sat a few yards away. As the loading ramp began to lower, Gearwire shoved his way to the front of the group.

Timothy walked down the ramp, followed by three others in strange armor, one of whom Jewel recognized as Timothy's long-missing brother, Maurice. A cheer rose from the waiting crowd when they realized who it was that was coming toward them. Timothy's smile widened when he saw Jewel. He ran over to her, enveloping her in a massive hug.

"How—how did you survive?" Jewel asked, her tears staining Timothy's shoulder.

"It's a long story," Timothy said, nodding toward the trio who still waited awkwardly on the ramp. "The important thing is, I'm here now. And I'm never leaving you again."

Author's Note

If you've enjoyed this story, please consider leaving an honest review on whatever platform you purchased this book from. It really goes a long way toward my ability to continue to release new titles in a timely fashion. And remember, if you haven't already, sign up for my e-newsletter at weston-fields.com to receive a free digital copy of "Quill's Box" and updates on upcoming stories!

Acknowledgements

This book would not be what it is today without the help and input of so many people who gave me support and advice throughout the process.

I would first like to thank my sister, Natalie, for reading through the early manuscripts for me on multiple occasions and allowing me to talk at her about the story when I got stuck. A special thank-you is also due to my mother for helping me iron out some of the remaining wrinkles in the story.

A few more rounds of bonus thank-yous: Dad, for letting me name my main character after him; Natalie and Elizabeth, for allowing me to use the characters of Crystal, Jewel, and Madison in this story. I hope I did them justice.

Last, but certainly not least, I would like to thank God for giving me the abilities and the resources to complete this project and for providing such an amazing world for me to gain inspiration from.

About the Author

Weston Fields is a student at Calvin Theological Seminary and Valdosta State University, where he studies theology and library science, respectively. When not considering adding yet another degree, he can be found working at the library or working on his latest book.

You can connect with me on:

🌐 https://weston-fields.com

Subscribe to my newsletter:

✉ https://tinyurl.com/WFieldsnewsletter

Also by Weston Fields

The Guardians of Kawts

Everything is not as it seems in Kawts. It's been nearly a year since Quill lost The Race, leaving his best friend Timothy with a mysterious wooden box and a host of unanswered questions. Although Timothy has tried to move on from his friend's death, the unusual circumstances of Quill's last days continue to haunt him. When Timothy is caught up in the middle of a raid on the Kawts Library, he realizes that there is more going on in Kawts than meets the eye.

The Weather Belt

In the months since the Council's exile, the Guardians of Kawts have been hard at work rebuilding the city, working to reverse the damage done by the Council's reign. The fragile peace is shattered by the arrival of an urgent message from Alpen - Ethos has taken over the capital in his search for a powerful ancient weapon. As the Council"s plans become clear, Timothy and his friends must race through a dangerous compound to reach the Weather Belt before the Council does. But all is never as it seems when the Council is involved, and this time is no exception.

www.ingramcontent.com/pod-product-compliance
Lightning Source LLC
Chambersburg PA
CBHW051222130726
47988CB00001B/190